SOME WOMEN

EMILY LIEBERT

THORNDIKE PRESS
A part of Gale, Cengage Learning

Farmington Hills, Mich • San Francisco • New York • Waterville, Maine
Meriden, Conn • Mason, Ohio • Chicago

LIBRARY OF CONGRESS CATALOGING-IN-PUBLICATION DATA

Names: Liebert, Emily, author.
Title: Some women / by Emily Liebert.
Description: Large print edition. | Waterville, Maine : Thorndike Press, 2016. |
    Series: Thorndike Press large print women's fiction
Identifiers: LCCN 2016019230| ISBN 9781410492579 (hardcover) | ISBN 1410492575
    (hardcover)
Subjects: LCSH: Female friendship—Fiction. | Large type books. | Domestic fiction.
Classification: LCC PS3612.I33525 S66 2016b | DDC 813/.6—dc23
LC record available at https://lccn.loc.gov/2016019230

Published in 2016 by arrangement with New American Library, an
imprint of Penguin Publishing Group, a division of Penguin Random
House LLC

Printed in Mexico
1 2 3 4 5 6 7 20 19 18 17 16

SOME WOMEN

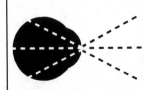 This Large Print Book carries the
Seal of Approval of N.A.V.H.

*For my Pop Pop,
my fifth book on April 5, what would have
been your ninety-ninth birthday.
You're in my heart always.*

ACKNOWLEDGMENTS

To my rock star literary agent, Alyssa Reuben — thank you for your endless support (and therapy). Heaps of gratitude to my editor, Kerry Donovan, who's put up with me through four books in less than three years (saint!). Kathleen Zrelak and Diana Franco — thank you for your tireless publicity efforts.

My parents, Tom and Kyle Einhorn, have never stopped telling me how proud they are of me, which is a gift. Thank you to my brother, Zack Einhorn, and my grandmother Ailene Rickel, for always being there. And also my in-laws: Peter B. Liebert, Mary Ann Liebert, and Peter S. Liebert.

Thank you to my Pure Barre Westport ladies for keeping me sane for at least fifty-five minutes a day!

Melody Drake, I love you for being my best friend for twenty years. You're my number one fan and my most authentic critic!

The most heartfelt thank-you to all of the amazing authors in my genre who support me and one another.

And to my friends — old and new — I'm so lucky to have you in my corner: Kerry Kennedy, Sara Haines, Shari Arnold, David Goffin, Devin Alexander, Jane Green, Tamra Judge, Zoe Schaeffer, Hyleri Katzenberg, Monica Lynn, Robin Homonoff, Emily Homonoff, Debbie Mogelof, Marni Lane, Allison Walmark, Jamie Camche, Danielle Dobin, Emily Rosnick, Amy Kallesten, Jen Scott, Karen Sutton, Jordana Eisenstein Gringer, Amy Falkenstein, Amy Lopatin, Heather Cody, Anne Epstein, Anne Greenberg, Heather Bauer, Jen Goldberg, Jenn Falik, and Julie Levitt.

To my three boys — my husband, Lewis, and our sons, Jax and Hugo. Lewis, I couldn't do any of it without you. Jax and Hugo — I love you to the moon and back.

"I get everything all beautifully planned out and it has to go and rain."
— *Wilbur,* Charlotte's Web

ONE

It started out like any other Sunday, as Annabel imagined most Sundays did — even the ones that ultimately bore the burden of cataclysmic news. She peeled one eyelid open, then the next, and sat upright. Already she was disappointed that any lazy tendencies, any desire to roll over and go back to sleep, had been supplanted by a breathless urgency to commence the household chores that confronted her.

Then there was Henry, lying next to her on his back, with his arms folded across his chest, one hand on top of the other, as his lungs filled with air and exhaled with the crackle of a sputtering carburetor. Deviated septum, he insisted. Extra thirty pounds was more like it. She watched silently as his nose twitched and his lips quivered. He barked a phlegmy cough and rolled onto his side to face her, his heavy arm landing on the pillow where her head had been just moments earlier.

Sleeping in the same bed with Henry had become a competitive sport — every man for himself. It was all about who could strategically gather the most sizable chunk of mutual real estate while, at the same time, guarding his or her own. All the while making certain not to relinquish an extra inch or two of sheet or comforter. How many times had Annabel awakened in the middle of the night, shivering beneath the frigid squalls of air-conditioning — because Henry insisted on air-conditioning 365 days a year — and been forced to wrestle her way back into the cocooning warmth that her husband had been monopolizing during their precious hours of REM? Too many times to count.

She wondered absently how long he would lie there if she let him. If she didn't launch herself out of bed with the determination of an Olympic pole vaulter to vie for a gold medal in domestic efficiency. There was always so much to *get done.* Seemingly endless check boxes to tick in her eternal pursuit to finally reach a point where she could relax.

That morning, in a rare state of affairs, her resolve was dulled, if only slightly, by the absence of their twin five-year-old boys, Harper and Hudson — names for which Annabel had endured interminable eye rolls and disapproving shakes of the head. Henry had wanted to know why they couldn't call them Ben and Scott or Matt and Jason. He'd even agreed, albeit begrudgingly, to Dylan and Taylor, until two other babies in the hospital nursery — two girls — had assumed the newly minted unisex monikers. In the end she'd convinced him that having sons with the same first initial as their father was an honor that he should embrace rather than rebuff. And then she'd prayed he didn't suggest Harry and Harvey or Hank and Howard.

Annabel plodded doggedly toward the bathroom, intimidated by the aberrant silence. Typically by this point, Harper would have been up for at least an hour. He'd have come stumbling into their room, barely alert, crawled into his spot between the two of them, and curled his body into hers. "Snuggle," he'd have uttered, almost imperceptibly, and she'd have cuddled him close, dotting his plump, rosy cheek with the softest kisses. Faultless indulgence at its finest.

No less than thirty minutes later, Hudson would have made his grand entrance, bursting onto the scene by catapulting all thirty-eight pounds of himself on top of everyone, thereby instigating indignant shrieks from his brother, grumbles of protest from his father, and roguish laughter from himself.

Harper and Hudson. Angel and devil. As different as any two children could be, especially identical twins, although they barely looked alike to her. Harper was Annabel's lover-not-fighter. Her sensitive thinker. The one who, at four years old, had reminded Henry to buy her flowers on Mother's Day. Not because he expected a reward or even a pat on the back for it, but because he'd wanted to make sure she was happy. He'd wanted to make sure that all of the efforts she put forth on any given day, the many strands of silk she wove to construct the intricate web that was their life, didn't go unnoticed. Hudson, on the other hand, was a silent manipulator. A child who had your number before you knew there was a number to be had. A child who could use any weakness to his advantage while making you believe *he* was doing *you* a favor. To know Hudson was to work for Hudson, whether you'd voluntarily initiated your employment or not.

Still, now, with the boys at her parents' house, where they'd slept the previous night so she and Henry could attend his assistant, Liberty's, wedding — *and he thinks Harper and Hudson are odd names* — it was hard not to miss them, devious behavior and all. That was the funny thing about children. When they were around, you wanted peace and quiet. A mere moment to yourself. You felt absolutely desperate to go more than three minutes without hearing the word *Moooooooom* echoing throughout the house. To go to the bathroom or — if luck was really on your side — to take an uninterrupted shower. Yet, when they were absent, no matter how infrequently that happened, it felt as though someone had amputated your limb and left a stinging open wound in its place. And you craved them like a cold beer on a blistering summer day.

Annabel brushed her teeth and splashed tepid water on her face before patting it dry and massaging a thick white cream around her eyes. *Deflates the puffiness,* read the bottle, a promise she trusted it would live up to. After all, no one wants to look like she's squinting until midafternoon. She pulled her robe off the hook by the shower, slid her arms into the sleeves, wrapped it around her body, and cinched it at her waist. Her waist, which was no longer as cinchable as it used to be. Unfortunately, when she'd attempted to zip up her favorite black dress for Liberty's big day, she'd had the unwelcome realization that any efforts to regain her prebaby figure had been infuriatingly futile. She'd danced. She'd jiggled. She'd even tried Vaseline — a tip she'd read in one of the women's magazines in her dentist's office. Until, finally, yesterday she'd resigned herself to donning a remotely flattering navy blue maternity dress, which she'd hoped no one would actually notice was a maternity dress. Unfortunately, Gary Blank's wife — who was, in fact, pregnant — had been wearing a strikingly similar one in a lighter shade of blue. Even more depressing was the fact that she'd carried it off far better than Annabel had.

Minutes later, she found herself downstairs in the kitchen, prepping the kids' backpacks for school the following day, making their lunches, loading and running the dishwasher, finishing a basket of laundry, ordering the week's groceries online, and emptying the garbage cans — which she'd reminded Henry to take care of before going to bed. Again, no such luck. As the clock struck nine, her groggy husband finally made his way downstairs, rubbing his eyes with his fists, then stretching his arms above his head before emancipating an onerous moan. Apparently, all that rest could really take it out of a guy.

"Look who it is." He'd barely come to life and already she was anxious for him to pitch in. "Did you make the bed?" *Seriously, let's get to the point.*

"Nope," he called from the family room, where she found him reclining on the couch with the television remote already in hand.

"Do you really need a rest after eight hours of sleep?" Hands on hips. *Hello? Do you see that? Hands. On. Hips.* Men could be exasperatingly oblivious.

"The race is on."

"What race?"

"NASCAR. It's just another forty-five minutes. *Relax.*"

There it was. The state of being that purportedly held the key to her infinite happiness: relaxation. Except how exactly was she supposed to kick up her feet and chill out when there were still three more loads of laundry to be done? Not to mention dinner to queue up for that evening — for them and the boys. Because God forbid everyone in the house should eat the same thing. Actually, it would be remarkable if even two people ate the same thing. Harper subsisted solely on a diet of peanut butter and jelly, fruit, and spaghetti with *no sauce,* while Hudson — who was allergic to peanut butter — preferred chicken, apples, and carrots at every meal. Every meal, including breakfast. Henry was on a diet, which he'd been on since Nixon was in the White House, so he was off carbs completely, save for the family-sized bags of Peanut M&M's he would devour after she'd gone to sleep at night. And although Annabel would have loved to shun bread, pasta, and rice for all eternity — perhaps then she'd be able to zip up that black dress — she'd found they were integral to both her sanity and her well-being.

"Right. Sure, I'll just do that. When does our slave arrive? Oh, wait a minute — she's here! And it's me!" Annabel laughed. Henry did not.

"Come on, stop it. No one thinks you're a slave," Henry groused, focusing his attention on a pack of shiny, sleek cars whipping around a track. It didn't make any sense to her. They were driving. That was all. Fine, so it was really, really fast driving. But where was the ball? The puck? The goal? There wasn't even a gritty fistfight to flinch through.

"Do you have any idea how much I've

already done today and how much there still is to do before my parents bring the kids back in a few hours?" Because once that happened, the house would turn into a circus. Quite literally. Okay, minus the live animals. Though Hudson had been begging for three dogs. Annabel wasn't sure why one wouldn't suffice, but he was pretty damn set on three. And, in thinking about it, hey, maybe they could charge for spectators. *Come one! Come all! Front row seats to see the crazy show at the Ford house!* She could even be convinced to throw in some microwave popcorn.

"I know, Annabel. You remind me every day." She didn't see him roll his eyes, but was fairly certain he had.

"I do not." Arms crossed. Affronted scowl.

"Whatever you say."

"Don't do that."

"What?" He sat up now, visibly riled.

"Placate me."

"How about this? Why don't you tell me what it will take for you to be quiet and let me watch my race?"

"Don't tell me to be quiet! All I'm trying to do is make sure everything gets done."

"I understand that, but does everything really have to be done before ten in the morning? We have the whole day."

"We do not have the whole day." Why didn't he see that? Didn't he know that it was impossible to even complete a thought when the kids were around? "Maybe, just maybe, you could set aside your race. And, wait — here's a revolutionary idea: help out!"

"Help with what?" Henry got up and tossed the remote onto the couch, as if to indicate *Now I'm up. I'm actually standing on my own two feet. I'm just that irritated. I've also paused the all-important race and thrown the remote. So, clearly, I mean business.*

"Everything."

"Annabel," he exhaled dramatically. "Unless you have something specific that needs to be done right now, please get off my back for once."

For once. "Well, you could start by making our bed."

"I'll make it when I go up to take a shower."

"Yes, of course. Why do now what you could do later?" *When we both know I'll have done it already.*

"For fuck's sake." He stomped back up the stairs, and for the next twenty minutes all she could hear was a lot of thumping about. Honestly, it wasn't that hard to make the bed.

■ ■ ■ ■

By the time Henry made a reappearance, Annabel had shoveled down half a bagel with butter and was surprised to find him showered, dressed, and toting a large suitcase. *Surprise vacation!* Maybe her parents were keeping the kids for another week while they jetted off to Cabo San Lucas for fish tacos and margaritas. She could already feel the warm breeze against her pallid skin and imagine her auburn highlights brightening beneath the blazing sun.

"Are you going somewhere?" She arched an eyebrow, which reminded her that she desperately needed to get them waxed. Hell, if they were heading to the beach, she'd throw in a bikini wax for good measure.

"I'm leaving." He looked down at their mahogany-stained hardwood floor.

"Leaving for what?"

"Nothing, Annabel. I'm just leaving," he said soberly, lifting his gaze to meet hers.

"You can't just run off for the night because you're annoyed that I want you to help out more around here rather than loiter about all day."

"It's not just that." He shook his head. "And it's not just for the night."

"Excuse me?" Instantly, she felt like her lungs had been pierced, stifling her ability to take in air.

"You're a miserable person, and I've had enough."

"Miserable? So, what? You want a *divorce?"* The word hung in the stagnant air like a marionette waiting for someone to coax it to life.

He nodded somberly.

"And you've packed all your things in the past half hour? You've just decided to destroy our life because you didn't want to make the bed? That's rich, Henry. Really rich."

"I've had the bag ready for some time." *Knife. Heart. All manner of blood and guts.*

"Some time?" Was her throat closing up? Was this what it felt like to be asphyxiated? "Exactly how long is *some time?"*

"I don't know, Annabel. Five, maybe six months?"

"Six months! You've been thinking about leaving me for *half a year?"* She shook her head frenetically. "We had sex last night!" Fine, so their last romp had probably been around the time he'd packed his divorce bag, but still. She suddenly felt icky. Had he been thinking about alternate accommodations as he'd nibbled on her nipples?

"On some level."

"This is ridiculous. I'm sorry but this is . . . It's just ridiculous." He inched toward the door, and panic set in. "What about the kids?"

"I'll call you later. We'll figure everything out." He was calm. Cool. Collected. He'd thought this through. Henry always thought things through. Important things.

"Wait." She lunged toward him. She wanted to pin him to the ground with her bare hands. To tell him he had to stay. To tell him that they were a family. And that no family was happy all the time. Marriages are work. Kids are tougher work. But they could work harder. She could work harder for all of them. Perhaps she had been complaining too much lately. It was just that she'd felt so exhausted and alone in her attempt to keep everyone's lives running smoothly. She'd force herself to relax more. Yes, that was it. Forced relaxation. Only none of those thoughts came out. Instead she said, "Are your brown slacks in that bag?"

"What?" He furrowed his brow.

"They've been missing for months. I thought maybe . . ."

"Jesus, Annabel." He shook his head disbelievingly.

23

"I'm just saying!" She'd searched high and low for those brown slacks. Why didn't he appreciate that?

"I'll be in touch." Henry walked toward the door without so much as a perfunctory kiss good-bye. Before leaving, he turned toward her. He was changing his mind. She knew it. He was going to sink his exhausted body back down into that sofa, put up his feet, and settle into his comfortable life once more. "And, Annabel, please don't try to manage this the way you do everything else. My mind is made up."

His mind was made up? What about her mind? Ten years of marriage and, just like that, he was prepared to toss her in the trash like a used tissue?

That was when it hit her. Beyond a shadow of a doubt. Henry was cheating. Because, honestly, why else would anyone leave someone who'd devoted her entire life to her family? Someone who worked hard every day with the interests of her husband and children at the forefront of her mind.

Suddenly Annabel had never been surer of anything in her life. The only question was, who was he cheating with?

Two

"I cleared out this whole chest and a big section of the closet, which really isn't that big, since the closet itself is tiny." Piper Whitley scurried around her bedroom, opening and closing drawers and shoving her own crumpled clothing haphazardly wherever it would fit. She wanted Todd to feel at home in her house, as if it was theirs together. "Do you think that'll be enough space? If not, I can probably purge some of my stuff."

She could definitely purge some of her stuff — most of it, actually, considering how half of it dated back to college, a time in her life when she was considerably fitter and at least ten pounds slimmer.

"There's plenty of room for my things," Todd assured her. She knew he hadn't brought over everything from his place. Not yet.

"You'd tell me if there wasn't, right?" she

asked anxiously.

"Come here." He waved her toward him and then placed one hand on each of her arms to steady her. "Relax. Take a deep breath. And remember this is a good thing."

"Says who?" Piper's ten-year-old daughter, Fern, appeared in the doorway.

"Who says what?" Piper turned toward her, hopeful that a quick but knowing glare would shut down her daughter's newly developed disdain toward her mother's boyfriend.

"Who says Todd moving in is a good thing?" She folded her arms across her chest petulantly. "I don't recall anyone asking my opinion."

Fern's apparent contempt for Piper's boyfriend was a new and unwelcome shift in their mother-daughter dynamic. Piper and Todd had been dating for over a year now and, at first, Piper had been pleasantly surprised by the ease with which he'd blended into their family of two. Fern had accepted Todd from the start. She'd been a willing and eager participant in the many activities he'd arranged in an attempt to form and later solidify their bond. Todd had taken her to see *The Nutcracker* last Christmas, only weeks into his relationship with Piper. He'd trailed Fern for hours at the library while she'd meandered up and down the stacks, showing him every one of her favorite books. And there were many. He'd even bought tickets to a New York Rangers game, making the hour-long drive each way into the city simply because she'd expressed a passing interest in the team. As it turned out, Fern was no more a fan of hockey than she was of any other sport. Like mother, like daughter.

Todd had fallen into the role of father figure with more grace and fluency than most real fathers Piper knew. And Fern had been his enthusiastic guinea pig, ready to try whatever new and interesting pursuit he suggested. Even eating rattlesnake, which, she'd confirmed, tasted just like chicken.

"No one asked your opinion? I'm so sorry about that. We definitely should have." Todd wasn't oblivious to Fern's distorted behavior. But, at the same time, it didn't make him uncomfortable and it hadn't scared him off. He was reasonable, rational, and evolved beyond Piper's expectations.

"Fern." Piper's tone was firm but not harsh. "We talked about this at great length."

"Yes, but telling someone something and asking their opinion are two different things. Am I right, Fern?" Todd winked at Piper when Fern wasn't looking.

"I guess," she grumbled. "I have home-work to do." Fern pivoted toward the door and stalked out with her arms still crossed.

"Dinner is in a half hour," Piper called after her, though she received no response.

"She just needs some time to process." Todd smiled, unruffled by Fern's ornery behavior.

Before Todd, Piper hadn't thought a man like him existed. And if he had, she certainly hadn't been involved with any of them.

There had been other boyfriends. A hand-ful who'd taken her out once, twice, even three times when Fern was a toddler. Still, Piper had been so young when she became a mother. Young enough that most of the men she'd met weren't keen on assuming the role of dad to a child who wasn't theirs. Of course, these were the same men who, a decade later, were probably divorced with a couple of kids of their own, and now it didn't seem odd at all to date a woman who was also a mom. Somehow her timing was always off. And, eventually, Piper had become perfectly content to be alone. Because, the fact was, with Fern by her side, she was never lonely.

When Todd had come along, things had felt different. Or maybe it was Piper who'd felt different. Either way, their connection had been instantaneous yet blissfully uncomplicated. He'd been so forthright that first night at a bar on Elm Street — the one that had been shut down a few months later, thanks to a rash of underage drinking. It was hard to remember why she'd even been out at a bar to begin with, even though it was only a year ago. Ah, yes, her colleague Kim's promotion party. How could she forget? Kim had been bumped up to features editor at the *Journal*, where Piper had been a crime-beat reporter for the past seven years. The new job had come with a lot of extra responsibility, which Piper had not envied, though she was well aware that Kim — a self-proclaimed lifelong bachelorette — was up for the challenge. What she had been jealous of was the bigger paycheck Kim could look forward to, which she'd maintained she was going to invest in a weeklong getaway to Cancún with twelve of her besties. Kim's declaration had only served to remind Piper that it wasn't easy being a single mom. Not that she really needed a reminder. There were no vacations to Mexico with her brood of besties. To be honest, there wasn't even a brood of besties to go anywhere with. Between working and parenting, finding time for friends hadn't been at the top of Piper's priority list.

That night Todd had sent her a vodka martini with three olives, her drink of choice. And then he'd waved from the other end of the bar, smiled genuinely, and pointed to himself and Piper, asking her permission to come introduce himself. She'd nodded and released a quiet squeal, because he was so distinguished-looking. Not her usual type, with his nearly black hair and equally dark eyes, but there'd been something so comforting about him. Something she knew she could trust.

Eleven months and a whirlwind romance later, Todd had moved in. He'd wanted Piper and Fern to come live with him in his three-story McMansion, which was at least four times the size of Piper's small yellow house with black shutters, but she'd explained that she could only subject Fern to so much change at once. He'd understood, but said he'd hold on to his house anyway. After all, he'd invested fifteen years in his private dentistry practice in order to be able to afford it. Maybe one day Piper would come around, or they'd sell it and buy a new home for all three of them. Until then, he'd insisted he was perfectly happy to move in with her and Fern, even if they didn't have flat-screen televisions in practically every room. It had finally felt like everything was falling into place.

Until things had shifted. Fern had started rebuffing Todd's offers to take her places, even to the bookstore, which was unheard of. She'd also begun ignoring him when he spoke to her, turning to her mother to reply instead. Her developing coolness toward Todd had been subtle at first, but ever since he'd taken up physical residence, things had gone from not great to downright intolerable far too quickly.

"I guess." Piper sighed. "I'm starving. How about you?"

"Famished. What do you say we go downstairs? I'll put the steaks in. You throw together a salad." Todd extended his hand for her to hold on to. Piper accepted it gratefully.

"Sounds like a plan." Her mouth curled into a smile, although she sensed it didn't really reach her eyes.

"Let's go around the table and say what we're thankful for." Piper straightened her posture, as her grandmother had taught her, and clasped her hands in front of her. "Why don't you start, Fern." She smiled affectionately at her daughter, whose shock of shaggy red hair framed her cherubic face, with its constellation of freckles. Perhaps the dark storm clouds surrounding her would begin to lift.

"Okay." She cleared her throat and sat upright, mimicking her mother. "I'm thankful for my book fair at school tomorrow. And my dog."

"Fern, you don't have a dog."

"Yes, I do. She's sitting right next to me. Isn't that right, Charlotte?" She nodded confidently before shoveling a heaping spoonful of rice pilaf into her mouth. "Just because you can't see her doesn't mean she's not real."

"Well, actually, it does mean that." Piper laughed effortlessly. Fern had been born with an overactive imagination, which — most of the time — worked to everyone's advantage. Like when they took long road trips, or at night when it was time to go to sleep. Unlike other children her age, her daughter was perfectly content to lie in silence, concocting convoluted stories in her head. Stories so elaborate that when she relayed them to Piper the following morning, it was hard to believe Fern hadn't pilfered them from an epic fairy tale. "But she seems like she's going to be a pretty easy pet, so I'm on board. Todd?"

"Absolutely! Can I get your little buddy a treat?"

Fern rolled her eyes. "She's not hungry."

"Okay. Well, then, we'll feed her later." Todd squeezed Piper's leg under the table.

"I'm thankful for two things," Piper spoke up, turning the attention away from Fern's satiated, not to mention bogus, dog. "Anyone have a guess?"

"I'm one!" Fern shouted, flaunting a punctured grin as she shot her arm to the ceiling. The tooth fairy had been working overtime lately. Teeth didn't come cheap these days. When Piper was growing up, she was certain that one dollar had been the going rate. Now the other kids in Fern's fifth-grade class were reporting cash earnings of twenty bucks a pop, which was way too steep for Piper's wallet. Of course, Todd always offered to pitch in, but they weren't there yet. She was more than happy to let him take on some of the household expenses, since they were, in fact, cohabitating now, but when it came to Fern, Piper still assumed the financial responsibility as hers and hers alone.

"You're right! How did you know?"

"Because you always say the same thing, Mom." She rolled her eyes again, though not in the same way as she had at Todd.

"What's the other thing?"

"The other thing isn't any more a thing than you are. It's Todd. I'm thankful that he's here with us and that we can all be a family."

Fern was silent. She'd always been a good girl. Never defiant or bratty, as so many of the other kids at her school were. Perhaps because of their circumstances, she'd matured faster than her years. If Fern's nose wasn't in a book, then she was researching something online such as brown recluse spiders or goblin sharks. She'd had an enduring obsession with Piper's favorite book since Piper had first read it to her as a child, mesmerized by the fact that she shared her name with one of the main characters — no coincidence there. To this day, Fern slept with the same stuffed pig she'd received as an infant and had named Wilbur as soon as she could speak. She'd declare to anyone who listened that *Charlotte's Web* was the key to all of life's most vital lessons, a hypothesis Piper never dared refute.

"I'm thankful for that too," Todd echoed. "But, most of all, I'm so grateful to have you in my life." He smiled at Fern.

"I'm not your daughter." She pushed her plate forward and stood up. "I'm tired. May

I please be excused?"

"Fern." Piper's voice was stern. "You have to finish your dinner."

"I'm not hungry." She stared down at her uneaten salad and a piece of steak with one bite cut out of it.

"It's okay." Todd nodded at Piper reassuringly. "If you want to go to bed, that's fine."

He may not have been the bearer of permission Fern had expected, but she seized the opportunity nonetheless, not bothering to say good night to either of them.

"I'm sorry." Piper placed her hand on top of Todd's.

"Go ahead." He motioned toward Fern's room with a tilt of his head. "She needs you."

"She can't just act this way."

"She can and she will. I'm pretty sure it's normal."

"You are amazing." Piper stood up, cupped Todd's face in her hands, and kissed him firmly on the lips. "What would I do without you?"

"You did just fine for thirty-plus years. Remember that."

"I love you. Give me five minutes."

Piper climbed the steps to Fern's room.

The door was slightly ajar. She'd expected to find Fern reading one of the many books that littered her shelves and the floor of the room. Again, like mother, like daughter. But she wasn't. Her body was coiled into a little ball, and all Piper could hear was the faint whistle of her breath. She moved toward her, sat down on the edge of the bed, and rubbed Fern's warm back. She would come around. She had to. They would find a way forward. Together.

"Mom?" Fern whispered.

"Yes, sweetie?"

She rolled toward her. "I need you to do something for me."

"What's that, baby?" Piper stroked Fern's flushed cheek and was quite certain, in that moment, that she would do anything to make her daughter happy. Anything at all.

"I need you to find Dad."

Anything but that.

It had been one of those mornings. The arctic chill from outside was too formidable an opponent for the heat, which was cranking and grinding tirelessly in an effort to overtake it. Piper had lingered under the steam of the shower until her fingers were shriveled like sun-dried tomatoes, all too aware that as soon as she turned off the

36

faucet there would be those grueling seconds, minutes even, between the refuge of the hot water and the insulation of her reliable black cashmere sweater.

Fern hadn't mentioned her biological father again. Maybe she'd forgotten all about it. About him. Was that what Piper really wanted? To erase him from their history? One dad out. Another, much more suitable and reliable "dad" in. It had all been going so well. There were even days she could almost forget he'd ever existed. Almost.

It wasn't as though she thought Fern deserved to grow up without knowing the man who was responsible for half of her genetic makeup; it was that she thought he didn't deserve to know her. Or to be a part of her life in any tangible way. Not that he'd offered. Not that she'd heard from him since last year around this time, just before Thanksgiving; three years had passed before that. He'd sent an e-mail saying he was on a ship in the South Pacific and that, if he had the opportunity, he'd try to send Fern something for Christmas. Piper hadn't bothered to mention it to Fern, since his promises were notoriously empty. And by the time she'd tried to write back a few days later, his account had been shut down.

Unfortunately, this was the most contact Piper had ever had with Max, since the day he'd left. For Fern's part, she'd never even seen her father in person. Not even a photograph.

When Fern was younger, Piper would purchase one elaborate gift each year and set it under the Christmas tree, affixing a tag that read, *Love, Daddy.* Without fail, it had always been Fern's favorite present. And, at some point, this had begun to irk Piper. Why should this man who'd never so much as changed a diaper or been projectile-vomited on in the supermarket get to be the hero? *She* was the hero. The heroine. *Whatever.* Either way, it was a lie. She was deceiving her daughter in order to dull the inherent pain that came with having a father who'd fled for the hills shortly after she'd been conceived.

She'd never told Fern the details. Only that her dad loved her and that he had important business traveling the globe. The business of having no accountability — she'd left that part out. And Fern, to her credit and possibly to Piper's, had never once showed any signs of feeling abandoned. Until now, she'd never even expressed an interest in meeting him. Sure, Piper had known the day would come, although she'd secretly hoped it would turn out to be years away.

Her sole purpose in life had been to make sure Fern always had enough love. To make sure that she loved her for both of them. But yet here they were. Fern's tortuous request. If only she understood it wasn't that easy.

Piper pushed through the front door of her office building, as Bernie the doorman came running toward her.

"Who's da bomb?" He held up his hand for a high five, and Piper slapped it, giggling at the same time.

"Me?"

"That's right, little lady." He smiled magnanimously.

"Not so little these days." She patted her stomach.

"You're crazy! You're one hot number!"

Piper laughed. Bernie had been working there for at least twice as long as she had. If he'd ever had a bad day, he'd never let on. She'd once asked him how it was possible that he was so happy all the time. He'd just shrugged and said, "I guess I got nothin' to complain about." Of course, Piper knew very little about Bernie's personal life, except that he had two teenage daughters and that his wife had passed away about five years ago, which couldn't have been easy. Not to mention that he probably wasn't commanding a hefty salary while opening doors and buzzing in visitors. Yet he always had a smile on his face and a skip in his step. Piper thought about her own circumstances. She was a single mom, but still. She had a steady job, only one child, and a significant other who was devoted to both her and Fern. Regardless, it seemed like there was always something to gripe about — whether the garbage disposal was on the fritz *again* or, you know, your daughter asked you to find her wayward father.

She took the elevator up three floors and headed straight for her office, bowing her head so that Chatty Jenny — her colleague Rachel's assistant — wouldn't try to cut her off at the pass for an exhaustive discussion about some trashy reality-TV show Piper would have to deny watching. She'd received an e-mail that morning from her boss saying there'd been a rash of robberies the previous night and that Piper had a lot of work on her hands to make sure all the details were in place for her article, which would go to press at five o'clock — not a minute later. She'd have to interview the victims, locate any witnesses, and pay a visit to each crime scene. For now, she shucked off her puffy winter jacket and wrangled her stubborn dark brown curls into a style she hoped resembled a ponytail.

"You look stressed." Her protégée, Lucy, stood in her doorway with a steaming mug of coffee.

"That's exactly how I feel." Piper motioned to the chair opposite her. "Come. Sit. Please tell me that's for me." She motioned to the cup.

"Of course." Lucy placed it on Piper's desk and sat down. "What's on the agenda today?"

"You don't even want to know." Piper circled her head slowly in either direction, straining to get rid of a crick in her neck.

"What's going on there, Stevie Wonder?"

Piper nearly spit out her coffee. "Funny. I must have slept on it in some weird way, during the few hours I actually slept."

"Uh-oh. That doesn't sound auspicious. Tired Piper equals cranky Piper."

"And I didn't have time to eat because I was late getting Fern to school."

"Oooooh! Double whammy. Tired and hungry Piper equals all hell breaking loose. Can I get you something at the food truck down the street? They make a mean breakfast burrito."

"Really? What's in it?"

"Who knows? Who cares? It tastes like heaven in a wrap."

"Good sell. I'm in." She reached into her purse for her wallet and handed Lucy a twenty-dollar bill. "Buy one for yourself too. My treat."

"Thanks, but I'm on a strict diet. Anything else I can do for you?"

She'd never heard Lucy mention trying to lose weight before, not in the two years they'd been working together. She was one of those people who wore her extra padding well. A little here, a little there, a little more in the rear. She had pretty features and nice long, thick wavy blond hair.

Piper cleared her throat. "Now that you mention it . . ."

"Yeah?"

"I was hoping you could help me out with something." Piper trusted Lucy implicitly. After all, she'd proved herself time and time again. "Something personal."

"Sure, anything."

"Excellent." Piper exhaled, releasing the tension that had her shoulders at her ears. "I need you to help me find Fern's dad."

THREE

Annabel sat, wearing only her underwear and a sports bra, on the edge of her bed with her pale, flabby legs flung over one side. All she had to do was wriggle into her workout clothes, lace up her sneakers, and drive to class. Seemingly simple tasks and ones that she'd been executing for the past eight weeks, ever since she'd committed to a new exercise regimen — every-other-day barre classes, a body-sculpting combination of ballet, yoga, and Pilates — come hell or high water. It was hard to say what had motivated her after so many years of doing absolutely nothing to raise her heartbeat beyond the mad rush of getting her boys off to school in the morning.

Today she'd cried when the bus had pulled away. Hot, bulbous tears. The kind that sprang without warning. The kind you couldn't squelch without diverting your mind to something benign, like getting dressed. This was new to her. Even on Harper and Hudson's first day of kindergarten she hadn't been nearly this distraught. And every day after that had felt like cause for a minor celebration — seven whole hours with no one to yank on her shirt, asking for more milk or begging her to help them construct yet another skyscraper out of Magna-Tiles. Only now their departure felt like an affront. Why did everyone have to leave her?

The kids had no idea what was going on with her and Henry. He'd wanted to explain things to them, but she'd balked, insisting it was way too early to involve them. What if Henry decided he'd made a mistake? He said he wouldn't. What if he missed his home? His children? What if he missed *her*? He'd reiterated that his decision was final and, surprisingly, the sting of rejection was no less excruciating the second time around.

That was when she'd gotten angry and started taunting him with threats they both knew she'd never follow through with. *I'll fight for full custody,* she'd avowed. Then she'd practically spit at him, *You'll never see your sons.* Annabel had cringed, detecting the pointed cruelty in her own voice. Was she capable of using their children as pawns to punish Henry? For no other reason than that he'd excluded her in his decision to bulldoze everything she'd worked so hard to construct? For him. For all of them. She didn't think so. But sometimes the depth of her indignation over being jilted so suddenly and definitively consumed her. And, in those moments, she thought she might be capable of just about anything.

Why had she promised Piper she'd meet her for class this morning? Her body ached from thrashing about restlessly in her king-sized bed, which had once felt like limited space. Now, without Henry by her side, she was like a tick on a horse's back: there was so much surface area that all she wanted to do was needle her way into a comfortable fold. Piper had been the one person she'd confided in about Henry's game-time exodus. They'd been friends for only about two months, since they'd met at the opening of the new barre studio in town. They'd hit it off immediately by grimacing and griping about the women whose emaciated physiques belied their inherent bone structures, and the ones who could drop down into a split with the ease of sitting in a chair. After their first session, Piper had asked Annabel to grab a coffee at the café next door, and they'd been doing so regularly ever since.

The thing was, Piper wasn't really the sort

of person Annabel was typically drawn to. She was often disheveled and, while she clearly loved her job as a crime reporter, Annabel had observed that Piper didn't possess the sort of ambition Annabel had once worn like a badge of honor when she'd been vice president of marketing for a fine-jewelry conglomerate. When Annabel had asked Piper where she saw her career headed, she'd replied that once upon a time it had been her dream to work as a producer on *America's Most Wanted* or some equally grisly show, but that the combination of her responsibilities to Fern and her ever-growing debt had forced her to set aside her own goals. Annabel had wanted to encourage her, though she'd realized it might appear hollow coming from someone who hadn't been employed by anyone other than her own family in more than five years.

She was practically a different person now than she'd been half a decade ago. She'd had nothing to focus on back then, beyond her career and a husband who'd toiled to build his technology company from the ground up. Those had been the days. Annabel had thrived on the pressure; she'd marinated in the Kool-Aid of shared misery with her colleagues. The workdays had stretched longer and longer until finally there'd been little distinction between one day ending and another beginning. The last-minute international flights out of Newark at six in the morning, which had required her to be up, alert, and out the door no later than three — an ungodly hour to inhale frozen waffles in a taxi cab. And, finally, the verbal abuse from a team of executives who'd always expected more, no matter how much of yourself you'd applied to the job.

How many Thanksgivings and Christmases had she and Henry willingly forsaken in the name of their skyrocketing careers? How many times had she let her parents down? Parents who'd said they understood, but could never truly fathom the intensity of her passion, the way it seared her from within, and the sudden rushes of handling marketing catastrophes that she metabolized like a ravenous pit bull.

In the early days, before Henry, even months after they'd been dating, the idea of marriage and children had terrified her. Annabel had viewed them as obstructions, even nuisances, that would inevitably stunt her ascending mobility. More to the point, she hadn't been remotely concerned about the internal clock that seemed to plague her female coworkers with its tick, tick, ticking until many of them had settled for their not-so—Prince Charmings, in exchange for an appropriately sized engagement ring and the promise of never being dubbed an old maid.

Then Henry had proposed. And she'd told herself they would wait years to have kids. Until she'd gotten pregnant after she'd quite unintentionally forgotten to renew her prescription for birth-control pills. The irony being that she'd forgotten because she'd been overwhelmed by a major project at work. When her obstetrician had announced, "Congratulations, you're having twins," Annabel had felt like her whole world was imploding, though she'd never let on. She'd mustered a wide smile and immediately started trying to piece together how she was going to make it all happen. Other women did it. Other women who had bigger careers than she did and more than two children, in some cases. She would hire a team of baby nurses and nannies. Whatever it took.

By the time Harper and Hudson had made their way into the world, she'd had an infallible plan in place, one that would entail comprehensive maneuvering and multiple hands on deck, but it was a plan nonetheless. Then she'd held her babies in her arms and, like the parting of the Red Sea, in an instant she'd recognized her plan was entirely wrong — a realization that had both delighted and frightened Henry. He'd admitted that all along he'd hoped she would come around. He'd said that he'd yearned for Annabel to be the kind of mother to their children that his own mother had never been to him. Not because she'd been married to her career, but because she'd been a raging alcoholic who could only be counted on to show up at school reeking of gin. Suddenly, and quite unexpectedly, she'd wanted to be the perfect mother *and wife.* For him. And for herself. That had been the unexpected part.

And now, after five years of devoting herself to her husband and children with the same fierce dedication she had to her burgeoning career, he'd up and left. Without so much as a thank-you for establishing and maintaining the beautiful life they'd built. The beautiful life *she'd* built for all of them. She was disoriented. Henry's abrupt departure had rendered her useless. The gaping fissure in her family structure had left her unsure of her role, not only as a wife and mother, but also as a person. And Annabel couldn't stand for that. She needed a whole new plan. A clear direction with which to forge ahead. Either that, or she feared she might stay lost forever.

"Okay, before we discuss what's going on with you, can we please talk about the chick in the front whose arms looked like Hulk Hogan's?" Piper slipped off her rain slicker as she spoke and hung it on the back of her chair.

"The ripped one with the fake tan and the white tank top?" Annabel smiled knowingly. They'd learned quickly that there were women in their class who had staked their claims to certain spots. Spots that were not meant to be taken by newbies. Piper had made that mistake early on. There'd been a real hubbub about it, including a few malevolent glares.

Piper motioned to the waitress. "I don't know about you, but I'm famished. I'm thinking eggs and bacon."

"They take forever with the cooked stuff. Don't you have to get to work at some point?" Annabel was well aware that Piper's hours were anything but regular, but somehow it still made her anxious that she didn't need to be at her desk before nine.

"At some point, yes. I was on location until two in the morning and then had to get up at six to help Fern get ready for school." Her stomach grumbled. "Thus these lovely black circles under my eyes."

"Please. Don't even talk to me about black circles. Do you see this puffiness?" She pointed to the socket under her eyes and then pinched the fragile skin between her thumb and index finger.

"Would you stop? That'll only make it worse!" Piper swatted at Annabel's forearm and then motioned to the waitress, who was standing idly in the corner, intermittently checking her cell phone.

"What can I get for you ladies?" She'd made her way over to them reluctantly.

"I'm going to do one of those fruit-smoothie things and a fat-free oat bran muffin." Annabel snapped her menu shut before noticing Piper's bulky hand-knit scarf, which was spattered in what appeared to be congealed food. She made a mental note to buy her a new one for Christmas.

"You're a better woman than I am." Piper looked up at the waitress. "I'll do the eggs Benedict with a side of honey sausage. And hash browns. Black coffee, please. As strong as possible."

"Good for you." Annabel nodded. She'd never been able to eat that way without inflating like a hot-air balloon. Piper, on the other hand, seemed to indulge in whatever she was craving at the moment and somehow managed to remain in decent shape. She wasn't quite thin, but she didn't need to lose more than, say, ten pounds — much like everyone else in the world — to achieve an enviable figure. If Annabel didn't like Piper so well, she might have felt resentful toward her.

"I wouldn't go that far, but I have too many other things to think about than dieting. Plus, doesn't this class burn, like, eight hundred calories? That should knock out the sausage and potatoes, no?"

"I'd say so." Annabel took off her own jacket now. She was always cold, but the heat generating from the close-packed quarters had warmed her. It was something she and Henry had always struggled over. He liked the thermostat at sixty-six. She preferred it at seventy-three, seventy-five if she really had her way. Unfortunately, the boys took after their father, so she'd been outnumbered for three solid years — since they, too, could express their penchants.

"Now that we've ordered, give me the scoop. How are you doing with everything?" Piper propped her elbows on the table and leaned forward.

"Better, I guess." Annabel shrugged.

"That's *great.*"

"Actually, that's a lie." Annabel covered

her face with her hands and then dropped them into her lap again. "I'm miserable. Angry. Hurt. Pissed. Furious. Sometimes even vengeful. It's a lot of fun."

"It sounds it." Piper exhaled. "How about the kids?"

"They don't know yet. Henry wants to tell them, but . . ."

"But what?"

"I just think it's too soon."

"You have to do what feels right to you." The waitress returned with her coffee and Annabel's strawberry-colored smoothie. "Although, haven't they asked where Henry is?"

"Not really. I keep making stuff up before they have the chance. And then I have to e-mail Henry to get him to corroborate, which he doesn't seem to appreciate."

"That sucks."

"Ya think?" Annabel bent her straw into her mouth and sucked hard to imbibe the dense liquid. "The worst part is that I don't really understand why he left in the first place. It was like everything was completely normal one minute, and then the next he was toting his already-packed suitcase out the door."

"He hasn't offered any explanation?" Piper sipped her coffee.

"Not much. He said he's sick and tired of living in my world. That I always have to control everything, and he feels like he can't breathe."

"Okay. Does that resonate with you?"

"No! Not at all. He thinks we live in *my* world? All I do every day is run around getting things done for him and the kids. How is it *my* world to be grocery shopping, picking up *his* dry cleaning, getting the kids on the bus in the morning, picking them up in the middle of the afternoon, and chauffeuring them around to their various extracurricular activities, only to come home and bathe them before making dinner?" Annabel huffed. "All he has to do is shower, dress himself, saunter out the door, and return ten hours later to a perfectly tidy house with everything in its place."

"Maybe he feels left out because he's not around as much as you are?"

"Is that cause to leave someone?" Annabel raised her voice and then, aware of her intimate proximity to their neighbors at the next table, lowered it again. "I'm sorry, but it's maddening."

"It sounds like it." One of the runners appeared with Piper's eggs Benedict and Annabel's muffin. "Don't forget the sausage and hash browns, please." He nodded vaguely and scurried off to relay her message.

"That's why I need your help." Annabel's expression hardened.

"I'm so sorry I've been distracted with work and stuff with Fern."

"Oh no. Don't get me wrong. You've been an amazing sounding board." She looked down. "It's something else. Something your line of work uniquely qualifies you for."

"What? Anything." Piper bobbed her head feverishly, and Annabel was buoyed by her new friend's immediate loyalty. It felt like so many of the other women she called friends — the moms at Harper and Hudson's school and the few former coworkers she still kept up with — were fair-weather. They were there when the sun was shining bright, but as soon as there was even a threat of rain, they scuttled away, pretending to be too busy with their own lives to take an interest in hers.

"I need you to catch Henry cheating on me."

"What makes you think he's cheating on you?" Piper's eyes widened.

"It's the only explanation that makes sense. And there have been a lot of late nights in the past few months." She'd been chastising herself for being so credulous.

Had she really become one of *those women*? The ones who went on talk shows and swore they'd had no idea their husband was stepping out on them, despite the fact that every shirt collar of his had been stamped with a lipstick shade that wasn't theirs.

"Annabel, you know I'd love to help you. It's just that . . ."

"What?"

"It seems like a conflict of interest, don't you think? I mean, wouldn't you rather hire a private detective or something? They're trained for this kind of thing. I can get you names."

"No. I need someone I can really trust. Someone like you."

"As much as I appreciate your faith in me, I'm not sure . . ."

"Listen, I know it's a tall order, but if there's any way you can see to help, I'd be forever indebted to you."

"I'm not saying yes, but, in theory, what if I did find something?"

"Right?" Annabel could tell that Piper was warming to the idea already.

"Are you sure you'd want to know?"

"Absolutely," she insisted. Although she hadn't given much thought to that piece of it.

"People always think they do, but then

they shoot the messenger. Or they regret it, like . . ."

"Like what?" Annabel leaned in closer, as if Piper was about to divulge a delicious secret.

"I was going to say like Fern will." Instinctively, Piper clenched her teeth.

"Fern, as in your daughter?"

"You got it." Piper sighed. "Apparently, she's decided she wants me to track down her father."

"Oh, wow." Annabel was momentarily distracted from her own onerous situation. She knew this couldn't be easy for Piper.

"*Oh, wow* is right! I mean, what the hell am I supposed to do with that?"

"That's a tough one." Annabel sympathized. "Kind of damned if you do and damned if you don't."

"Right. And that's exactly what I'm saying to you. Are you certain beyond a shadow of a doubt that you'd want to know if Henry is cheating? I just think some things are better left —"

"Piper." Annabel cut her off.

"Yeah?"

"I've never been so sure of anything in my entire life."

"Okay," Piper conceded.

"Then you'll do it?" Annabel's heart was

already thumping in anticipation.

"Let me look into it."

"Thank you! You have no idea how much this means to me."

"I'm not making any promises, though." She smiled slyly. "But if there's something to find, I'll find it."

"That's what I'm counting on."

FOUR

Mackenzie scrutinized her reflection in the antique vanity mirror suspended above her tempered-glass sink. She cupped one breast in each hand, balancing them in her palms like cantaloupes, and then applied the slightest pressure, as if to gauge their ripeness. Could they be tender? She poked and prodded some more. It was early yet — only day twenty-four of her cycle — but she had a feeling. A woman's instinct, if you will. This month would make nearly three full years of trying.

"Lucky number three," she whispered, even though there was no one around to hear her. Perhaps releasing it into the universe would be enough.

Trevor was already in the kitchen, reading the morning edition of the *Journal,* one of the many newspapers and magazines his family business, Mead Media, published. Any minute now, she'd catch him shaking his head and grimacing over yet another careless typo. She wondered if the errors actually niggled him the way they seemed to or if it was more about the fear instilled by his mother, Cecilia, that everything must be polished to perfection. *I will not have the good name I've worked so hard to build be tarnished by incompetent people.* It was her trademark refrain, especially when barked in that familiar husky voice with her finger pointed high in the air and an obdurate expression shrouding her ageless face.

Mackenzie clasped her eyes shut and, this time, squeezed her breasts even harder. Next she inspected her nipples. All of the pregnancy websites she'd referred to for research had listed darkening of the areolas as one of the early signs of conception. They did look a shade browner. Maybe.

Finally, fed up with speculating, she surrendered to the unknown. After all, she couldn't test for a few more days. Or maybe she could. She shuddered at the thought of how much money she'd spent on those little cardboard boxes, so full of promise. There were so many women out there who couldn't afford to simply pop into their local drugstore and buy a dozen tests at a time. She'd been one of those women before Trevor. But he didn't seem to mind. If anything, he'd encouraged her to do whatever it took to have a belly full with the heir to the Mead fortune.

How many times had she envisioned that moment? The one where she'd finally get the answer she was so determined to have: two straight pink parallel lines as clear as a cloudless day. She'd always been so close with her own mother that having a child would continue that same cherished bond, and was something Mackenzie had been looking forward to for as long as she could remember. She planned to teach her daughter (or son) how to cook and sew, the way her own mom had taught her. And to read and snuggle with her kids every night in bed until they were too old to cuddle, if that day ever came. For her part, whenever Mackenzie went home, she still relished curling up with her mother on the couch. It had been their way since she was old enough to abandon her crib. She'd also vowed to be a present and attentive parent, as had her own mother, someone her kids could come to with anything, without fear of being judged. Wasn't an open line of communication the most important thing in any relationship?

Mackenzie willed herself not to reach into the cabinet, to hold out at least one more day. The sheer anticipation of waiting while the hourglass contemplated her fate was enough to fracture her tenuously positive disposition. She couldn't cope with a negative result today — she had a desk at the office piled high with papers and reports, all of which would need her immediate attention. Then there was a stream of conference calls leading up to a late-afternoon meeting with her mother-in-law. And for that she'd need to be at the top of her game. Every encounter with CeCe — whether personal or professional — required razor-sharp attentiveness and the focus of a brain surgeon performing a lobotomy.

She pulled a black ribbed tank top over her head, coiled her wavy blond hair into a knot, and wandered downstairs to the kitchen, hoping to distract herself with sustenance.

"Hey, honey." She smiled at her husband, who was predictably hunched over the *Journal,* which was splayed in front of him on their oak pedestal table, a wedding gift from her parents.

"Would you believe this?" Trevor grumbled, flattening a crease in the page with his hand. "They switched the headlines. Unbelievable. My mother is going to be apoplectic."

"Let me see." She walked over and sat

down beside him.

"Right here." He indicated one article and then the next.

"Oh, wow." She couldn't help but laugh at the irony, even though she concurred with Trevor that CeCe would be outraged. "They used 'A Walk in the Bark' for the beauty-pageant piece and 'Gowns and Crowns' for the one about the annual dog show. Not good."

"That's an understatement." He pressed his fingertips to his temples.

"How about some eggs and grits to make you feel better?" Mackenzie had long prided herself on her culinary skills. Having grown up in the Deep South — Georgia, to be precise — she knew her way around corn bread, fried chicken, dumplings, peaches, and most every kind of seafood. When she and Trevor had first started dating, he'd gained at least fifteen pounds and had insisted he'd be absolutely fine with being a fat old man, as long as she kept on cooking. And there was nothing a chef appreciated more than some good, old-fashioned flattery.

"That sounds great. Maybe a little turkey bacon?"

"Sure, no problem." *Turkey* bacon. She'd come around to accepting it as a suitable enough replacement for the real thing, even though she'd been raised rendering fat. At some point, Trevor had decided that indulging in the many delicacies she whipped up would not be an ideal recipe for lifelong health. Unlike her, he didn't know how to eat in moderation; it was either all or nothing. Surprising, given that CeCe certainly did not approve of gluttony.

"Glass of orange juice too, please." He looked up at her for just a moment and then went back to dissecting the paper.

Mackenzie smiled at him affectionately. Theirs wasn't a rip-your-clothing-off, all-consuming kind of love — she understood that. Still, she cared for him deeply and he for her. He never raised his voice or questioned a single decision she made. Trevor could always be counted on to produce a sparkling bauble at Christmas-time, two dozen of the reddest roses for Valentine's Day, and a fur or cashmere something or other when her birthday rolled around. He was a good husband. Solid in every way. So what if she wasn't desperate to pin him to the bed and have her way with him?

There had been too many jerks like that before him. The guys who lured you like an addiction and then discarded you when someone younger and perkier — someone more eager — emerged.

When she'd been introduced to Trevor by her college roommate, Zoe — another trust-fund baby — at a posh charity gala in New York City shortly after graduating, she hadn't been interested at first. Sure, he was cuteish, in a Michael J. Fox sort of way, with his shaggy brown hair and affable blue eyes. Still, he'd lacked that sensual, brooding posture she'd become accustomed to. Mackenzie had given him her number when he'd asked politely and, as she'd expected, he'd called the next day and every day after that, until he'd proposed with a six-carat cushion-cut diamond ring over a four-hour-long dinner at Le Cirque, one of Manhattan's finest restaurants. A month later, he'd announced that they were moving to the suburbs — to a five-bedroom home on six plush acres. Mackenzie would have to leave her position as an assistant producer at ABC News, but — not to worry, he'd assured her — there would be a job waiting for her at Mead. A job that, despite her initial hesitation to shift career paths, she'd come to both love and take great pride in.

Their wedding had been one for the storybooks, with everything executed by a celebrity planner to meet CeCe's meticulous stipulations and desires. Mackenzie had been so swept up in the glamour and extravagance of it all that she hadn't even thought to express her own needs and wants on anything beyond the dress, a Vera Wang strapless ball gown with intricately woven beading covering the satin bodice and with an abundance of lace and tulle.

It hadn't been until about a month or two after their honeymoon in the south of France that CeCe had started talking about a grandson. Oddly, the fact that no one had any control over the sex of their unborn child didn't seem to matter. She never once spoke of tutus, bows, or ballet classes. Only of a shrewd little boy to preserve the family name, a name she herself had married into.

Mackenzie carried a full plate of food and a glass of juice over to the kitchen table and set it down in front of Trevor.

"This looks delicious." She leaned over so he could kiss her on the cheek. "You've always known the way to my heart is through my stomach." He picked up a piece of bacon. "How *do* you manage to get it so crispy?"

"I'll never divulge my secret." She rubbed his back. "I'm going to get dressed."

"You're not joining me?"

"I'll grab a bagel on our way out." The truth was, she wasn't that hungry. And even the enticing smell of her own home cooking hadn't been enough to distract her from the inevitable.

She headed straight upstairs to their bathroom, retrieved the pregnancy test from the cabinet, and tore it open before she could convince herself otherwise.

Maybe today she'd get her two lines.

Mackenzie stood outside CeCe's office with the poise of a saluting officer and rapped loudly on the door. Her mother-in-law had informed her on day one of the job that a firm knock was like a firm handshake and that anything short of that was *unacceptable.* It was probably the word she used most often. *The quality of the lettuce in this salad is* unacceptable. *So-and-so's snarky attitude and unwillingness to be a team player are* unacceptable. *Everything and everyone, with the exception of those I approve of, are* unacceptable. Mackenzie wasn't sure how she'd managed to fall within CeCe's classification of what was, in fact, acceptable, but she felt grateful.

"You may enter." Her gruff roar pierced the feverish rumpus in the newsroom, and Mackenzie complied, closing the door quickly behind her.

"Hello, CeCe." She'd once — and only once — made the mistake of calling her Mom, as her own mother had asked of Trevor. All CeCe'd had to do was widen her buglike eyes and purse her glossy lips in order to convey to Mackenzie the error of her ways, further indicating that a second gaffe would be *unacceptable.*

"Hello, darling," she rasped, and swiveled around in her high-back chair. She was wearing an all-white, figure-hugging Chanel suit with crisscrossed gold Cs for buttons. Her straight red hair was cropped into a chin-length bob, and her heavy bangs evoked Anna Wintour — not an easy style to carry off.

Mackenzie thought back to the time in tenth grade when the barber in the small city she'd grown up in had convinced her to get bangs. He'd said they would complement her heart-shaped face. He'd been wrong. And she'd cried for three weeks leading up to the school dance, when her mother, in a fit of desperation, had found a way to clip them to the side. She still cringed whenever she looked back at the photos.

"You wanted to meet with me?" Mackenzie couldn't help but notice CeCe's four-inch, nude patent-leather stilettos with their gold spiked heels, no doubt coordinated to the buttons on her suit. Not to mention the scintillating pair of gold and diamond stud earrings piercing her lobes. And then there was Aspen, her miniature poodle, situated on his plush dog bed beside her. Despite Aspen's size, he'd taken it upon himself to adopt the personality of a hundred-pound guard dog, snarling at anybody who came within three feet of his master. Not that anyone would dare to complain. Sometimes Mackenzie thought CeCe loved Aspen more than she loved her own son.

"Yes. Sit down." She motioned to one of the smooth leather chairs on the other side of her sleek lacquer desk. Mackenzie had often wondered how she kept everything so immaculate — from her clothing to her furniture.

"If this is about the marketing report," Mackenzie started, well aware that she was ahead of schedule on delivery, as she always was. She was dedicated to her job. Wholly devoted, actually. While she'd probably have been a great television producer, Mackenzie savored the hands-on creativity involved in cultivating a nugget of an idea into a comprehensive plan. She thrived on the pressure of managing a large team, ingesting their feedback, and then working together to realize their ultimate goal: to shepherd Mead Media into the twenty-first century. Although some people probably speculated otherwise, Mackenzie was more than the wife of Trevor or the daughter-in-law of CeCe. She may not have earned her position in the traditional way, but she worked as hard as anyone else at the company.

CeCe held up her hand, and Mackenzie stopped speaking abruptly. "This isn't work related." She cleared her throat.

"Oh?" Mackenzie noticed a new snapshot of Aspen bedecked in a fur coat on the credenza behind CeCe. She'd placed it front and center, upstaging a glossy photograph of CeCe flanked by Gwyneth Paltrow and Madonna, their arms entwined like best girlfriends. And an eight-by-ten of her dancing with Barack Obama.

"I was at the American Cancer Society gala at Cipriani last night."

"Oh, right. I'm sorry we missed that," she lied.

"Yes, as am I." CeCe pressed her lips into a thin line. "At any rate, I met a lovely gentleman — Dr. Stanley Billingsly. Very charming. We got to talking, and it just so happens he's the leading fertility specialist in New York City."

"Oh?"

"I'm certain he could help you." She slid Dr. Billingsly's card across her desk.

"Thank you."

"I'm concerned," CeCe continued. "As I'm sure you're aware, or at least I hope you are, it's been three years, and here I am, still without a grandson to spoil."

"I know." Mackenzie's hand went instinctively to her stomach. "We're working on it." It was a slippery slope deciding how much information to divulge to CeCe.

"Well, if there's a *problem* . . ." She strummed her manicured red nails on the desk as she awaited Mackenzie's response.

"I don't think there is." Although she had wondered the same thing.

"Have you thought about" — she paused, presumably searching for the most clinical word she could come up with — "intervention?"

"Not really. I mean, I'm still pretty young. You know, I'm not even thirty yet."

"Youth may not have anything to do with it." She took a small sip from her glass of Perrier with three limes. Always three limes. Two bobbing around in the Perrier; one on the rim. "Call Dr. Billingsly."

"I'm not sure that'll be necessary. I bet we'll have good news very soon."

71

"Well, I certainly hope so." CeCe stood up, indicating that Mackenzie should do the same and that their brief conversation was over.

"Me too." She smiled, well aware that the gesture wouldn't be reciprocated. Having been dismissed, she walked toward the door to leave.

"Oh, and, Mackenzie."

"Yes?" She turned back around.

"I hope you realize that anything else would be" — she cleared her throat — *"unacceptable."*

FIVE

Why on earth had Piper ever told Annabel she'd help investigate her husband? *Why?* Nothing good could come of it. Nothing at all. If she did, in fact, catch him in the act of cheating or anything resembling it — which she would, if there was any truth to Annabel's speculation — Piper worried Annabel would unwillingly resent her. Of course she'd *said* she wouldn't shoot the messenger. That she would be profoundly grateful if Piper uncovered something — *anything.* It had almost sounded as if she'd wanted her husband to be an adulterer. Still, Piper had been down this road before. Not with a friend, and certainly not with someone she'd met only months earlier, although she and Annabel had clicked immediately. But with her own aunt — her mother's older sister — who was practically like a second mother to Piper.

She'd never forget the day her aunt Claire

had shown up at their front door, her face stained with tears, her hands balled into tight fists, wearing an expression that conveyed fear, anger, shame, and bewilderment. They'd later found out that her husband, Bob, Piper's favorite uncle, had been having an affair with her aunt's best friend of fifteen years and that there was a distinct possibility that her friend's youngest daughter was Bob's child. Fortunately, DNA testing had later proven otherwise, but her aunt didn't care. All she could focus on was the lacerating betrayal. She'd lived with Piper's family for six months until the divorce had been finalized, sleeping in the bedroom next to Piper's. If ever she'd actually slept. All Piper could remember was overhearing her heaving sobs and occasional cursing fits through their thin walls. She'd felt powerless in her desire to ease her aunt's pain, to put an end to her misery.

Perhaps that was part of the reason she wanted to support Annabel now. Even though she'd never been able to rescue her aunt, she was suddenly in a position where she could help someone in a similar predicament.

Annabel didn't seem like the sort of person who would direct her wrath at Piper. She was much too refined and uptight for

that, though it was hard to say what someone would do in the heat of rage. For her
own part, she'd lost her temper with Fern
on a few occasions when a sudden swell of
frustration had gotten the best of her. Now,
in hindsight, she realized that in those moments she'd felt out of control, unable to
prevent herself from snapping at her daughter. Of course, she'd never laid a hand on
her and never would. Still, the realization
that a switch could be flipped just like that
was humbling.

She sat cross-legged at her computer.
Todd was downstairs, watching some legal
drama, and Fern had gone to sleep hours
earlier, clutching her tattered copy of *Charlotte's Web* — with its many earmarked
pages, highlighted passages, and notes in
the margins. Tonight Piper had sat at the
edge of Fern's bed and watched her until
she'd fallen asleep, inching closer to stroke
her cheek and then her head. Finally, as
she'd felt herself drifting off in an upright
position, she'd placed the softest peck on
Fern's button nose and resigned herself to
her office to get some work done. Only she
hadn't been able to concentrate. Instead,
she'd started looking for Max. Her Max.
Not anymore, though he was still Fern's
father, at least by blood. He was also the

only man who'd shredded her heart with his absence.

Two hours later, she'd turned up nothing — a galling reality for someone who prided herself on being able to find anyone, anywhere, at any time. Exasperated, Piper turned her attention to Annabel's husband. Before she could really start staking out his movements, she needed to arm herself with more information. Who was this man? What types of places would he frequent to meet this mystery lady, if he met her in public at all? She typed *Henry Ford* into her search engine. It didn't help that he shared a name with possibly the most prominent American industrialist of all time and the founder of the Ford Motor Company. Had his parents done that intentionally? It had always seemed cruel to Piper when people forced their children into the shadow of someone famous. If her last name had been Streisand, she certainly wouldn't have named her daughter Barbra.

Once she'd weeded through the articles on the legendary Henry Ford, she'd come upon a number of links related to Annabel's husband, who was quite a success story in his own right. As a technology entrepreneur, he'd launched his first start-up company in late 2003, after scaling the corporate ladder at Amazon.com by playing a fundamental role in the growth of their e-commerce. Since that time, he'd negotiated major deals with an assembly of other tech giants, including Apple, Microsoft, Dell, IBM, and Google. Most recently, he'd presented a TED Talk that had been hailed as "genius" by Mark Zuckerberg. The funny thing was, Annabel hadn't mentioned any of that. She'd said only that he ran a business in the Internet space and that he made a lot of money. Piper had no idea how sizable his paycheck actually was, but judging from the scant research she'd done, Annabel stood to come away with a substantial chunk of change, especially if she could prove that he'd been unfaithful.

Just what Piper needed: more pressure. She stretched her arms above her head, leaned back against her chair, and yawned. She checked the clock on her laptop, which read just past midnight, and then shut it down. Exhaustion had set in somewhere in the neighborhood of ten thirty, but, as usual, she'd pushed through it, too ensconced in her sleuthing to surrender to sleep. Todd was probably already in bed. She crept downstairs to pour herself a glass of water and noticed that the living room light was still on.

"Hey, you," Todd whispered, so as not to wake Fern, who'd been a light sleeper since the day she was born.

"Hey. I thought you'd be down for the count already." She sat next to him on the couch, curling her body into his and resting her heavy head against his chest. She'd always found his heartbeat strangely soothing.

"I probably should be, but I got to reading after my show ended and I couldn't put it down." He held up a thick hardcover novel with a judge's gavel on the cover.

"Wow, Fern's really rubbing off on you, huh?" She smiled and then kissed him on the lips, caressing his bristly face with her hand.

"So have you." He smiled and kissed her back, lingering for longer this time. "What has you burning the midnight oil?" He looked at his watch. "Literally."

"Just work stuff." She sat up, propping herself against the sofa cushion with her elbow. She hadn't told him about Annabel's request. In part because he'd met her only one time, when he'd picked up Piper from her exercise class. But also because she knew he'd tell her what she already suspected: that it was a really bad idea to rummage through a friend's dirty laundry. Even

78

if you planned to wash, dry, and fold it for her.

Todd was far more practical than she was. It was one of the many things she loved about him. He made comprehensive lists. He categorized his socks by type — casual or dress — and color. He kept a schedule and followed it. He thought about dinner before his stomach was already grumbling. And he bought gifts in advance of every holiday. All things that Piper had neither an affinity for nor an interest in. Prior to Todd, the inside of their house had looked like the aftermath of a hurricane. Hurricane Piper. She wished she could say it had been organized chaos. But there had been nothing organized about it. Weeks' worth of mail had been stacked into towering piles on the kitchen counter. Clothing had been flung over the backs of chairs, where it would remain for anywhere from a week to a month. Food had remained in the refrigerator well past its expiration date. And credit card receipts had been crumpled into balls and shoved in drawers or cubbies. It wasn't that she'd enjoyed living that way. It was just that because there had always been so much to do, orderliness had never taken priority.

When she and Todd had determined that

he was going to move in with them, he'd gingerly broached the subject of Piper's pigsty. She'd never forget how he'd twisted his face and gesticulated with his hands as he'd attempted to arrive at the best way of conveying his feelings about the shambolic environs he was readying to inhabit. He must have started his first sentence four or five times until she'd finally told him to spit it out, for fear that he'd changed his mind. For fear that he'd decided to remain at peace in his uncluttered world.

Todd had been visibly surprised when Piper had said she'd be thrilled if he hired a cleaning service to come in and whip the place into shape. He'd then taken it a step further and suggested that someone come regularly, maybe once a week, and stressed that he'd be footing the bill for it. He'd been worried, he'd admitted, that it would be too much, too soon for him to arrive and overhaul things. But Piper had reassured him that it was his home now, as well as theirs, and that he had to be just as comfortable as she and Fern were living in it. Not to mention that everyone would benefit from occupying a cleaner, neater space.

"You work too hard." He raked his fingers through the spirals in her dark brown hair — she'd wrestled them into loose waves that morning, but they'd since coiled back into tight corkscrews, thanks to the damp weather outside. "And they don't appreciate you enough."

"You get paid to say that." She smiled at him adoringly. He was the only man she'd ever been with who wanted to protect her. The only man who'd put her well-being and the well-being of her daughter before his own. After so many years of taking care of herself and Fern, it was like she didn't know how to let someone take care of her. Todd had told her she would have to learn, because he planned to tend to her and spoil her for the rest of their lives. She often asked herself how she'd gotten so lucky to have met such a gift of a human being. Because she wasn't the sole beneficiary of Todd's goodwill. There was his mother, Berta, and his sister, Sally, who lived in Florida. Not only did he cover many of their bills, but he spoke to them almost every day, checking in to ensure that they didn't want for anything, either financially or emotionally.

It was a shame Todd had never had the opportunity to become a father. No one was better suited for the job than he was, which was why it was so important to Piper to get to the bottom of Fern's apparent change of heart.

"I wish I did." He laughed. "Is it so wrong that I want to be able to take my wife on vacation once in a while?"

"Wife?" Piper grinned. They'd discussed the prospect of getting married on a number of occasions. Of getting married *one day.*

Sure there'd been a period in Piper's life when daydreaming about her wedding had been a preferred pastime. She'd never been one of those women who desired something over-the-top, with three hundred people she didn't know and a dress so heavy she could barely walk. Instead, she'd pictured a beach setting. Bare feet. A garland of daisies and baby's breath fashioned into a white halo around her head. Her groom in khaki pants and an untucked white linen shirt.

Her groom. In her reveries, his face had always been Max's. Even after he'd left. Because nobody ran out on their girlfriend and child forever. Right?

"Wishful thinking, I suppose." He pulled her onto his lap.

"Is that so?" She curled her arm around his neck.

"If I have anything to say on the matter."

Of course it had crossed her mind that he would propose eventually. To be honest, though, she hadn't given a whole lot of thought as to when that would be. Had he looked at rings? Would he ask her father's permission? Suddenly her heart was stampeding in her chest.

"Well, let's just hope Fern comes around by then."

"She will." Todd nodded confidently.

"How can you be so sure?" How could he always be so sure about everything? Piper could spend forty minutes vacillating on what to order for dinner. But if you asked Todd, he could answer without a moment's hesitation. Chinese. Pizza. Sushi.

"Because I know her. And I also know that this is a completely normal reaction to having your mother's boyfriend move into your home, when it's been just the two of you for as long as you can remember."

"It sounds funny when you call yourself my boyfriend. I feel like I should be wearing your class ring or your letterman jacket. You know, the ones with the white leather sleeves. God, those were cool."

"You may be in luck. I think my mother still has mine from varsity baseball."

"No!"

"Yup. Have you ever known my mother to throw anything out?"

"Is that why you love me so much, because I'm a pack rat like she is?"

"I believe the politically correct term is

hoarder. But that is definitely not why I love you so much. Although I do love you a hell of a lot." He pressed his lips to hers, kissing her eagerly this time, as their mouths opened and tongues entwined. "What do you say we take this up to the bedroom?"

"I say, 'Yes, please,' " she panted as he stood up and hoisted her into his arms.

"And I say, 'That makes you one very smart lady.' "

As he carried her up the stairs and down the dimly lit hallway, neither of them noticed the crack in Fern's door and the silhouette of her body, cloaked in the shadows, up long past her bedtime.

Six

"That was brutal." At the end of class, Annabel stretched her aching arms through the sleeves of her camel-colored shearling coat — the one Henry had bought her for her thirty-fifth birthday. Another gift from her husband. *Her. Husband.* She hadn't allowed herself to contemplate not being able to call him that anymore, even though the divorce proceedings had commenced just days earlier.

Had Henry already stopped calling her his wife? Annabel hadn't bothered to ask. Whenever they spoke, which was still once or twice a day, there was always so much to go over. What time he'd be picking the kids up for dinner — for now they'd agreed that twice a week seemed fair. Plus every other weekend he'd take them to visit his sister, Lisa, and her family in New Haven. As it stood, Henry had rented a small apartment near his office on a monthly basis — until they finalized things, he'd said. What did that even mean? Nothing would ever be *final* in her mind. Even if they signed a document saying that they were no longer legally committed, they'd still be bound to each other indefinitely through the kids.

Henry had insisted that they tell the boys something. He'd said it wasn't fair to him for them to think he was suddenly gone so often. In an effort to be concise, he'd proposed the following one-liner: *While Mommy and Daddy love each other and you very much, it's in everyone's best interest for us to be apart.* Annabel had agreed. Only when the time had come, she'd instinctively tagged a *for now* onto the end.

Before leaving, Henry had delivered the news that he wanted to take Harper and Hudson to Lisa's house for Thanksgiving. Suddenly it had hit her like a mallet to the head, that the clearly defined road map that had once been her life was about to be shredded into meaningless relics. There would be lonely, dead-end streets. Diverging paths. And just enough intersecting trails to make the whole thing as convoluted and muddled as possible. The ground felt unsteady beneath her feet. Everything had been stable and predictable for so long that now she was left to wonder what would change, go wrong, or surprise her next. Annabel had never been one to appreciate surprises. She felt dizzy, breathless, and choleric all at once. Henry was single-handedly obliterating everything she'd known. He'd robbed Annabel of her security and raided her inner peace like they were engaged in guerrilla warfare. She'd told him she'd think about his Thanksgiving proposal. Then she'd slammed the door behind him and called her lawyer.

"Completely brutal." Piper sighed. "I wonder if it'll ever get easier." She followed Annabel to the café next door, where they were seated at their usual table by the front window. They both relished the sport of people watching and, before Annabel's divorce had devoured their conversations, they'd taken great pleasure in pointing out random strangers and concocting comprehensive backstories, which would have them occupied for hours.

There'd been the time when Annabel had chosen an attractive woman with dark brown hair slicked into a neat chignon. It had been raining that day, so she'd been wearing a tan trench coat belted at the waist. "Stripper," Annabel had announced, chortling aloud. Because that was about as dirty as it got with her. She'd then gone on to explain that said stripper was taking her clothing off only to put herself through a master's degree program in education. So she could be a teacher. That was when Piper had given the woman a closer look and realized that she was, in fact, already a teacher. At Fern's school. This had launched them both into a fit of hysterical laughter.

"I hear it doesn't. My friend Amanda has been taking the noon barre class five days a week for about a year. She claims she's perpetually sore."

"Well, that's great to hear."

"I guess it means it's working. At least I hope it is."

"What, now that you might have to dip back into the dating pool?" Piper's hand flew to her mouth. "I'm so sorry, Annabel. I didn't mean that the way it sounded."

"It's okay." Only it wasn't. The idea of having dinner with another man was terrifying enough. The very last thing she wanted to entertain was someone other than her husband seeing her naked. Just the thought of it was enough to make her slink down in her chair. Where would she meet someone anyway? It wasn't as if she was about to hit the bar scene or jaunt into Manhattan for a night of clubbing with her girlfriends. She didn't even have single girlfriends anymore.

Unless you counted Piper, who these days was closer to calling herself married than Annabel was.

Would she have to sign up for one of those ghastly dating websites? Annabel wouldn't. She couldn't. The whole thing would be far too humiliating. Plus, what would she even say about herself? *Annabel has no job and two young kids. She likes to shop and has currently taken up working out in order to get her fat ass into shape. Oh, and her ex-husband thinks she's a miserable person. Let's grab a cocktail, shall we?*

"No, it's not. It was insensitive. I'm sorry." Piper handed Annabel her cell phone. "If it makes you feel any better, I just got this text from my assistant. She was able to track down where Henry has made dinner reservations on Saturday night. It's a reservation for two at Nellie's Tavern."

"He loves that place." She shook her head in disbelief. Henry had taken her there for their fifth wedding anniversary. And their seventh. Not to mention for various birthdays. Annabel could predict his order faster than her own — filet mignon medium rare with a side of creamed spinach and an order of potatoes gratin. What she couldn't predict was whose mouth he'd be spooning that creamed spinach into. She shuddered involuntarily. "It's so strange."

"What?"

"That he has plans I don't know about. I used to be able to see his schedule online. Until he changed his email password."

"It doesn't mean it's a romantic thing."

"I bet it is, though." Her eyes stung with the threat of tears. It didn't take much lately for her to erupt into uncontrollable sobs. Fortunately, to this point, she'd avoided public blubbering.

"Let's not get ahead of ourselves. I'm going to check it out and report back."

"You'll take pictures?" Annabel despised the desperation in her voice. She'd never imagined it would come to this. She barely recognized herself anymore.

"This isn't my first rodeo, my friend."

"Thank you." She nodded gratefully.

"Don't thank me yet. I haven't found anything."

"Yes, but you're trying. And that's more than anyone else has done for me." She swallowed her anxiety. "Did you know that when you get divorced people immediately become allergic to you? It's like they're worried it's contagious."

"I'm not surprised in this town. Try being the only never-been-married single mom in Eastport, Connecticut. Most of the women don't want to associate with me, for fear I'll sink my claws into their husbands. As if I'm some major dish." She snorted.

"Speaking of which, did you see that hot little number in the back right corner of class this morning? When we did that leg-stretch thing against the wall, she could practically touch her nose to her knee. And she was prancing around like it was nothing during the cardio section."

"No, I didn't. I'm afraid that if I look at anyone other than myself in the mirror, I'll topple onto the floor. If you haven't noticed, my sense of equilibrium leaves a lot to be desired."

"Well, she couldn't be a day over thirty. Bitch."

"She could be a lovely person, for all you know."

"She could be." Annabel watched as the door to the café opened, allowing a gust of cold air to stream through. "Oh, shit. Don't look now, but she just walked in." Piper turned around. "I told you not to look!"

"Yeah, sorry. *Don't look now* means *Look right now* to me."

"And you call yourself a private investigator."

"Actually, no, I don't! You're the one that came up with that idea, remember?" Piper focused on the woman, who was every bit as perky as Annabel had described. "Oh, my God, I know her!" She whipped her head back around to face Annabel. "That's Mackenzie Mead. She's married to CeCe Mead's son and she runs the marketing department at my company."

"Oh yeah. I think I've seen her before in *Eastport Magazine*." Annabel appraised the woman as a jeweler would a diamond. "She's even prettier in person. You should say hello."

"Are you crazy? She has no idea who I am. Plus, I'm half an hour late to work. Don't even look in her direction." Piper held the menu in front of her face.

"She'll never see you now!" Annabel smirked.

"Put your menu up too. Come on."

"Why? She doesn't know me." Annabel did as Piper said regardless. "This time, really do not turn around. She's coming this way."

"Piper?" Mackenzie stood at the side of their table in black capri-length Lycra yoga pants with a figure-grazing white tank top under her distressed-leather, motorcycle-style jacket.

"Oh, hi. Mackenzie, right? I didn't see you come in."

"We were in exercise class together just now."

"Really?"

"I always stand in the back. I feel like such an uncoordinated fool in there."

"*You* feel like an uncoordinated fool?" Annabel interjected, in an attempt to rescue Piper from her awkward discourse. "I thought you might be one of the teachers at first."

"Ha!" Mackenzie laughed, and Annabel noticed how straight and white her teeth were. "I just started. I've always been more of a runner, but I wanted to find a workout that wasn't as hard on the body. I'm, um, trying to get pregnant." She massaged her belly in a circular motion, and Annabel couldn't help but wonder if she already was. Women always said they were going to make major lifestyle changes in advance — give up things like coffee and alcohol. But, the truth was, most of it was crap. And anyway, Annabel's obstetrician had once told her that he'd heard of more kids conceived on drunken nights than at any other time.

"Good for you." Annabel smiled. She remembered being Mackenzie's age, likely twenty-seven or twenty-eight, if she guessed correctly, when the future had held the promise of *everything.* Back when she hadn't given any thought to divorce agreements or custody battles over the children she didn't even have yet. She'd viewed the world through the rosiest glasses and had occupied a bubble that even the sharpest needle wouldn't have been able to burst. And she imagined Mackenzie's bubble was even sturdier, given the family she'd married into. At least she hoped it was, for her sake.

"Thanks. It's early yet. I have a hard time keeping my big mouth shut."

"Your secret is safe with us." Annabel signaled to Piper, who was staring silently at Mackenzie, no doubt thankful that Annabel had hijacked the conversation. "Right, Piper?"

"Oh yeah. Absolutely. My lips are sealed."

"I really appreciate that. You know how my mother-in-law is."

"I don't even know her that well." Piper shook her head.

"Don't worry. I'm fairly certain no one knows CeCe that well. Except maybe her dog." Mackenzie smiled slyly. "I know she thinks very highly of you, though."

"Me?" Piper pressed her palm to her chest.

"Yup. Remember when you and Lucy helped her and my husband with that big project a few months ago? She still talks

about how sharp you were with your obser-
vations."

"Wow, that's nice to hear."

"Especially coming from the boss lady."
Mackenzie grinned. "Even Santa has a hard
time making it onto her 'good' list." She
held up her cup of steaming tea. "Gotta run
to work. Will I see you ladies in class again?"

"I'm afraid so." Annabel sighed.

"Well, nice to meet you . . ."

"Annabel."

"And nice to see you, Piper. I'm sure we'll
run into each other in the halls at Mead."

"Absolutely."

Mackenzie waved and weaved her way
through the crowd and back out the door.

"Hello? Earth to Piper." Annabel passed
her hand in front of Piper's face. "Are you
starstruck or something?"

"Honestly? Kind of. No one at the company really talks to Trevor or Mackenzie. I
didn't even think she knew my name. Much
less Lucy's. I mean, she really pulled that
out of her ass."

"She seems like a genuinely nice person."

"See, I told you she wasn't a bitch."

"That was when you didn't know who I
was talking about!"

"Still, it'll teach you not to judge a book

by its cover." Piper rounded a brown eyebrow.

"That's unlikely. Nine times out of ten, the cover says it all. Speaking of which . . ."

"Yeah?"

"Did you see the look on her face when she was talking about getting pregnant?"

"No, why?"

"For God's sake. Aren't you supposed to be observant?"

"Apparently, according to CeCe Mead."

"I'm telling you she's already got a bun in the oven."

"Mackenzie?"

"No, Madonna."

"Very funny."

"Mark my words. That girl's eating for two."

"You think?" Piper considered this for a moment. "That would actually be big news. Everyone at the office knows CeCe has been dying for a grandson. Plus, she's talked about it in every interview I've read with her."

"And yet we're the first to know." Annabel's lips curled smugly.

"Well, she didn't actually come out and say it."

"She didn't have to."

"Maybe you should be the one doing the

sleuthing."

"Believe me, I would if I could."

"Okay, I have to get to work." Piper stood up.

"You'll call me if you find out anything else about Henry?" She'd forgotten about him for a few blissful moments.

"Yes."

"Promise?"

"Promise."

Once Piper had left, Annabel sat for a while, gazing out the window at the passersby — a middle-aged mother with a triple stroller packed with two toddlers and a screaming baby; an elderly woman hobbling across the street, pushing a metal cart full of groceries; and a young couple with their arms linked and their sides fastened to each other's like Siamese twins. Without warning, the lump that had been residing in her throat erupted into a wretched howl she just managed to suppress in time. After throwing some cash down on the table, Annabel raced out of the café toward her car, where she hunched her body over the wheel and released a torrent of savage wails.

If this was what it felt like to be alone, she wasn't sure she'd survive it.

Seven

Everything felt different when there was life growing inside of you. Even if it was only an embryo, somehow Mackenzie knew she was no longer responsible for just herself. And each decision she made — even the ones that had seemed trivial before — suddenly necessitated the vigilance of an air-traffic controller.

She hadn't told anyone yet. Not her mother. Not her childhood best friend, Trish. Not even Trevor. She'd expected she'd want to scream the news from the rooftops, maybe issue a press release — she knew one would be forthcoming anyway, if CeCe had anything to say about it. Which, inevitably, she would. But, instead, she'd felt instinctively protective of the new life — a natural maternal impulse, she'd decided, allowing herself to keep her delicious secret for just a day. At most. Only one day had tumbled into a few, and eventually she'd started to feel guilty for depriving her loved ones of the joyous news.

She'd thought about telling Trevor the previous evening, until he'd announced that he was leaving first thing in the morning for a quick business trip to Boston — there and back by dinner. *Perfect.* She'd call her mother and get the recipe for the Southern fried chicken Trevor had swooned over last time she'd visited them. And those mashed potatoes. Had she used cream cheese and cheddar? If Mackenzie was feeling especially ambitious, she'd bake her famous peach cobbler, its aroma so potent it permeated every square foot of their home. Weeks later, she could swear she still smelled it, sunk deep into the fabric of their curtains and couch cushions.

When Trevor arrived home, she'd have their dining room table dressed in their finest linens with the elaborate china place settings, heavy silver flatware, and delicate crystal glasses they'd received as wedding gifts but had yet to have occasion to use. She'd pop a bottle of champagne and pour herself a full glass, so as not to let on at first, although she knew she'd barely take a sip, if that. Mackenzie had heard of women who drank their way through pregnancy, allowing themselves a conservative helping of wine here and there. It wasn't that she judged them or even begrudged them this small indulgence; it was that she'd waited for this for so long. And nothing — *nothing at all* — would stand in her way of carrying a full-term, healthy baby. At least not if she could help it.

She sat down at the kitchen table with a tall glass of orange juice and a plate of eggs. Typically, she craved coffee in the mornings. Strong, black coffee. Three cups by noon, accompanied by a bagel or muffin. Carbs and caffeine. But not anymore. Mackenzie needed sustenance, vitamins, protein. She grimaced at the whole-grain toast, smeared with avocado she'd prepared on the side. As soon as she was done eating, she'd set things up for dinner, call her mom for a list of ingredients, and head to the supermarket, all before her late-afternoon appointment with her gynecologist. It was Friday, but she'd taken the whole day off, well aware that she wouldn't have been able to get anything done at work in advance of hearing her child's heartbeat for the very first time. Come to think of it, would she be able to hear the heartbeat yet? Probably not. She'd read somewhere that this milestone came later on, maybe seven or eight weeks in. There was so much to learn. A trip to the bookstore was definitely in order. She could already envision the thick parenting tomes splayed on her bed, while she scoured each chapter, absorbing as much useful knowledge as there was space in her head. She'd try to remember to pick up something for Trevor too. Weren't there whole books targeted toward fathers-to-be?

Mackenzie lifted a forkful of eggs to her mouth just as the phone rang.

"Hi, Mom." She swallowed quickly. "I was just about to call you."

"Oh, that's funny, sweetheart. Daddy and I were talking about plans for Thanksgiving, and I thought I'd give you a jingle. It's just a few weeks away."

"Wow, I forgot it was so soon." The truth was, between work and trying to conceive, she hadn't focused on much else in a while. "Do you think you guys want to come up here?" She knew the answer before she asked.

To say that Mackenzie's parents were out of their element in Eastport, Connecticut, was tantamount to declaring that Ozzy Osbourne had never used drugs. Their excursions into Manhattan were even worse. The first time she'd introduced them to Times Square, she'd thought her father was going to keel over in front of the entrance to the

St. James Theatre in the middle of Forty-fourth and Broadway. Of course, that had been nothing compared to the reverberating yelp her mother had released at the American Museum of Natural History, upon sighting the *Tyrannosaurus rex,* with its four-foot-long jaw, six-inch-long teeth, and hulking thigh bones.

"I don't think so, sweetheart. It's just" — she cleared her throat — "too much for us."

"I understand." She did. But it didn't make her want them there any less. For so long, Mackenzie had been focused on the prize of becoming pregnant that she hadn't given much consideration to how she'd feel — beyond being thrilled — when the time actually came. Now, though, she wished her mother lived closer. She wished she could hug her tight when she told her the news. And that she could be there to accompany her to doctor appointments and when she went shopping for maternity clothes.

Mackenzie didn't have many friends in Eastport. Initially it hadn't bothered her. She'd been so consumed by her new married life — new job, new husband, new world — and by the many events that they were not only invited to but expected to attend. She'd talked to Trish on the phone every day, convincing herself that that would be enough until she had kids in school and met all of the other mommies in town. Trish already had three kids. Three kids in four years. That was how they did it in Bowman, Georgia. Only eventually, she started to realize that she had little left in common with Trish, and while their phone calls were still filled with laughter, there wasn't much of substance left to discuss. Before long, their daily chat sessions had dwindled to once a week, then biweekly, and ultimately they'd resigned themselves to catching up whenever time permitted, which — as of late — seemed to be never. How was it, Mackenzie had pondered, that the very person who had been able to read her mind from the smallest expression could abruptly become someone with whom she had to grapple for something to gossip about? She could tell Trish felt the same way, as was evidenced by her rush to "jump off" the phone every time Mackenzie spoke of a complication at work or another charity gala.

Sometimes she wondered how she'd ever lived in Bowman, a painstakingly rural city in Elbert County, Georgia. Although it was a stretch even to call it a city, with its 2.6 miles of land and population of fewer than one thousand people.

"Perhaps you and Trevor would like to

come down for the holidays. Maybe stay through Christmas?" she asked hopefully.

"I wish we could, Mommy. But you know . . ." She didn't have to say any more than that. The chances of CeCe relinquishing either holiday were about as good as Santa Claus appearing in the flesh to roast the Thanksgiving bird. Of course, Mackenzie's parents were always invited, if not welcome, to join the festivities at the Mead estate.

"I know." She detected the disappointment in her mother's wilted tone. And all at once she wanted to make it better.

"I have some great news, Mom."

"What's that, sweetheart?" Her mother's attempt to sound buoyant fell flat. She was probably expecting word of another professional accolade — something that had never held intrinsic importance to her, even though she'd always been genuinely proud of Mackenzie's accomplishments.

"I'm pregnant!" It was the first time she'd said it aloud, and it surprised her almost as much as it had when she'd seen those two precious pink lines.

"Oh, Mackenzie. That *is* great news! Arthur! Arthuuuuuur!" Her mother bellowed. "Wait until I tell your father. He's probably out in the backyard. Well, this is just fantastic! When did you find out? When are you due? I'll have to plan a few trips up immediately. And then, of course, when the baby is born . . ."

"Mom."

"It's a lot to think about, you know," she continued. "You'll need a crib and bedding and lots of onesies, because infants spit up all the time, and . . . bibs . . . And what do they call those playthings you can travel with? There's so much more these days than back when I had you."

"Mom, slow down." She laughed. "I haven't even told Trevor yet."

"Oh?" A nuance of concern crept into her voice.

"There's nothing to be worried about. I have something special planned for tonight. I just . . . I wanted you to be the first to know."

"My lips are sealed. Except . . ."

"Yes, you can tell Daddy."

"Thank goodness, because you know I'm not good at keeping secrets from him."

"I know, Mom. And I love you for that. Minus the time you told him that I'd gotten my period in the middle of science lab at school."

"I don't remember that."

"Really? Because I'm pretty sure Uncle

Joe does, since he was standing right there."

"Oh, sorry."

"I've let it go." Mackenzie smiled to herself, aware that her mother's apology was both authentic and unnecessary. "Listen, I have to run, but can you please e-mail me your fried chicken and mashed potato recipes? The ones you made last time you were here?"

"I'll do that right after I wash the breakfast dishes."

"Thanks."

"And, sweetheart."

"Yeah?"

"You're going to make a wonderful mother."

"Annabel, right?" Mackenzie pulled her jacket over her workout gear. The doctor had confirmed that exercising within reason while pregnant was not only safe, but encouraged. "Piper introduced us on Monday at Café Crunch next door."

"Yes, of course, I remember you." Annabel smiled tentatively.

"Are you going over there now? I'm starving and I'd love some company." She couldn't quite figure out how old Annabel was, but her best guess was mid-thirties. She probably had kids in school already and a strictly defined clique of friends in place, but so what? Mackenzie could tell by her prowess in their exercise class, even though she wasn't the most athletic-looking person, that she had a strong personality. An attribute she appreciated in other women, since so many of them she'd met or worked with in Eastport tended to be riddled with insecurities. Never thin enough. Never rich enough. Simply never enough in any way. That wasn't Mackenzie's style.

"Sure, that sounds fine." They walked over to the café together, bemoaning how tough the morning's class had been, and then took a seat by the window.

"I'm completely ravenous. You?" Mackenzie looked up from her menu.

"Oh, me? Unfortunately, I'm always hungry. But I'm trying to lose some weight."

"Why? You look amazing."

"No, *you* look amazing. I'm fifteen pounds from looking decent." Mackenzie's mouth bent into a frown. "Don't worry, I'm not one of those psycho chicks with the juice cleanses and starvation diets. I'm just honest. I gained sixty pounds with my twins, and five years later I've still got a Goodyear around my waist and more junk in my trunk than there is at a yard sale."

"Well, I think you should eat whatever

you'd like. We must have just burned at least five hundred calories in there." The waitress appeared beside the table, poised with pad and pen. "Can I have a ham and mushroom omelet, a side of sausage, and some fruit, please?"

"Wow, you don't mess around." Annabel scanned the menu. "I'll have what she's having, minus the omelet and sausage." The waitress twisted her face in confusion. "Just some fruit, please," she clarified, handing her the menu.

"Just fruit? I thought you weren't one of those psycho chicks." Mackenzie laughed.

"Don't worry. This is my second breakfast."

"Let's call it a midmorning snack."

"I like that." Annabel looked down at Mackenzie's stomach. "So, when are you due?"

"Excuse me?"

"When's the baby coming?"

"I don't understand. How did you know?" Mackenzie shook her head.

Had her gynecologist leaked something to the press? She thought she'd made it very clear to her the previous afternoon at her checkup that *no one* — with the exception of her mother, father, and Trevor — was to find out before they had the chance to tell

CeCe in person. Could it have been the nosy nurse who'd peppered her with questions under the auspices of being kind? Or the receptionist who'd complimented an article in the recent issue of the *Journal*? She'd never fully adjusted to the concept that people followed her husband's life and that — by association, when they were in public together — it meant they occasionally cared about hers.

"I could tell the other day. Something in your demeanor." Annabel smiled as the waitress placed their plates of fruit in front of them. "Don't stress. Your secret is safe with me."

"What about Piper? Does she know too?" Mackenzie's head was spinning like a revolving door. "God, I'm such a blabbermouth."

"She definitely doesn't *know,* but I did mention that I suspected it."

"Shit."

"You can trust Piper. I promise."

"That's good to know." She exhaled, feeling at least somewhat relieved. "You guys must be old friends."

"Actually, no. We met a couple of months ago when the barre studio opened. We clicked immediately and made a habit of coming here after class. It's funny — I spend more time with Piper than any of the old friends I've had for much longer, not that I'd really call most of them true friends. She gets me."

"I only know her a little through work, but everyone at Mead thinks very highly of her. And someone told me her daughter is some kind of prodigy."

"I'm not sure about prodigy, but I understand she's extremely smart, always with her nose in a book." Annabel pierced a hunk of cantaloupe with her fork and raised it to her mouth to take a bite.

"That's great. I wish I'd been like that as a kid."

"I bet you were head cheerleader or something like that."

"Not exactly. There wasn't much in the way of team sports in Bowman, Georgia."

"You're from Georgia?"

"What? You didn't detect my Southern twang?"

"Not so much." Annabel took a sip of water. "So, you still haven't told me when you're due."

"Oh, right. July third. Summer baby."

"No way. My boys were born on July ninth!"

"How old again?"

"Five. And the most delicious things you will ever lay eyes on." Mackenzie watched as Annabel beamed with adoration. "Though they sure do give me a run for my money sometimes."

"I'm sure. Is your husband helpful? That's the one thing I'm worried about, you know. Okay, that's a lie! There's a ton of stuff I'm freaking out about. It's just that Trevor is a great husband, but I'm not sure how he's going to be with an infant."

"Henry is a good father." Annabel's eyes shifted downward. "But we're actually in the process of getting divorced."

"I'm so sorry." Mackenzie placed her hand on Annabel's. "I'm sure that's not pleasant."

"That's an understatement." Annabel took a deep breath.

"I didn't mean to pry."

"It's okay. I need to get better about saying it out loud without feeling like someone's tearing my insides out. You know, it's a funny thing. You devote your existence to this person. Your days, weeks, months, and years revolve around them. You think about how to make his life easier at every chance you get. You worry about what he's going to wear, what he's going to eat, even how to make him feel like he spends enough time with the kids, despite the fact that he works overtime. And then, just like that. Just like fucking that . . ."

"Annabel?"

"I'm sorry. I'm rambling." She looked up to see Mackenzie's face grow ashen. "Are you okay? Did I say something? What's wrong?" Suddenly tears were streaming down her face. "Mackenzie? What's happening?"

"I think I'm bleeding." She looked down at the red fluid that had soaked through her pants.

"Oh, my God." Annabel shot upright. "Don't move." She rifled through her purse, handed Mackenzie a pack of tissues, and slapped thirty dollars on the table.

"I don't understand what's going on! Am I losing the baby?" Mackenzie clasped her arms around her stomach and felt ready to collapse.

"Let's go!"

"Where?" Mackenzie couldn't think straight. This couldn't be happening. All she could hold on to was the idea of the precious life inside of her.

"To the hospital. We have to get you to the hospital right now." And with that, Annabel helped Mackenzie to her feet, rushed her to her car, and sped as fast as she could to Eastport Memorial, with Mackenzie sobbing violently beside her.

EIGHT

She'd left behind one very irate ten-year-old with a scowl on her freckled face and her arms folded across her chest. Most recently, Fern did not appreciate when Piper worked late into the evenings or went out to dinner without her, forcing Todd to fend for the two of them. She'd become whiny, petulant, even, sulking around the house, muttering insults under her breath. Was this the gateway to her teen years? It seemed too soon for that, but who was she to say? She'd heard horror stories from women with docile, even-tempered daughters who'd morphed into obnoxious, entitled brats as soon as puberty and its inherent hormonal swerves had arrived. But she'd never believed it would happen with Fern. Her unflappable, wise-beyond-her-years little girl.

From the early age of two, Fern had accompanied Piper on work assignments, sitting contently in her car seat, gnawing on a bagel. While Piper had questioned witnesses, furiously taking notes, Fern hummed along to the theme song from *Sesame Street* blaring from the CD player. She'd taken Fern to hair appointments and doctor visits, even to the office on a few desperate occasions. And, without fail, everyone had remarked that Fern was the most easygoing child they'd ever been in the company of. It was as if she'd understood Piper's plight as a single mother. Apparently, not so much anymore.

Piper had spent the past few weeks lying awake in bed at night, wondering where she'd gone wrong and how to reverse it. Just the other day, she'd tried to sit down with Fern and talk to her about what she was feeling. Piper had reassured her that Todd was neither a replacement for nor a barrier to what they had. She'd told Fern that their bond was unbreakable. That it was so special, there wasn't a person or circumstance that could come between them. Fern had remained quiet, ostensibly listening to what Piper was saying. Seemingly absorbing the significance behind her words. She was certain she'd made headway. Until tonight. When Fern had stomped her feet. Hurled invectives. And even threatened to run away if Piper left her alone with Todd one more time. That had been a first.

Piper had considered calling Lucy to ask if she could stalk Henry Ford in her place, but Lucy had gone home to her parents' house in Massachusetts for a long weekend. Not to mention that she couldn't do that to Annabel. Piper had made a promise and, if there was one thing Piper was good for, it was staying true to her word. Sure, she'd left the house in shambles — with dirty dishes from dinner piled high in the sink and the contents of the family-sized carton of Goldfish she'd spilled still littering the pantry floor — but it'd been all she could do to pry herself from Fern's grip before swearing she'd be back to tuck her into bed. Henry and his companion had better not linger over dessert.

Piper perched on a stool at the bar and ordered a glass of white wine. She'd need more than one to ease the tension that had set up camp in the spot where her neck sloped into her shoulders. Annabel had told her to order whatever she wanted, on her, but when she'd checked out the menu online and noted the offensively exorbitant prices, even for Eastport, she'd settled for the leftover lasagna Todd had made the previous night and a promise to treat herself to a chocolate soufflé, courtesy of Annabel. After all, if she was going to be spying for her, the least she could do was pay her in sweets.

She scanned the restaurant in search of Henry. Luckily, Nellie's Tavern was an intimate spot with only a dozen or so tables, all of which were in plain sight. And, fortunately, Henry had no idea who she was or what she looked like. Thanks to the Internet and a few pictures Annabel had showed her, Piper now knew that Henry was tall with dirty blond, receding hair; large, oval-shaped light blue eyes, and about thirty extra pounds on his sturdy frame. He was attractive, though not her type, and definitely not what she'd pictured for Annabel. She wasn't sure why, since they'd spoken very little of him before he'd announced that he was leaving. Still, she'd imagined Annabel with someone darker, more ominous — someone who looked more like a technology mastermind than a football player. In the meantime, he was nowhere to be found inside the restaurant. If he'd canceled his reservation, she'd be legitimately pissed. Although Lucy had texted Piper at noon to confirm, even though she was out of town.

"Come here often?" She felt an arm heavy

on her back and whipped her head around like Jackie Chan.

"Excuse me?" Piper snapped, prepared to effectively shut down whatever loser thought that line still worked. If ever it had. "Oh, my God — Dan!" She laughed. "What are you doing here?" Dan was one of the copy editors at Mead. He'd worked at the company for longer than she had, and was the kind of guy she could always count on to tackle eleventh-hour corrections.

"Celebrating ten years with Ginny." He smiled.

"That's so great!" Piper couldn't help but think about Annabel and how she'd lamented the fact that Henry was dining at the very restaurant where they'd celebrated multiple joyous occasions, including more than one anniversary. "Looks like a nice place."

"Never been, actually. Ginny picked it. I almost went into shock when I saw the prices. I mean, thirty dollars for a salad?"

"Maybe it's gold-leaf lettuce."

"It had better be." Dan motioned to the bartender. "I'll take a gin and tonic, and the lady will have . . ."

"Another Pinot Grigio. Thank you."

"You want to see what I got her?" Dan

looked over his shoulder. "Before she gets here."

"Definitely!" Piper swallowed the remaining wine in her glass before gratefully accepting another. She was appreciative for the impromptu company. Something to distract her from dwelling on the upheaval at home and the uncomfortable task at hand.

"Okay, now, be honest." He pulled a small black velvet box from his pocket.

"Why? What are you going to do now if I don't like it?" She smirked.

"Good point. On second thought, don't be honest. Just tell me it's perfect." He opened the lid, and Piper gasped at the delicate pearl bracelet with its figure-eight diamond clasp.

"It's perfect."

"For real?"

"For real. She's going to love it. And if she doesn't, I'll take it!"

"If she doesn't, I may not have to remortgage our home. So there's that."

"I believe your bride has just walked in." Piper gestured toward the door and waved at Ginny, who was already walking in their direction.

"Hi, Piper." She smiled warmly. Ginny was a slight thing, barely exceeding five feet in high heels, with short, spiky brown hair and sparkling green almond-shaped eyes. "Don't take this the wrong way, but I hope you're not joining us!" she chirped.

"No offense taken. That would be a little awkward, huh?"

"Hello, sweetheart." Dan pulled Ginny into a tight embrace. "Ready to sit down?"

"Yup!" She looped her arm through his.

"Are you waiting for Todd?" Dan looked around.

"Um, no."

"Drinking alone?"

"Something like that." What else could she say? *Actually, no, I'm here to trail my friend's husband. You know, see if he's been screwing another woman behind her back.*

"Well, enjoy." He patted her on the back.

"You too! I hope you lovebirds have a fantastic night."

Piper swigged some more of her wine and checked her watch. It was already a quarter after eight. She smiled at an attractive woman at the other end of the bar, noticing how well put together she was in a tailored red suit, with long, sinewy legs and an elegant swanlike neck. Her thick, shiny black hair fell just below her shoulders, swishing effortlessly every time she turned her head. *What would it feel like to look like her, if only for a day?* Piper wondered, and ran her fingers through her tangle of brown curls and gazed down disapprovingly at her own wrinkled black slacks and untucked white silk blouse with a coffee stain on the cuff.

She sighed. It appeared as though Henry wasn't coming. She rifled through her purse for her cell phone. She'd call Annabel first to tell her that their mission had been aborted. And then Todd to say she was on her way home, and to make sure that Fern didn't fall asleep before she'd had a chance to say good night.

"Welcome, Mr. Ford. It's so nice to see you again," Piper heard the hostess announce before looking up to find Henry standing less than ten feet away. "Your guest is waiting for you."

"Thank you, Linda. I'm sorry I'm late."

"Not to worry, Mr. Ford. We always have room for you at Nellie's."

He nodded, following the hostess to the other end of the bar, where the lady in the red suit greeted him with a demure smile and a chaste peck on the cheek. Then she led them to their table for two in the corner by the window.

Piper squeezed her eyes shut, praying that what she'd just seen wasn't leading down the path she thought it was.

The path to Annabel's worst nightmare.

"Hey, you." Todd greeted her at the door, drawing her close to him.

"It's freezing out there." Piper stomped her boots forcefully on the floor mat. "I thought it wasn't supposed to be this chilly until January."

"It's just a quick cold front passing through this week. Then we should be good for another month." He helped her slip out of her jacket and walked it directly to the closet to hang it neatly in line with the rest of their coats. Most likely because he knew Piper would have tossed it on the closest piece of furniture. "Do you want a cup of coffee? Decaf?"

"That sounds amazing right now." Especially since she'd had two glasses of wine. Gratefully, Nellie's Tavern was only a mile from their house.

"How's Lucy?"

"Huh?" Piper sat down at the kitchen table, feeling a little tipsy. She'd always been such a lightweight.

"Lucy. Your assistant. The one you just met for drinks."

"Right, yeah. Sorry." She'd nearly forgotten her own lie, which was precisely the thing about lying. Too many details to keep straight.

She hated being dishonest with Todd. She'd scolded herself more than once for not having been up front with him from the start. Fine, so she knew he'd disapprove, but she was an adult, perfectly capable of making her own decisions. Regardless, stalking your friend's soon-to-be ex seemed so juvenile. Probably because it was. And she didn't want Todd to view her that way. Piper wanted him to regard her as someone with a strong moral compass, a woman of virtuosity. A role model. Of course, she was entirely comfortable with him watching her go to the bathroom, standing beside the toilet while he brushed his teeth. Still, though, that fell safely within the confines of intimacy, whereas snooping around where you weren't supposed to just made her appear childish.

"So, did you guys have fun?" He set a steaming mug in front of her and sat down across from her with his own. Todd and Lucy had hit it off immediately. After Todd and Piper had been on three dates, Lucy had declared that she was *absolutely certain* that Todd was Piper's Prince Charming. Because at Lucy's ripe age of twenty-five, she still believed in things like soul mates and happily ever after. She'd never been burned by an ex who'd decided to sow a prettier pasture or, even more galling, take off to find himself and not return for more than ten years. Lucy had survived two and a half decades unscathed. Come to think of it, Piper had never met anyone she'd dated.

"Oh yeah, for sure. Lucy's the best. Though we did have to get some work done." Piper felt the guilt rise in her chest. The guilt from protracting the lie and from leaving her family so she could do so. "Was Fern pissed that I wasn't here to put her to bed?"

"Hard to say. She didn't speak more than two words to me all night. And those words were *Get out* when I attempted to enter her room."

"I'm so sorry. I thought things would be getting better with her by now." Piper dug her elbows into the table and pressed her face into her palms.

"I've told you you don't have to apologize. I still think this is pretty normal."

"But it's getting worse."

"I have to agree with that." Todd slid his chair next to hers and began stroking her back. "Do you think maybe we should make an appointment for her to see someone? Like a counselor. Even if it's nothing to be worried about, it might set your mind at ease."

"That's a really good idea." Piper looked up and around the room for the first time. "You cleaned everything. Again."

"I couldn't help myself." He shrugged perfunctorily.

"I feel awful. You should have left it." She cupped his cheek in her hand. "You're too good to me, you know that?"

"Too good? Nah. I just knew you wouldn't want to do it when you got home tonight. And I had the time, what with being ostracized by the only other person in the house."

"You really sure you want to commit to us lovely ladies? One slob and one diminutive bully." She laughed feebly. "I'd be running for the hills as fast as my legs would carry me."

"I think I'll stick around. I prefer to think of you as eccentric and Fern as a work in progress. She's a good kid. She'll come around."

"Eccentric? Eeew. That makes me sounds like a crazy old lady who confides in her cats and knits everyone wool scarves."

"A scarf would be cool." Todd leaned in and kissed her on the lips, and she inhaled the sweet and spicy aroma of his aftershave. "Especially if you knit it for me."

"I would love to. Only one small problem."

"Don't know how to knit, huh?"

"Not even a little."

"Well, in that case, I'll settle for you accompanying me to bed." He clasped her hand in his, entwining their fingers. "I'm sure you can find a way to make it up to me. My nonexistent scarf, that is."

"Can I meet you up there in ten minutes? I just need to send an e-mail and then I'm all yours."

"I like the sound of that." He stood up. "The *all mine* part."

"Well, then, I'll see you soon." She attempted her best seductive grin and watched him go before carrying their empty coffee cups to the sink. Then she climbed the stairs to her office, dragging her tired body the whole way.

She hadn't been able to reach Annabel on the way home. Her cell had gone straight to voice mail, which was strange, since she'd made Piper swear on her life to call her as soon as she'd left the restaurant.

She sat down at her desk, switched on her computer, and opened a blank message, then typed a quick e-mail to Annabel to let her know she'd see her in the morning at barre class and that they'd talk afterward. Not wanting to leave her hanging, she'd added that there was nothing scandalous to report. Although she wasn't so sure Annabel would see it that way. Just as Piper was about to get up and join Todd in the bedroom, she noticed a small envelope taped to the inside of her office door with "Mommy" scribbled on the front in Fern's handwriting. *That's sweet,* she thought. She'd probably decided to leave her a little good-night note, since Piper hadn't made it home in time to say so in person. She unfolded the piece of white computer paper, which Fern had clearly pilfered from her desk, along with the envelope.

Her daughter had written three words.

Only three words.

Three words that felt to Piper like they could change the course of their lives forever.

I found Daddy.

NINE

Annabel watched the rise and fall of Mackenzie's chest. She looked so peaceful, as still as Sleeping Beauty, only in a hospital bed with a battery of wires, and monitors blinking and beeping around her. There'd been complications, the doctor had said. It wasn't simply a chemical pregnancy, which so many women endured at this stage. Nor could it be considered a full-blown miscarriage, since she hadn't been far enough along. Still, something wasn't right, and they needed to get to the bottom of it before they could even think about releasing her. Annabel had felt like an imposter being the sole person on the receiving end of such woeful news. They'd only just met, and now here she was, sitting beside her like she was part of the family.

She'd stayed all day and all night. How could she not? When the doctors had asked Mackenzie whom they should call on her behalf, she'd looked perplexed — mentally unable to engage in making what, for most people, would have been an obvious decision. Her husband, Trevor, she'd said, had been stuck in Boston because of a snowstorm. She hadn't even had the chance to tell him about the baby yet. Her parents lived a plane ride away in Georgia, and she didn't have any close friends to speak of in the area. Annabel had gently suggested reaching out to her mother-in-law, desperate to share the burden of such classified information with someone. *Anyone.* But as soon as she'd seen the fearful look in Mackenzie's eyes, she'd dropped it immediately. Then she'd taken Mackenzie's hand in hers, as a nurse had wheeled her stretcher down a long hallway, so they could hook her up to some more machines for testing. Annabel had promised to remain there as long as Mackenzie needed her and, in turn, Mackenzie had vowed to alert Trevor as soon as she was awake and lucid again.

Now that Annabel really had the chance to look at her, she noticed just how breathtaking Mackenzie actually was. If she didn't feel sorry for her, a part of her would have been jealous. That was the thing about Mackenzie. Typically, her warm and outgoing demeanor actually distracted you from noticing her natural beauty.

She'd never know what it was like to be that woman. There'd been a time when Annabel had been ten pounds thinner, her hair had been thicker and glossier, before clumps of it had fallen out in the shower after she'd given birth to Harper and Hudson, and she'd been whistled and hooted at by construction workers on the streets of New York City countless times, not that that necessarily indicated much. Regardless, anyone who said it didn't feel good was a liar. Now that she was a mother, those days were long gone. She rarely had the time or impetus to blow her hair out in the morning or wear more makeup than was essential to look passably attractive.

She couldn't help but recognize the irony. What she wouldn't give to look like Mackenzie, with her full head of wavy blond hair, penetrating green eyes, and a body so toned and sleek it would give any actress in Hollywood a run for her money. And what Mackenzie wouldn't give to have two healthy, adorable five-year-old boys to love and care for. Annabel suspected she'd make a great mom. One whose diaper bag would always be fully stocked with wipes, a change of clothing, and nutritious snacks. One who'd be unruffled by being awakened in the middle of the night, no matter how many times or for how many months. One who would wear parenthood as a badge of honor, a gift, rather than parading her child around like a trophy or dressing it up like a doll. It was hard to say what gave her this impression, considering she barely knew her, but in some strange way, Mackenzie reminded her of her former self. Bright. Ambitious. *Optimistic.* The person Henry had fallen in love with.

Henry. She sighed. Annabel hadn't thought about him since the moment she'd rushed Mackenzie to the hospital, until her cell phone had registered a call from Piper and a subsequent — and irritatingly vague — e-mail saying that there was nothing scandalous to report. What was that supposed to mean? Any report of her husband dining out with another woman was inherently scandalous. After all, Piper would have said if he'd been at the restaurant for a boys' night. Fortunately, she hadn't been able to obsess over it, given the current circumstances. Here she was, with a woman who'd just lost her baby. A woman who'd had "complications" that had yet to be defined. What if she could never have kids? What if Annabel had been able to do something differently? They'd hit traffic on the way to the hospital. Could she have taken an alternate route? Attempted a shortcut? Would that have saved the fragile life inside of Mackenzie?

The doctor had told her of her loss. In his compassionate yet clinical tenor, if that combination was possible. He'd seen this so many times. That was obvious. Women who were in car accidents. Or who'd fallen down a flight of stairs. Women who, like Mackenzie, had done nothing at all, but were just unlucky. That was what he'd called it: "an unlucky situation." She'd cried quietly at first, allowing Annabel to hold her close. But they'd already plied her with painkillers, and while Mackenzie had understood the spoken words conveying her "unlucky situation," she wouldn't sustain the full breadth of her pain until she woke up to a less-bleary existence. That much Annabel knew. She also knew that she'd be right there beside her to ease her into the reality of such a lacerating blow.

Mackenzie shifted in the bed, her eyes fluttering like the wings of a weakened butterfly. Then she clawed at her left arm where they'd inserted the IV.

"Try not to do that, sweetie," Annabel cautioned, whispering so as not to fully wake her. Because then she'd have to figure out what to say. And she wasn't sure she was prepared for that. Not that she ever would be.

She checked her watch. It was nine o'clock. Henry had already dropped the boys at the door to their kindergarten classroom, with its colorful letters cut from construction paper and adhered to it. Fortunately, her babysitter had been able to stay the night, and Henry had been thrilled at the opportunity to pick them up and bring them to school. It felt strange not having to explain herself to him. Had he wondered why she hadn't slept at home? If he had, he certainly hadn't pried. Or maybe he just didn't care anymore. Piper would be finishing exercise class in fifteen minutes — the one they were supposed to go to together — and there was no doubt she'd be calling directly after. She'd have to tell her something. Would it be insensitive to ask Mackenzie if she could bring Piper into the fold? After all, they certainly knew each other better than she and Mackenzie did. Still, she worked at Mackenzie's husband's corporation and that could present an issue.

Annabel's stomach growled. It was probably time to brave either the vending machine or the cafeteria. She'd just run downstairs and come right back up; Mackenzie wouldn't have the opportunity to miss her. The very last thing she wanted was for her new friend to wake up alone. She grabbed her purse from on top of the windowsill and crept toward the door.

"Hello?" Mackenzie's raspy voice startled her, even though it was barely audible, and Annabel's heart tightened in her chest.

"Hey there." She set her purse on the floor and moved toward Mackenzie in what felt like slow motion.

"Where am I?" She rubbed her eyes and then homed in on her surroundings. "What's going on?" She tried to sit up quickly, but instantly fell back against the flimsy foam pillow.

"You're in the hospital. You're okay." Annabel tried to keep her tone level and aimed for soothing. "Try to relax."

"Relax?" Her ashen face was awash with panic and confusion, as the events of the past twenty-four hours began to stumble into place. "Did I . . ." Mackenzie croaked, and her hand went immediately to her stomach. "Did I . . ." She couldn't finish the sentence, but Annabel knew exactly what she was asking, and she nodded mournfully. "No!" She cried. "Please tell me it's not true." Tears plunged down the sides of her face without warning.

"I'm so sorry." Annabel sat on the side of her bed, taking Mackenzie into her arms as her shoulders shuddered and her body heaved with the cavernous, guttural sobs. "I'm so sorry," she repeated over and over again.

Because what else was there to say?

Finally, four hours later, Mackenzie's gynecologist had granted permission for her to go home. She'd insisted that Mackenzie take it easy. No work. No exercise. As little moving around as possible for at least a week. The results of the various tests they'd run had come back inconclusive. A good sign, her doctor had said, adding that she saw no reason why Mackenzie couldn't get pregnant again and carry the baby to term. "Such great news," Annabel had encouraged, but Mackenzie had just nodded dully and then stared absently at the blank white wall in front of her.

"Your friend is right," the doctor had corroborated, but Mackenzie hadn't looked at either of them. She'd said only, "Please get me out of here," and Annabel had complied, driving her back to her house, helping her into pajamas, and setting her up in bed with a stack of fashion magazines she'd purchased in the hospital gift shop, a tall glass of ice water, and an array of snacks. "Stay with me for a little while," Mackenzie had pleaded, "at least until Trevor gets here." Annabel had said she wouldn't have it any other way.

"Are you sure you're comfortable?" She was hovering over her as she would Harper or Hudson when one of them was sick — a fundamental maternal instinct.

"Yes." Her eyes were glazed with grief.

"Okay. I have something to tell you." Annabel adjusted Mackenzie's pillow instinctively. "Please don't be upset with me."

"I'm pretty sure I'm drained of emotion at this point. So you're in luck."

"I had to tell Piper what happened. I'm so sorry. It's just that she did this thing for me last night, and then I was supposed to meet her this morning, and when she called for, like, the fourth time . . . I had no idea what to say. So . . ."

"Annabel." Mackenzie held up her hand. "It's fine."

"Oh, thank God. I really thought . . . Well, I don't know what I thought, but I was worried."

"I said, it's fine. Seriously. As long as she doesn't say anything at work."

"I made her swear."

"Well, then, that's good enough for me."

135

"There's more."

"Yeah?"

"She should be here any minute. But if that's not okay, I'll tell her. She really wanted to see you. To, you know . . ." Annabel sat down on the edge of the bed.

"Feel sorry for me." Mackenzie closed her eyes and took a deep breath.

"No, no. Definitely not. Unless that's what you want."

"Not particularly. Come to think of it, I have no idea what I want." She reached for the glass of water on her nightstand. "There were a bunch of books here. Parenting books."

"Um, yeah. I put those away. I just thought . . ."

"Thank you."

"It was nothing, really."

"No, thank you, Annabel. For everything. You barely know me, and you stepped up in a way I could never have expected you to. It means a lot to me."

"You would have done the same thing in my place." Annabel smiled. It felt nice to be acknowledged for doing something nice for someone. She was half tempted to drop into conversation with Henry a detailed account of her goodwill. *See? I'm not such a miserable person. That's right. Just call me Flor-*

136

ence Nightingale.

"Maybe so, but most people would have called me an ambulance or dropped me at the emergency room and cut out." A look of genuine concern crept across her face. "Wait — what about your kids?"

"No worries. I took care of it."

"I bet you missed them."

"Eh." She shrugged. "Once you have your own, you'll see that a night away isn't the end of the world."

"A night at the hospital?"

"A night anywhere!" Annabel laughed, as the doorbell rang. "That's probably Piper. I'll be right back."

A few minutes later, all three women were sitting together on Mackenzie's king-sized bed.

"I brought muffins from Le Pain. Orange juice. Chocolate. More chocolate. And jelly beans." Piper riffled through a series of plastic bags. "I read once that jelly beans are your favorite. Does that sound stalker-ish?"

"A little." Mackenzie smirked, and Annabel could tell she was feeling at least somewhat better, if not pleasantly distracted.

"Speaking of stalkers . . ." Annabel arched an eyebrow.

"Does she know?" Piper mouthed without

speaking.

"Does she know what?" Mackenzie perked up. "By the way, the invalid can still read lips."

"Not yet, but at this point . . ."

"I'm kind of trailing Annabel's ex-husband," Piper blurted.

"He's not my ex yet. But she is completely trailing my husband." Annabel admitted. "I know what you're going to say."

"That's awesome!" Mackenzie's cheeks flushed with color.

"Okay, that was not what I thought you were going to say."

"I *love* shit like this." Mackenzie bobbed her head eagerly. "Is it to see if he's cheating or something?"

"You got it."

"Can I help?"

"I don't think you're going anywhere for a while. But, hell, if I'd known it would have made you so happy, I'd have told you sooner."

"I've always been super into those crime shows."

"Me too," Piper echoed. "Angela Lansbury is my hero."

"Mine too." Mackenzie reached for the bag of jelly beans Piper had opened. Then she popped a couple into her mouth. "I want in on this when I'm back on my feet." She paused. "Sorry. I didn't mean to sound insensitive."

"It's quite okay. I think we're past the formalities at this point."

"Who else knows?" Mackenzie stuffed another handful of jelly beans in her mouth.

"Just Lucy." Piper bit into a Hershey bar. "So, do you want to know what happened or not?" She turned to Annabel.

"You tell me."

"He was with a woman." She spoke deliberately.

"Great." Annabel's eyes stung and her throat felt suddenly parched.

"But, as far as I could tell, there was nothing physical. Nothing really romantic."

"Nothing *really* romantic?"

"Nothing at all. I mean, except that they were having dinner together at an expensive restaurant."

"Henry doesn't do cheap dining, so that's nothing to write home about." Annabel flicked her wrist in the air. "How did he greet her and say good-bye?"

"Kiss on the cheek. No more." Piper spoke decisively.

"Was she pretty?" Annabel narrowed her eyes.

"Attractive." Piper didn't hesitate.

"Well, what did she look like?" Annabel pressed.

"Shoulder-length black hair. Simple features. Nothing that stood out."

"What was she wearing?"

"A red suit."

"Was it slutty?" Annabel dug deeper.

"Not really," Piper answered uneasily.

"Not *really*?"

"No, it wasn't slutty." Piper panted, trying to keep up with Annabel's rapid-fire interrogation.

"Did you take a picture?"

"I couldn't. That restaurant is tiny. I was afraid to blow my cover."

"Ooh, good crime speak," Mackenzie interjected.

"I thought so." Piper smiled. "Listen, it's just a start. I'm on it. I promise."

"Correction." Mackenzie held up her index finger. "*We're* on it."

"Thank you." Annabel sighed. "Looks like I'm going to need all the help I can get."

"We all do." Mackenzie bowed her head and placed her hand gently on her stomach. "Anyway, isn't that what friends are for?"

TEN

Sometimes the only answer was to go home. There really was no place like it, as Dorothy had said. After losing the baby, Mackenzie needed an escape. A familiar setting where she could be herself without any of the pomp and circumstance that came with the lifestyle she had married into. Where she could breathe the uncontaminated air down South and eat food that wasn't polluted with preservatives. Cue the ruby slippers.

She'd told Trevor that she needed to be with her family for Thanksgiving, maybe even Christmas, if he could see to being without her for a whole month. More to the point, if he could convince his mother to permit something so out of line with her expectations, both professionally and personally. Of course, they'd told her what had happened. "She's my mother; how can we not?" Trevor had asked when Mackenzie had gently suggested that they not burden her with their problems. Translation: *The last thing I need is more guilt.* Ultimately, though, she'd relented. He was probably right, after all. If it had been anyone else in CeCe's position, she wouldn't have given it a second thought. She'd never have considered concealing their loss from her own parents. The thing was, she knew that CeCe would count it as yet another strike against her. Not Trevor, but her. Because wasn't the woman always to blame when a couple had difficulty conceiving — even if it wasn't actually her fault?

Come to think of it, CeCe had never once suggested bringing Trevor in for testing. What if his sperm were slow swimmers? Or the count was low altogether? But it felt pointless to even broach the subject. Mackenzie knew Trevor would feel emasculated and, more so, that if anything did turn up, it would launch CeCe into a ferocious tailspin. So instead of focusing on the real issue at hand, she'd decided that getting away from the stress at home for a while would be the most cathartic course of action. If CeCe had put up a fight, Trevor hadn't mentioned it to her. He'd said only that he felt awful that he couldn't join her and that he would miss her terribly, though she suspected as long as someone fed him and washed his clothing, he'd be just fine without her for a few weeks. And then he'd handed her a long, thin box covered in thick gold paper with a bright red bow — her Christmas gift, he'd said — and made her swear not to open it until December 25. In turn, she'd said his present was on the way and would arrive wrapped and ready with plenty of time. *As soon as I find something and order it online.*

The real surprise had come when she'd shared her plans with Annabel and Piper, and Annabel had said she was going to be all alone for Thanksgiving, since she'd agreed, albeit begrudgingly, to let Henry take Harper and Hudson to his sister's house. It would be the first holiday apart from her children. And further evidence that Henry wasn't going to change his mind about the divorce. "Come with me to Georgia!" Mackenzie had exclaimed, assuming Annabel would decline. Only she hadn't. Instead, she'd agreed readily, explaining she could come only from the Wednesday before Thanksgiving through the weekend, but that she'd be delighted to join her if that was okay.

It had been nice to have the company on the airplane. She'd never traveled with someone like Annabel, who planned everything from the moment they got into the cab to the airport to the moment they'd set foot on Georgian soil. She'd toted just one carry-on bag, insisting that it was the only way to fly. If ever she needed anything more, she'd clarified, she shipped ahead, though that obviously wasn't necessary for such a short trip. And she'd packed her bag with the efficiency of a soldier in training, allowing her to sail through the security check, where she waited patiently on the other side with everything back in its place, while Mackenzie struggled to shove her laptop anywhere it would fit and retie her sneakers. "You should really wear slip-ons," Annabel had commented, shaking her head at Mackenzie's disheveled appearance. "Rookie mistake." Then she'd directed them to the gate, where she'd handed Mackenzie two blueberry muffins and told her to hang tight while she ran to the sundries shop to get them drinks. "Thanks, Mom," Mackenzie had called after her, wondering if she approached everything in life with the same manic compulsion. Although by the time they'd reached her childhood home, she was fairly certain she had her answer.

"Good morning, love." Mackenzie had awakened to the ring of her parents' telephone and Trevor's soothing voice easing through the line as she picked up the receiver. "I tried your cell, but it went straight to voice mail."

"Yeah, sorry. We have little to no reception here." She sat up in bed. The same bed she'd slept in during elementary, middle, and high school.

"How are you feeling?"

"I'm okay. It's nice to be home."

"I miss you." She could hear the concern in his tone. He'd been so kind in the wake of the miscarriage, not that he wasn't always kind. It was just that, since they'd lost their baby, he'd been more overprotective and attentive than usual. "I wish I could be there to take care of you."

"I know. Me too."

"Did you get my notes?"

"I got one note." She smiled to herself. She'd found it in her toiletry case the previous evening. He'd written *I love you* at least twenty times in his crooked handwriting. "But I haven't unpacked entirely yet."

"Well, there may be a few more."

"There may be?" She laughed.

"Fine, there are six more," he admitted. "Or was it seven?"

"You're the best." It felt nice to be doted on, especially when she was still in such a fragile emotional state.

"I wanted to make sure you had a piece of me with you, since I can't be there in person." He paused. "I love you, Mackenzie."

"I love you too."

"I want you to take it easy down there, okay? Let your parents and Annabel do the heavy lifting. You hear?"

"Loud and clear!" she teased. "I'm going to have some breakfast now."

"Okay, my love. Have a relaxing day, and I'll check in on you later."

"You too." She blew a kiss into the phone before hanging up. Then she slid her feet into her slippers and headed downstairs.

"Hello, sweetheart," her mother greeted her, as she ambled groggily into their small kitchen, which hadn't seemed constricting when she was growing up. She'd never forget the first time she'd returned home with Trevor after they'd moved in together. Everything had appeared so tiny. Like a life-sized dollhouse. She'd had to arrange the six chairs at their dining room table so the four of them and her parents' next-door neighbors could squeeze around it, their elbows knocking together every time they'd lifted their forks to take a bite of food. Even the blue-and-white checkered curtains framing the windows in the living room looked to have shrunk into wisps of fabric that barely obscured the penetrating rays of the morning sun filtering through them.

"Hey, Mom." She kept her voice low. "Annabel is still sleeping."

"Good for her." She smiled, brushing a graying tendril of hair off her face. It was already eight thirty. There was no doubt that her mother had been up for hours. She'd probably finished four loads of laundry. Scoured the countertops. Vacuumed the rugs. And fed the animals — three dogs, two cats, and a hostile turtle she'd won at a local fair and refused to get rid of because it would be, in her words, "inhumane." That in and of itself spoke volumes about Loretta Jane Baker, who'd aged naturally and beautifully into a marginally puckered version of her former self, still with long blond hair and the purest ivory skin.

"Something smells amazing." Mackenzie moved toward the stove.

"That would be tonight's dinner casserole. I hope Annabel likes beef and beans. If not, I can make her something else."

"I'm sure that'll be fine, Mom." Although, for all she knew, Annabel could be a vegetarian.

"I figured what with tomorrow night's turkey, I'd do something simple."

147

"If I'm sure of one thing it's that she'll never have eaten such delicious home cooking in her entire life." Mackenzie came up behind her mother, who was scrubbing plates and glasses at the sink, and hugged her tightly. The word *dishwasher* was not part of her mother's lexicon. Quite the opposite, in fact. Her motto was and had always been, *Why waste money on appliances when you can do it just as well, if not better, yourself?* Which she truly believed she could.

"I'm so happy you're here, sweetheart." She squeezed Mackenzie's arms, which were wrapped around her waist. "Dad is too."

"Speaking of which, where is he?" Mackenzie released her grip and walked toward the table to sit down. Sure, she could have offered to help, but to know her mother was to understand that the kitchen was her domain and she'd shoo away anyone who made an advance.

"Fixing something on that stupid old shed."

"Do you think maybe it's time to get a new one?"

"And then what would your father do?" She laughed. "I'm pretty sure it's more of a hobby than a necessity."

"You're probably right."

"So, tell me about this friend of yours. She seems lovely, but you've never mentioned her before."

"She's actually kind of a new friend."

"Oh, that's nice." Mackenzie had confided in her mother how hard it had been to meet people she connected with in Connecticut. There weren't many women her age with no kids in their neighborhood.

"Yeah, it is. She was the one who drove me to the hospital and stayed with me all night."

"Then I like her even more. Although . . ."

"Although what?"

"She seems" — her mother paused — "troubled." She placed a basket of warm biscuits on the table and then went to the refrigerator, returning with a tub of butter.

"Your instinct has always been spot-on." Mackenzie helped herself to a biscuit, unaware of how ravenous she'd been until the scent that was so evocative of her childhood permeated her senses. "She's going through a divorce."

"That's a shame."

"And, from what I can tell, it was unexpected."

"Even worse."

"I know. I'm really happy she decided to

come with me. She needed a break. We both did." Mackenzie focused on the faded metal sign hanging above the back door to their patch of a yard. The one that had been there for as long as her memory stretched back. It read: *Home Is Where the Heart Is.* And she couldn't help but feel, in that instant, that nothing had ever been more accurate.

"I have never eaten more in my life or been this happy about it." Annabel massaged her stomach in a circular motion.

"Welcome to my world." Mackenzie stretched her legs down the length of her parents' plaid wool sofa, each stain and tear in the fabric evidence of a useful existence.

Sometimes she thought about what it would be like to return to Bowman for good. To give up all of the frivolities she'd become so accustomed to. Because when she was there, all of a sudden weekly manicures and monthly hair appointments seemed like nonsense. Not to mention the blow-outs and professional makeup applications that were expected every time she attended an event. Things felt so much simpler at home. So much easier. When you walked down the street, people actually said hello, even waved, while bearing a wide grin. Imagine that! In Eastport, you were lucky if

150

someone didn't run you over in a parking lot or shove past you to get one spot ahead at the grocery store.

Growing up, she'd never thought that way. Living in New York City or even a suburb of Manhattan had held the promise of glitz and glamour. Opportunity and culture. It was sophisticated. It was a challenge. And Mackenzie had never been one to shy away from a challenge. After all, as Frank Sinatra had famously crooned, "If I can make it there, I'll make it anywhere." Her father, on the other hand, had begged her not to go. Probably because he knew she'd never come back if she did. He'd been right. Manhattan had been her first true love. In the months immediately after she'd moved there, Mackenzie had seen three Broadway shows — waiting in long lines to snag the cheapest tickets available. She'd sampled every variety of cuisine, from the ducks hanging in the windows in Chinatown, to the hot dogs from the street vendors in Central Park, to the illustrious black cod at Nobu, where her roommate had taken her on her father's black American Express card. She'd never seen a black American Express card prior to that. But, nothing — *nothing* — had compared to the sight of the towering and shimmering Christmas tree presiding over the skating rink at Rockefeller Center. A friend of hers had accompanied her to the lighting and had told her afterward that she'd never witnessed an expression of such untainted joy on anyone's face.

Why was it that she didn't do any of those things anymore? Somehow real life had interfered with experiencing it. *Really* experiencing it.

"I like your world." Annabel smiled, lying opposite her, their bodies in line with each other's.

"I'm surprised to hear you say that." Mackenzie adjusted the throw pillow behind her back and tossed one to Annabel.

"Really? Everyone here has been so nice and accommodating." She shook her head. "I think your mom has offered me three snacks since breakfast. And I'm fairly certain that in addition to making my bed, she washed my clothes from yesterday too. It's like being at the Four Seasons, without the hefty price tag!"

"I'd hardly compare it to the Four Seasons! But my mom definitely likes to take care of people. It's her thing."

"Well, it's a great *thing*." Annabel considered this for a second. "You must have had a blissful childhood."

"I did." Mackenzie nodded, though she'd

never thought about it in quite those terms before. Perhaps she would have given it more consideration had it not been. "What about you?"

"It was fine. My parents loved me, provided for me — you know, all that stuff."

"But?"

"But nothing. Your mom is special, that's all. I can tell."

"She definitely is," Mackenzie agreed, full of pride.

"It feels good to be away from everything." She pulled the navy wool blanket that was draped over the back of the sofa across her torso, nestling under it.

"Are you cold?"

"Nope, it just looked comfy." Annabel gazed around the room. "That's what it is. Everything here is comfy. It's a house you want to live in. Do you know what I mean?"

"Sure."

"I mean, if my kids spilled something on this rug, it probably wouldn't be the end of the world as we know it."

"Ain't that the truth!"

"It's refreshing, is what it is."

"You needed a break." Mackenzie exhaled. "We both did."

"And how." Annabel stared out the window.

"It's not my intention to pry, but — if you feel comfortable talking about it — what happened between you and your husband? I mean, what impelled him to leave so abruptly?" she asked cautiously, well aware that despite the intimate situation Annabel had been unwillingly thrust into, they were still in the getting-to-know-each-other phase of friendship. Teetering on the line of what was appropriate to inquire about and what might cross it.

"You know, it's funny. I keep asking myself the same exact thing."

"So you have no idea?"

"Well, I know he thinks I'm a miserable person."

"What?" Mackenzie was incredulous. "How could anyone say that about you?"

"He thinks I like to control everything."

"That I can see." She scrunched her nose as she realized what she'd said. "Sorry."

"It's okay. He's right. But what's so wrong with that? When you have kids, you'll understand." Annabel shook her head. "Now I'm sorry; that was insensitive."

"Not to worry. What say we give up on trying to tiptoe around two very unfortunate subjects?"

"Yes, please. I'm not particularly good at tiptoeing around things anyway, as you may have noticed."

"So, you're controlling. And? That doesn't seem like a reason to give up on how many years of marriage?"

"Ten. And thank you. I said precisely that to Henry." Annabel wrinkled her forehead. "That's why I'm sure there has to be more to it."

"Like another woman."

"Yup."

"Seems like a logical conclusion." Mackenzie hesitated. "Do you think Henry is the type to cheat?"

"Who knows?" She shrugged. "I didn't until he decided to up and leave; that I can tell you. Is there really a type anyway, beyond the obvious lechers?"

"I guess not."

"What about Trevor?"

"What about him?"

"Do you think he'd ever be unfaithful?"

"Ha!" Mackenzie snorted. "Are you kidding? I once found an empty box of cookies hidden under a paper towel in our garbage can when he was trying to lose weight, and he couldn't even lie about that with a straight face. Believe me, it's not that I think my shit doesn't stink. He's just . . . a little immature in that way. He'd be way too scared someone would find out. Plus his mother would throw a hissy fit if it ever leaked."

"I'm sorry my mother-in-law isn't a high-powered publishing magnate, then."

"Don't be. It comes with its own set of problems."

"I have no doubt."

"Hey, how about we abandon this uplifting conversation and I take you for a spin around Bowman? It won't be a long spin, but at least it'll get us out of the house."

"That sounds fun. Let me go change."

"Oh no, we're staying in our pajamas!"

"Can I wear my slippers too?"

"I wouldn't have it any other way." Mackenzie smiled. The last thing she'd expected when she met Annabel was to be cruising around Georgia together in her dad's beat-up brown Oldsmobile. But somehow it felt right. Somehow she felt right. And she was beginning to think Annabel did too.

ELEVEN

Annabel had awakened the day after Thanksgiving with a vaguely familiar feeling. One she hadn't been able to identify at first. She felt rested and refreshed, more so than she had in the past five years and possibly another five before that. Her stomach was pleasantly full, but not so full that the honeyed scent of Loretta's buttery biscuits wafting up the stairs and into the guest room couldn't lure her out of bed and down to the kitchen.

Her phone buzzed and she lifted it off the nightstand without the nagging urgency that typically compelled her to find out who it was at that very moment. And what they wanted from her. It was a text from Henry. A series of them, actually. The first had said "Happy Thanksgiving," with a photo of Harper and Hudson wielding caveman-sized turkey legs and bearing wide satisfied grins. The next few had just been pictures of her boys. *Their boys.* There they were tumbling around with their cousins in the backyard — without their winter coats on! There they were again tackling Henry to the ground in the middle of Lisa's living room floor, which was littered with a deluge of colorful plastic kid and dog toys. It was hard to distinguish between the two, save for the layer of saliva that would coat your palm if you dared to pick up one of Dusty's "chewies." She'd unwittingly made that mistake more than once. Of course, the slick layer of spittle wasn't visible in a snapshot, thus leading Annabel to consider what else she'd missed. What else had her children experienced on the one and only holiday she'd ever spent without them? What had they eaten? What had they talked about? Had they missed her? Had they wondered why she wasn't there to share such a special day with them? If so, exactly what had Henry told them?

Annabel dialed his cell number. She needed to hear their voices. Only it went straight to voice mail.

This is Henry Ford. I'm unable to take your call right now. Please leave your name and number and I'll get back to you at my earliest convenience.

"Hi, um, it's me." She cleared her throat.

Surely he'd still know who *me* was. "It's Annabel. I'm here in Georgia. Really missing the boys. Can you give me a call when you have a chance? So I can talk to them. Please. Okay. Thanks."

The formality of it felt so clumsy. Here was a man she'd seen naked. Wait — forget that. Here was a man who'd asked her to pop a pimple on his naked ass. A man who'd thrown up in her lap after a night of partying too hard with his college buddies. A man who'd gazed into her eyes and promised to love her always and forever. So much for that. Now they'd been relegated to — what? Acquaintances? It seemed preposterous, but she certainly wasn't about to call Henry her *friend*. No. A friend was someone who gave you a heads-up before shattering your entire world into painful shards and leaving you in a state of agony and bewilderment. A friend was someone who accepted you for who you were, looked beyond your shortcomings, perhaps even loved you for your imperfections, and stuck by you. Or, at the very least, tried to work out the knots before becoming completely untied.

She pushed any thoughts of Henry from her mind, slid her legs over the side of the bed, slipped her feet into her fuzzy sheepskin slippers, and tracked the aroma of bacon and eggs right down to the kitchen, where Mackenzie was seated at the table with a full plate of food in front of her.

"Good morning, sleepyhead!" She smiled and patted the chair next to her, signaling Annabel to join her. "What can I get you?"

"Whatever you're having," Annabel blurted, amazed by her eagerness to indulge. Again. At home she'd never allow herself to eat this way or this much. It was a daily battle — counting calories, offsetting those calories with enough physical exercise, all while making sure that everything she consumed had at least some nutritional value. Of course, living with five-year-old twin boys and a husband who liked to eat had made this mission more challenging than she would have liked. There were always bags of cheddar cheese Goldfish and packages of Oreos in the pantry. Not to mention those evil snack bars, which gave the impression of being healthful when they were actually little sticks of sugar dotted with barely-there nuggets of fruit. For a while she'd eaten at least three a day. Until she'd bothered to read the ingredients.

"That's what I like to hear." Mackenzie stood up and made her way to the stove, where a collection of pans were warming.

Pans that had definitely been cleaned post-dinner and were already being put to good use again this morning. Something that never happened in Annabel's home, and a foreign concept altogether to a girl who felt the same way about cooking as she did about scrubbing a public toilet with her toothbrush.

"Thank you. This looks unbelievable." Mackenzie placed a large plate in front of her, which was overflowing with fluffy yellow eggs, crispy bacon, a cottony white biscuit, and a generous scoop of cheesy grits. The gluttony was simultaneously terrifying and exhilarating. But not in the same way as all those nights she'd submerged her face in a carton of Breyers mint chip and then castigated herself with a bout of self-loathing. No, this was very different. It was a decision. A decision she wouldn't regret, even on the heels of a southern Thanksgiving feast that could have put Paula Deen to shame. Not that Paula Deen needed any more shame.

It was hard to even recall each dish Mackenzie and her mother had turned out, all while refusing to let Annabel lift a finger, despite her repeated overtures. There'd been the twenty-pound deep-fried turkey — the main attraction, with its perfectly golden skin — silky-sweet corn bread pudding, spicy okra pickles, deviled eggs, buttermilk biscuits, green bean casserole, collards with onion and garlic, sausage stuffing, and the most delightfully pungent cranberry sauce that had ever crossed her lips. As if that hadn't been enough, Loretta had capped off the banquet with her award-winning pecan pie and a rustic peach cobbler topped with homemade vanilla ice cream. And she definitely did not have one of those fancy Cuisinart ice-cream makers from Williams-Sonoma.

Her instinct had been to call Henry as soon as she'd thanked Loretta profusely and resigned to her bedroom. *You would have inhaled the sausage stuffing,* she'd imagined herself gushing. *Oh, and the corn bread pudding. Out. Of. This. World.* But she'd stopped herself, aware that the three glasses of red wine she'd imbibed had made her feel perilously bold.

"What should we do today?" Mackenzie tore her biscuit in half, releasing a rush of fragrant steam. "I warn you, the options are limited."

"Honestly, I don't really care. Whatever you want."

"Wow, relinquishing control, huh?" Mackenzie goaded, then snapped a piece of bacon between her front teeth.

"Imagine that." Annabel laughed. "Maybe we should take a walk or something."

"You mean, burn off some of the ninety zillion calories we've consumed in less than twenty-four hours?"

"I guess. That certainly couldn't hurt, but I was thinking more about breathing the fresh air. Clearing my head. You know?"

"I do know. And I think that sounds like an excellent idea." Mackenzie swallowed a gulp of orange juice. "Are you sad about not being with your kids for the holiday?"

"I am." Annabel nodded. "But, surprisingly, I'm more okay with it than I expected."

"Are you sad about not being with Henry?"

"Same answer." She nodded. "Though, I have to say, I thought it would be excruciating." She paused to chew a mouthful of eggs and then turned toward Mackenzie, whose natural beauty took her breath away yet again. "Thank you."

"For what?"

"For saving me from my own misery."

"I'd say you saved yourself."

"Maybe a little of both," Annabel mused, as the cuckoo clock chimed from the other room. And then it struck her: that vaguely familiar feeling she'd awakened to had been contentment.

"Please tell me we're almost there and that I'm not truly in such awful shape," Annabel panted, and then winced as droplets of sweat trickled from the nape of her neck down to the small of her back.

"Just a few more feet. You can do it. We're almost there," Mackenzie encouraged, and Annabel noticed she wasn't even perspiring.

Somehow their plan to take a leisurely walk had translated into a two-and-a-half-mile hike up the Blue Ridge Railroad Historical Trail. There were three tunnels along the way, adding an intriguing element to the climb, though they tended to seep water, which Annabel wasn't a big fan of. Fortunately, Mackenzie had remembered to bring a flashlight, so they could at least see what was dripping on them.

"Can we please sit down now?" Annabel hadn't realized quite how clement it would still be at the end of November. She'd noticed online that it was a chilly thirty-five degrees back in Connecticut, which was a little over half the daytime temperature in Northern Georgia and the surrounding areas. As someone who detested cold weather and would be overjoyed to eschew winter altogether, it felt nice to spend a few days in such a moderate climate.

"You got it." Mackenzie pointed to two big rocks. "How about there?"

"That's fine." Annabel rested her hands on her knees, hunched her body, and inhaled and exhaled until she'd regained her equilibrium. "Honestly, I'd sit on a bed of needles right now if it was the only option."

"You did great!" Mackenzie smiled, her neat blond ponytail whooshing back and forth with her effortless movements.

"Are you kidding? I'm about to die." She dropped herself onto the rock next to the one Mackenzie was already occupying. "Clearly, those exercise classes aren't doing the trick."

"Sure they are. I bet you wouldn't have been able to do that a few months ago." Mackenzie unzipped the backpack she'd lugged for the extent of the hike and handed Annabel a fresh bottle of water.

"I want a dancer's body like yours." Annabel grimaced. "Unfortunately, that will so never be me."

"Well, at least you have nice boobs. Flat as a board over here." She raised her arm in the air with a flourish.

"Gee, thanks! Trust me, I'd trade a tight ass and chiseled abs for big breasts any day."

"We always want what we can't have." They sat quietly for a minute, allowing the late-morning sun to warm their bare skin.

"I wonder if that's how Henry felt." Annabel's musing fractured the silence.

"How so?" Mackenzie pulled a bag full of nuts and raisins from her backpack and held it in front of Annabel.

"Thanks." She scooped a handful into her palm. "What if Henry was just sick of the status quo? You know, boring old me. I mean, how many times can you see someone tweezing their eyebrows or suctioning their hips and thighs with a pair of control-top panty hose before there's the urge to look elsewhere? That's the thing about meeting someone new. Someone whose unattractive habits are not part of the fabric of your daily life. Someone who doesn't fart in your presence or wake up next to you with frizzy hair and eye boogers."

"Eye boogers?" Mackenzie laughed.

"The sleep stuff that gets stuck in the corner."

"I get it. You're just funny."

"Seriously, though. This woman he had dinner with . . . maybe she's the greener grass and I'm merely the muddy old sod. The miserable muddy old sod."

"You are not a miserable muddy old sod.

Stop it." Mackenzie took a swig of water. "Did you ask Henry about it?"

"No way. How could I do that? Then he'd know I had someone following him." Of course she'd wanted to. In fact, it had taken all of her willpower not to assault him with the third degree. Who the hell was this woman in the not-really-slutty red suit with shoulder-length black hair and simple features? And what did she want with Henry? More to the point, did she think she was going to sail in and take over Annabel's life, become a second mother to her children? Oh no, no, no.

"You could have said a friend had seen him. Or just asked what he'd done that night."

"Nah, we're not really in that place right now. Not to mention that it would have seemed a little suspicious." Annabel wiped her damp brow with the back of her hand. "I'm in this for the long haul. However long it takes to get to the bottom of it."

"In that case, I have an idea."

"I'm all ears."

"Since you've been obsessing about Henry and who he's screwing around with, *if* he's actually screwing around with someone —"

"He is. I'm sure of it."

"Okay. Why don't you let me and Piper

pursue that while you concentrate on moving forward?"

"How am I supposed to move forward until I know why Henry left?"

"Think about it, Annabel. Does it actually matter why he left?"

"Fuck, yeah, it does!"

"I'm going to have to disagree with you there." Mackenzie passed the bag of trail mix back to Annabel. "He's left. Right? He's said he's not coming back. So the writing is on the proverbial wall in big, bold font."

"Really driving the point home, aren't you?"

"I'm sorry — as your friend, I think you need to hear this. More than that, I know it's for the best. For you." She rested her hand on Annabel's back. "We will find out why he left. I promise you that. If you promise to let us do our thing while you work on *not* dwelling on Henry and what he's up to. You need to find something that makes you happy — for your own sake and no one else's. I'm not saying he's going to change his mind about leaving you. But if there's one thing I know, there's nothing more attractive to a man than an independent woman who doesn't nag him about every minor detail or fixate on what he is or isn't doing when she's not around."

"You might be onto something," Annabel relented. "It's not going to be easy, though."

"The best decisions rarely are. But you're stronger than you think."

"I don't feel strong."

"Well, you are. I can see it."

"What if you find something? You're going to fill me in, right?"

"Absolutely. As long as it's concrete. I will not let speculation stunt your progress."

"Has anyone ever told you you're wise beyond your years?"

"That would make me — what? About as smart as you are?" Mackenzie smirked.

"Oh, you little bitch!"

"Perhaps. But you'll be thanking this bitch in no time!"

They laughed together, and Annabel noticed that the tight grip on her heart was gradually beginning to release.

TWELVE

Every year, without fail, Christmas snuck up on Piper like a mugger in a dark alley, thudding her over the head with the reality that she hadn't given a moment's consideration to buying a tree, stringing lights, hanging ornaments and stockings, or even what she was going to buy for Fern or Todd. Fortunately, Todd had ignored her overture that they all find a time to pick out a tree together. Instead, he'd said he was going to take Fern with him — just Fern. Maybe they could make it an annual ritual. This sentiment had imbued Piper with hope. And when Fern had willingly agreed to accompany Todd without her, Piper had felt that *finally* things could be turning around. After all, it was the season for forgiveness and family. So what if their family didn't fill the traditional mold?

In the past few weeks, Fern hadn't spoken much of her father. On the heels of the cryptic note she'd left in Piper's office, Fern had come to explain that she'd found Max on Facebook via one of his third cousins, whom she'd located through a website that tracked genealogy. She'd admitted to opening a Facebook account, despite the fact that she was legally too young to have one, and writing him a message, which — to her profound disappointment — he had not returned. Like mother, like daughter. Wasn't it natural for Fern to want to follow in Piper's professional footsteps, since she'd spent years accompanying her on work assignments? On the one hand, Piper was proud that Fern had made use of her innate investigative instincts to track down Max, and she knew those inherited skills were important to Fern — though perhaps not as important as luring her father back into their lives.

Piper had assumed she'd feel relieved by the reliability of Max's failure to reply to Fern. That it would be some sort of unspoken *I told you so,* after having been cast as the eternal cynic in Fern's eyes. But she'd derived no pleasure from watching her daughter's expectation wilt into sorrow once she'd realized that he was never going to answer her. Instead, Piper had felt indignant. Resentful. And protective. It was one thing to walk out on her, but to leave a child behind like this was not okay. It never would be. Yet it was Piper who'd been expected to pick up the pieces and to make sure that those pieces didn't come unglued.

Piper had asked Fern if she wanted to talk about it. About him. If there was anything she needed to know. She'd even offered to pull an old shoe box from the top of her closet, one she was certain contained a few outdated photos of Max. Photos she hadn't dared to look at for as long as she could remember. But Fern had shaken her head and said nothing. What was there for her to say? For so many years, Piper had waited for the day that Fern would be old enough to understand. To digest the fact that Max wasn't the superhero she'd imagined him to be. There was no cape. No gleaming "D" for Dad emblazoned on his chest. Because a father was someone who was present, and if, for some valid reason, that was impossible — for example, if he was serving his country overseas — then he was in touch. He sent letters. He did his best. That was what parents did: their best. Piper knew this to be true because she'd been doing her best for the past decade. And, if she did say so herself, she'd done a damn good job.

Only now — now that Fern was coming

to the realization that Piper had been forced to arrive at all those years ago — instead of feeling gratified, she felt scared. Scared that her daughter's comprehension would breed a fear of abandonment. An unwillingness to trust people. And, ultimately, a brand of self-loathing that had haunted Piper, possibly until she'd met Todd.

She hadn't told him about Fern's note. Or the fact that she'd found Max. What was the point? He was a ghost, and, as far as Piper was concerned, unless she saw one with her own two eyes, ghosts were categorically a figment of one's imagination. Continuing to allow Max to be part of their conversation wasn't fair to Todd. It wasn't fair to her. And it certainly wasn't fair to Fern.

By the time Piper arrived home at eight o'clock, the house was pitch-black, which was odd, because Todd always left a light on in the kitchen and it wasn't even that late. She'd spent the past two hours racing from store to store, trying to procure as many "perfect" presents as she could find, slapping down her credit card without a second thought and therefore spending way more than she'd planned or could really afford. Why hadn't she ordered everything online months ago, *before* Christmas Eve? *Before* the black Uggs Fern had asked for had been available only in brown, for thirty dollars more than they'd cost on Cyber Monday — when Fern had e-mailed her the link with a giant smiley-face emoticon next to it. All she would have had to do was click three or four times, and they'd have been delivered to her doorstep weeks before the holiday was upon them.

Why couldn't she be more organized, like Annabel, who'd declared with a proud grin the other day after they'd worked out together that all of her gifts had been wrapped, labeled, and hidden in a closet in her guest room since a week before Thanksgiving?

It was just that whenever she tried to set aside a block of time to attend to things like Christmas shopping or scheduling a long-overdue waxing appointment, something work related always got in the way.

"Hello?" Piper cracked the front door. "Anyone here?" she called out into the darkness.

"Mom! You're home!" Fern shrieked from somewhere in the distance. "Todd! Mom is home! Hurry!"

"Could someone maybe turn a light on?" Piper felt her way through the living room and into the dining room, where suddenly she noticed the table was lit with flickering candles, surrounding a succulent whole ham, bowls of roasted potatoes and green beans, and a loaf of homemade bread. There was a tall, bushy evergreen filling the corner of the room and draped from top to bottom with sparkling threads of white lights. At the top was a large red star constructed from paper, with a photo of Piper, Todd, and Fern in front of the Lincoln Memorial tacked to the center. They'd asked another tourist to snap that shot the previous summer when they'd decided to visit Washington DC for a long weekend. It was one of the last times Piper could recall them all being completely happy. As a family.

"Do you love it, Mom?" Fern was practically trembling with excitement.

"I don't know what to say." Piper's eyes brimmed with tears. "This is" — her words caught in her throat — "this is the nicest thing anyone's ever done for me."

Fern wrapped her arms around Piper's waist and Piper hugged her close. She smiled at Todd, who was looking rather pleased with himself.

"You've been working so hard lately. Fern really wanted to do something extra special for you." He came toward them and helped Piper out of her jacket and set her purse to the side.

"Thank you." As she held Fern's face in her hands, she noticed that she was wearing one of her favorite pink party dresses. "Thank you, my sweet girl. You have no idea how much this means to me." Then she turned to Todd, who was utterly dashing in a dark jacket with a red-and-green striped tie. "And you. Thank you for whatever part you had in this." She winked over Fern's head.

"Honestly, Mommy, Todd did most of it."

"Well, I certainly couldn't have done any of it without you." He stroked the back of Fern's head affectionately. As a father would. "For example, I would never have picked this perfect Christmas tie without you."

"That's true." Fern nodded. "And I did get the lights untangled for you."

"You absolutely did," he confirmed.

"You're both amazing." Piper kissed Todd on the lips and, for the first time in a long time, Fern didn't flinch or feign a gagging sound.

"Shall we eat?" He motioned to the mouthwatering feast.

"But I look like such a slob." The clean pair of blue jeans she'd worn to work that morning had been sullied at the knees when she'd slipped on a patch of ice and fallen forward into a puddle of muddy slush. Her shirt was wrinkled and mostly untucked. And her hair, which she'd blown into manageable waves more than twelve hours ago, was now slicked back into a sweaty bun after all of her running around. "Let me go change into something nicer. Maybe shower."

"No way, Mom! We're starving. We've been waiting for, like, an hour."

"And you look beautiful just the way you are," Todd added, guiding her to her seat next to him and across from Fern. "Now, who wants to say grace?"

"I do!" Fern's hand shot up into the air and she let it drop, blushing slightly at her own eagerness.

"I think that's an excellent idea." Todd smiled at her and then at Piper. "The floor is yours."

Fern sat up straight and cleared her throat. She clasped her hands, resting them on the table in front of her, and hooked her head downward, as Piper and Todd followed suit. "Thank you for this beautiful dinner. Thank you for my mother." She paused. "And for Todd." Piper and Todd exchanged knowing glances. "Thank you for the roof over our heads and all of the nice things we have that so many other people do not. Thank you for my friends and my teachers. And thank you in advance for my new Uggs!" She giggled like the ten-year-old girl she was.

"Well done!" Todd raised his wineglass, as did Piper, and they clinked theirs with Fern's water glass and then with each other's.

"Thanks." Fern smiled and then frowned.

"What's wrong, sweetheart?"

"I didn't get you anything, Mom. I wanted to, but . . ."

"Oh, baby, that's okay. I've got you, and that's the best present I could ever dream of."

"Maybe next year." She shrugged.

"Well, the way I always celebrated was that the kids get all the gifts. So there," Todd chimed in.

"Don't worry. Mom helped me buy you that new razor you wanted." Fern's hand flew to her mouth. "Oops! I just spoiled it."

"Um, actually, not really." Piper laughed. "I may have forgotten that particular item."

"Who needs a razor anyway?" Todd scooped a large spoonful of potatoes onto Piper's plate. "I'm thinking of going for the Santa Claus look this year. What do you guys think? Would I be debonair with a big, bushy beard?" He rubbed his chin with his fingers.

"Eeew, no!" Fern crumpled her face. "On second thought, maybe that would be good, because then Mom wouldn't want to kiss you all the time!"

"Sorry — I vote no beard!" Piper bit down on a string bean. "These are delicious!"

"There was a lot of butter involved. You may not want to look at the bottom of the bowl."

"I helped melt the butter!" Fern inserted. "These are much better than the ones you microwave in the bag, Mom."

"Yes, well, my culinary skills pale in comparison to Todd's. I'd say we're lucky to have him." Fern nodded in agreement, and Piper felt like her heart might burst with joy.

For the next hour, they lingered at the table, finishing dinner and then moving on to dessert — a stunning crème brûlée, concocted by Todd, with its rich custard base topped with a layer of crunchy caramel. They reminisced about the fun times they'd spent together and the few long-weekend trips they'd taken — sightseeing in Washington DC, skiing in Vermont, and whitewater rafting on West Virginia's Gauley River. Finally, after they'd all declared themselves stuffed like mushrooms, Fern was granted permission to stay up extra late to watch *It's a Wonderful Life,* while Piper and Todd retreated to the kitchen to clean up.

"You sit. Do not lift a finger," Piper insisted. "You've done more than enough already."

"Don't be silly. It'll take twice as long that way." He rubbed her shoulders from behind, where she was standing at the sink. "And then I'll just have to wait for you to come upstairs, like I always do."

"Fair point." Piper drizzled dish soap onto a plate and started scrubbing it with a sponge. "Did you hear what Fern said during grace?"

"Which part?" Todd took the plate from Piper, along with a handful of silverware, and loaded it into the dishwasher. "I ran and emptied it earlier so we'd have room for all the dinner dishes."

"Smart man." Piper turned to kiss him on the lips and then back toward the sink. "The part about the Uggs."

"Yeah? I think that's to be expected. She's a kid."

"Oh, I know. I don't mind that she said it. I mind that I couldn't get the ones she wanted. They only had brown by the time I got there tonight. I think that qualifies me as the worst mother ever."

"You are not, nor could you ever be, even close to a bad mother. Second of all, I got the Uggs a month ago when she sent us that link."

"You did not!"

"I did!"

"You are a god among men." Piper stood on her tiptoes to give him a proper hug. "Wait — how did you know I wasn't going to get them too?"

"Let's see . . . perhaps because I know you." He grinned.

"I guess she'll have two pairs now."

"Not the worst thing in the world. She's a good kid."

"That's true." Piper handed him the platter that had held the ham. "Have you noticed that things are getting better with Fern? She seems suddenly back to her old self. Not angry toward you or me anymore. I'd be skeptical if I wasn't so happy about it."

"I have noticed." Todd dried off the last bowl and placed it in the cabinet below the oven. Then he took Piper by the hand, drew her close, and enfolded her in his arms. "I think kids can be funny that way. Not that I have any prior experience, but they probably go through phases, and Fern might have been experiencing something we weren't necessarily aware of."

"I hate that."

"I know you do." Todd brushed an errant strand of hair off Piper's face. "But she's getting older, and she's not always going to tell us everything."

"Have I mentioned I hate that?"

"I believe so," he laughed softly and kissed her firmly on the mouth. "Things are great now, Piper. We're great. We're better than great. Fern is great. There's nothing to worry about. Just a whole lot of greatness."

"You make it all sound so simple." Their eyes met and, in that moment, Piper knew there wasn't a man on Earth who could make her feel safer and more loved than Todd did.

"That's because it is simple. All I need is you and Fern."

Just as Piper was about to reply with a similar sentiment, the doorbell rang. "Who the hell could that be at this hour?"

"That's for me!" Fern shrieked, racing into the kitchen as fast as her fuzzy slippers would carry her. "Oh, my God, I can't believe it! Mom! Your present is here! It must be him!"

"Him?" Piper looked at Todd, confused,

and he returned the same perplexed expression.

Until Fern flung open the front door. "Dad! It's really you!"

Piper's body froze and her mouth dropped open. The only word that escaped was "Max?"

THIRTEEN

When Henry had asked to have the boys for Christmas, Annabel had held firm. He had wanted to bring them back to his sister Lisa's, so they could spend the morning tearing through gifts with their cousins, but Annabel had said she preferred to have them home. After all, he'd taken them for Thanksgiving, and while her time in Georgia had been rejuvenating, she'd still missed her sons terribly. In the spirit of compromise, she'd suggested that perhaps Henry could pick them up the following day after dinner, even though they'd normally have stayed with her. Surprisingly, he'd agreed without protest.

"Mom . . . Moooom?" Harper stood by her side, gazing up at her with an angelic grin.

"Yes, sweetie pie?" Annabel smeared one piece of cinnamon raisin bread with peanut butter. There would be no elaborate Christmas feast for the kids — just their favorites. At some point, Annabel had resigned herself to the fact that it was better for them to eat *something,* even if Harper's sole source of protein was peanut butter, than for her to spin her wheels piecing together a healthful meal that they wouldn't take one bite of.

"You're in my way. And my fire truck has to get to an emergency over there." He pointed toward the dining room, where Hudson — purportedly the victim of said burning flames — was now flailing his arms and screaming, "HELP ME!" at the top of his lungs.

"I am so sorry. Looks like a real crisis." She took a step or two back.

"It is." He smiled, flashing his grassy green eyes at her.

"Do you know how much I love you?" Annabel leaned over and kissed him on the cheek before he scurried off to play with his brother. "So delicious!" she called after him.

She couldn't help but notice how nicely the kids had been getting along lately. And she wondered whether it was merely a stage they were passing through or if it had something to do with her and Henry's separation. There was a different dynamic in the house, to be sure. Strangely, while Annabel had assumed things would be more challenging with Henry gone, that even more responsibility would come to rest on her shoulders, it was actually quite the opposite. Naturally, when the kids were with her, she was the one who had to do everything. But hadn't it mostly been that way when Henry was around? Only now she could do it on her terms, without having to nag Henry to get up off the couch and help her. Not to mention that she no longer had to clean up after him. There were no dirty glasses left on the coffee table. No half-full bottles of water scattered about the house. No sullied laundry flung in the direction of the hamper that never ended up actually falling inside it. Not to mention that when Harper and Hudson were with Henry for the weekend, even for a night, it felt like someone had gifted her a mini-vacation.

How many times over the past five years, come six o'clock in the evening, had she been able to pour herself a glass of white wine, put her feet up, call for sushi delivery, and watch an uninterrupted episode of *The Bachelorette*? Not once. Yet lately she'd come to learn to appreciate her "breaks," as she referred to them. It was completely new to her to have time at home where she wasn't running around after the boys. Of course, there were moments when the stabbing pain of being without her children — and sometimes her husband — was more than seemed possible for her to endure. Still, she'd managed to find a way to push through it. To tell herself that this was all part of the acclimating process to life after divorce, and that it wouldn't ache this profoundly forever.

The doorbell rang just as she was slicing a carrot for Hudson, and Annabel darted into the downstairs powder room to check her appearance in the bathroom mirror. It was a funny thing. While Henry had lived at home, she'd never thought twice about gathering her hair into a messy topknot and lounging around in sweatpants and an oversized T-shirt, which may or may not have been stamped with yellow sweat stains at the armpits. However, now it somehow felt important that she look halfway presentable when he came around. Maybe she wanted him to feel like he was missing out on something. Maybe she wanted him to think about her instead of the woman in the red suit. Or maybe she was just deluding herself into believing that he still looked at her in that way at all.

Annabel raked her fingers through her hair, flattening the flyaway strands with the palms of her hands. She took a deep breath, twisting her rear end toward the mirror, so she could make sure her jeans still looked as flattering as they had moments earlier when she'd changed into them. She sighed. It was as good as it would get until she dropped a little more weight. Unfortunately, her marathon of indulgence in Georgia hadn't helped that effort. She walked deliberately toward the front door, thinking how silly it was that Henry couldn't simply enter his own home anymore without announcing his arrival.

"Hey. Sorry. I was in the bathroom." She greeted him, immediately regretting the decision to share that information. The last thing she wanted was for him to imagine her sitting on the toilet, with her pants around her ankles, although he'd seen it many times.

"Sure, yeah. No problem." He stood shivering on the front porch. "Can I come in?"

"Right, yes, absolutely." She backed up, holding the door open for him, and then pushed it closed behind him with a thud. "Can I take your coat? I was just about to feed the boys, and then they're all yours."

"Oh." He looked confused, and handed her his black puffer jacket to hang in the entryway closet.

"What's wrong?"

"For some reason, I thought I had them for dinner. I was going to take them to Luciano's for pizza."

"I'm pretty sure I said after dinner." Annabel wasn't pretty sure. She was 150 percent positive — and a month ago, it would have grated on her last nerve that Henry hadn't bothered to pay attention to the plans they'd set. Because Henry never bothered to pay attention to details that were integral to the way Annabel mapped out her days. In fact, a month ago, she probably would have gone so far as to retrieve the e-mail she'd sent him, which had outlined those very details. Only suddenly, it seemed petty and not worth the effort. "I can save this stuff if you want to take them now."

"No, no. It's okay. I'll bring them to Luciano's for lunch tomorrow. It's just . . ."

"It's just what?"

"Nothing. It's fine."

"Tell me."

"I haven't really eaten anything all day, so I'm kind of hungry myself." He wrinkled his forehead. "I'm working on a major deal and it's taking up all my time."

Normally Annabel would have assumed he was fishing for her to offer him something. But he didn't seem to be coming from that place tonight. Plus, she'd noticed he'd lost some weight — at least ten pounds. Of course, she'd jumped to the conclusion that he'd done so to impress Nellie's Tavern Lady or any other suitors he might be courting. Although now it occurred to her that he probably wasn't feeding himself as often as she had or stocking his apartment with quite the assortment of snacks, if any, that were perpetually available in her house.

"I have a frozen pizza I can heat up for you," she offered.

"Nah, that's not necessary."

"Are you sure? It will literally take seven minutes." Annabel made her way into the kitchen, and Henry followed. She opened the freezer and checked the back of the pizza box. "Oh, wait. It's actually eight minutes."

"Well, then, if it's not too much trouble."

"Nope." Annabel opened the box, placed the pizza on a piece of aluminum foil, and preheated the oven.

"So, how was Christmas?" Henry hoisted himself onto one of the barstools lining the center island with its black granite countertop. The black granite countertop they'd both fallen in love with the minute they'd walked into this very room all those years ago.

"It was nice. The boys made out like bandits."

"I bet. I have a few more things for them too."

"I figured you would." Annabel smiled guardedly.

"Don't worry. I didn't go crazy or anything." She could feel him watching for her reaction. And she knew exactly why. Every year, Annabel would go to great lengths to get the kids some of what they wanted and all of what they needed in the way of gifts. And every year, Henry would descend upon the toy store at the eleventh hour, like a gluttonous child, and purchase a cart full of extravagant toys, games, action figures, and so on, thereby obliterating her carefully executed strategy to indulge them, but not to turn them into spoiled brats.

"I'm not." She shrugged. "You're their dad. You can get them anything you want." She smirked. "Although I did nail it this year."

"I have no doubt." He was really looking at her now.

"What?"

"Nothing."

"Come on."

"I don't know. You seem different." He tilted his head to one side, as if he were seeing her for the first time.

"Same old Annabel." She slid the pizza into the oven and finished plating Harper's and Hudson's dinners.

"Maybe. But there's something . . . different."

"I just got highlights."

"No, it's not something physical." He thought for a moment. "You seem more relaxed."

"That's because you're not around to nudge me all the time." She laughed.

"Right." He snorted. "That'll take years off anyone's life."

"Can you call the kids?"

"Where are they?"

"I think up in the playroom."

"Sure." Henry stood and headed toward the stairs. "Hey, guys! Come on down. Dinnertime!"

"Coming, Dad!" Harper shouted back.

Annabel closed her eyes, allowing the sound of their plodding footsteps to soothe her. It was easy to fall back into the comforting embrace of her old life. The problem was, if she allowed herself to falter, she knew she'd come crashing to the ground.

■ ■ ■ ■

"You were completely right." Annabel broke off a piece of her fat-free blueberry muffin and popped it in her mouth. She'd suffered through another grueling barre class as she'd watched Mackenzie bounce around like her feet were affixed to a pogo stick. They'd then retired to their usual spot — the café next door — a ritual which had become far more about the company than the sustenance.

"Music to my ears." Mackenzie smiled before sinking her teeth into a chocolate croissant. "About what?"

"Okay, first of all, this muffin is disgusting." Annabel pushed the rest of it aside.

"I told you not to get it. *Fat-free* and *muffin* might as well be an oxymoron." She rolled her eyes. "Here, take half of my chocolate croissant."

"Thank you, but I can't. I'm really trying to lose ten pounds."

"You know, I think that's ridiculous, but if you insist, then I'd suggest an egg-white omelet with some veggies and protein. It'll fill you up for hours." Mackenzie took a careful sip from her steaming mug of tea. "So, what was I completely right about? I'm dying to know."

"That thing you said in Georgia when you forced me to hike a zillion miles. About how I should act more independent, you know, not nag Henry or obsess over every little detail."

"Ah yes, one of my many pearls of wisdom." Mackenzie smiled cheekily. "So, what's going on?"

"It's nothing major. But Henry came over last night to pick up the kids, and we actually got along." Annabel helped herself to a small section of Mackenzie's croissant, allowing the chocolate to melt on her tongue. "Oh yeah, this is much better than my muffin."

"Imagine that." Mackenzie cocked her head. "Seriously, though, in the way of Henry, that sounds like a step in the right direction. Maybe I've got a second career in marriage counseling."

"I wouldn't get too excited. It's not like he moved back in. It was just nice not to work myself into a tizzy over the small stuff."

"Tizzy?"

"Shut up. You know what I'm saying. We didn't bicker or snap at each other. I even made him a frozen pizza."

"You *didn't*!" Mackenzie feigned shock.

"I did." Annabel stuck out her tongue.

One of the things she'd come to love about Mackenzie was that she didn't take herself too seriously. She made Annabel feel comfortable, perhaps even more youthful — save for the fact that she didn't look any younger these days. "He said something was different about me. That I'm more relaxed."

"Are you?"

"Not really." Annabel laughed. "Perhaps slightly more tolerant. When he's not around all the time, there's not as much resentment over the day-to-day stuff."

"So maybe the split is for the best?"

"I didn't say that. I mean, he's still cheating on me." Annabel arched an eyebrow. "Speaking of which . . . any progress on that front?"

"Jeez, guilty before proven innocent, huh?"

"Let's call it a wife's instinct, shall we?" Annabel motioned to the waitress, who began making her way over to their table at the pace of a tortoise wading through honey. "The service here really leaves something to be desired. Anyway, you were saying . . ."

"Actually, I wasn't saying. You were asking. But, if you must know, we found out about another engagement on Henry's calender. Piper and I are planning to see what's what."

"Fucking bastard." Annabel shook her

head, and the waitress appeared by her side. "I'm going to need one of those chocolate croissants, please."

"Why? He's not allowed to dine out?"

"He is. It just better not be with that whore."

"Easy there, tiger." Mackenzie straightened her posture like the proper Southern girl she was. "Breathe in; breathe out." She demonstrated, placing her hand on her abdomen. "Have you ever tried meditation?"

"Do I seem like someone who's tried meditation?"

"Good point. By the way, where is Piper?"

"I don't know. She said she couldn't make it to class, but that she'd meet us here after." The waitress reappeared with Annabel's chocolate croissant. "Please tell me not to eat this."

"Don't eat that."

"Screw you."

"Okay, eat it."

"You are no help at all."

"Hey, now. I am stalking your husband for you." Mackenzie turned toward the door as it swung open. "There's Piper! Otherwise known as my partner in crime."

"Hi, guys. Sorry I'm late." Piper dropped her overflowing purse on the floor, shucked off her coat, and hung it on the back of the empty chair next to Mackenzie before sitting down.

"Are you wearing makeup?" Annabel asked incredulously. She'd never seen Piper with so much as a smear of lip gloss, even when she was going directly to work.

"Yeah, why? Does it look weird? Is it too much?"

"No, you look really pretty." Annabel smiled reassuringly.

"You're dressed up too," Mackenzie added, noting her simple black shift dress. Piper *never* wore dresses unless she had to attend a wedding. "What's the special occasion?"

"Oh, um, you know. I just have to meet someone after this." She checked her watch. "In an hour."

"Is this someone scouting thirty-something mommy models?"

"I wish." Piper propped her elbows on the table and buried her face in her palms. "Actually, I don't wish. But just about anything would be better than this."

"What's wrong?" Mackenzie shot Annabel a perplexed look while rubbing Piper's back. Annabel shrugged to indicate that she hadn't a clue what was going on either. "You can trust us."

"What's wrong?" Piper parroted. "What's wrong is that my ten-year-old daughter somehow found her father through the amazing world of social media and invited him to our house on Christmas! Apparently, somewhere in her twisted mind, she thought he'd make a wonderful present for me!"

"Oh, boy." Annabel widened her eyes at Mackenzie.

"Shit." Mackenzie widened her eyes back, before Piper lifted her head. "So, what did you do?"

"I asked him to leave! That's what I did. I told him that his surprise visit was not welcome. And that if he thought he was going to stay at our house — which, apparently, Fern had offered — he had another thing coming to him."

"And?" Annabel treaded carefully.

"*And* my daughter hasn't spoken to me for the past two days. Just when I thought things had finally calmed down at home after Fern's odd behavior when Todd moved in, now she's angry again *and* I have to deal with the sudden reappearance of the man who ditched us. *And* Max ended up texting me, which I can only assume means that Fern gave him my cell number. I guess he got a hotel room not far from here, and he asked me to meet him at a diner across the street so we could talk."

"Clearly, you said yes," Mackenzie interjected.

"Clearly. And clearly I'm a glutton for punishment. I mean, what the hell is there to talk about? He walked out on me and our as-yet-unborn daughter over a decade ago. He's barely been in touch. He hasn't sent money. He hasn't lived up to one single promise he's ever made. And now what? NOW WHAT?" She raised her voice on the last part. The women at the table next to them turned to stare, and then one of them murmured something to the other under her breath. "Oh, good. Now they think I'm crazy."

"Who cares what they think?" Mackenzie leaned forward so the women couldn't hear. "I know the one on the left. Not personally, but I know who she is through my mother-in-law. Her husband spent five years in jail for tax evasion, during which time she apparently screwed every single man over fifty in Eastport. And a few married ones."

"Lovely." Annabel rolled her eyes and then turned to Piper. "So, what are you going to do? What if he wants to get to know Fern?"

"I'm praying that's not the case, that this is just a short stop on his way out of town. Forever."

"And if it's not?"

"If it's not, I honestly don't know." Piper shook her head. "I'm finally happy. Eleven years later, and I'm finally fucking happy. Don't I deserve at least that?"

FOURTEEN

Piper hadn't thought about that day in years. Correction: she hadn't dwelled on that day in years. Yet every now and then, she'd look at Fern and see Max's penetrating eyes staring back at her. And a stitch of resentment would needle her from deep within.

She'd fallen asleep the past two nights counting the number of hours, days, weeks, and months she'd cried once she'd finally admitted to herself that he wasn't coming back. "It's not good for the baby for you to be this distraught," her mother had cautioned. "You're better off without him," her father had insisted. And then added, "If he shows his face around here again, I can't promise I won't punch him in the nose." As for the few friends she'd had, they'd scattered like a bag of marbles tumbling onto a hardwood floor.

After all, there weren't many twenty-four-year-olds who wanted to navigate the bar scene with a knocked-up wingman. Or hit the clubs with someone to whom waddling had become the closest maneuver to a respectful dance move. More than that, she'd had nothing to talk to them about anymore. They weren't concerned with what size diapers to buy or which formula would do the best job at diminishing a newborn's gas pain. And an afternoon spent perusing the baby store for crib bumpers and changing tables definitely was not at the top of their priority lists. In the same vein, Piper hadn't been terribly interested in hearing about their wild nights out in New York City — which new hot spots they'd checked out, how much liquor they'd consumed, or how many hot men they'd taken to bed. That wasn't her life anymore, and as if the writing on the wall wasn't glaring enough, Piper's growing belly was a tangible indication that everything was about to change in ways she couldn't even begin to imagine.

Of course, she knew she wasn't the first woman in the world to be with child at what felt like such a young age — whether by mistake or by choice. There were teen pregnancies cropping up all over the country like those pesky weeds in her mother's flower garden. There were girls who were practically children themselves, in countries where birth control wasn't an option, who were already responsible for two or three kids. How could she have been so stupid? She'd asked herself that same question so many times that it felt like a constant echoing in her head. They'd been together for a year. They were *in love.* He'd begged her to see what it felt like without a condom, vowing he'd never done it without one before. *Just once. Please, just once.* How could she have said no?

That was just the thing, though. She could have said no. It would have been so simple to say no. He wasn't some random guy pressuring her to make a decision she wasn't comfortable with. He was Max. *My Max.* If she'd said no, he would have been okay with it. Disappointed, perhaps, but still okay with it. And that would have been that. There would have been no pregnancy. There would have been no Fern.

In retrospect, it was easy to say she wouldn't have done anything differently. That having Fern was, overwhelmingly, the best thing that had ever happened to her. Still, it would have been a whole hell of a lot more manageable if Max had bothered to stick around. If he'd bothered to step up and be a father. Fern deserved the kind of father who fell in love with his daughter the moment he laid eyes on her, as her own dad had sworn he had. The kind of father who was willing to wake up in the middle of the night and warm a bottle, not because he had to, but because he knew it was a privilege to cradle a beautiful, healthy baby in his arms, no matter the hour. The kind of father who would eventually escort his little girl to a school dance or cheer in the audience when she recited her one line as an orphan in her elementary school production of *Annie.* The kind of father who would know who his daughter was — what she liked and disliked. That she was an avid reader, for example. Or that she could eat raw carrots every day for the rest of her life, but never cooked ones. He could have been the kind of father who'd cared enough about any of those things.

Now, sitting in her car in the parking lot of the diner across from Max's hotel, all she could do was linger on the memories of that day when he'd walked out on her, wallow in the old pain that suddenly felt fresh and raw. She'd been reclining on an old leather chair in the bedroom she'd grown up in. She'd yet to leave her parents' home since college, for lack of funds to rent an apartment in Manhattan — at least a passably clean apartment. No matter how many roommates she'd been willing to take on, her measly salary from working at the local newspaper was barely enough to cover the cost of furniture, much less the space to put it in. And, unfortunately, given the fact that her mother didn't work and her father had opted for early retirement, they weren't in a position to subsidize her living arrangements, outside of offering for her to stay in her old room for as long as she needed. They'd said they would feed her, even wash her clothing while she was at work, but that any incidentals — such as meals out, clothing, and the occasional concert at Jones Beach — were up to her.

She'd been reading a book in that old leather chair. She couldn't remember which book anymore — ironic, since she could recall almost every other detail of the day. She'd had one hand on her belly and another holding the creased paperback in front of her face. Just as she'd started to talk to the baby — to ask if he or she would love reading books just as much as she did, there'd been a knock at the door. "Come in," she'd called out, hoping it was Max. She'd shared the news of her positive pregnancy test with him just two days earlier. He'd then accompanied her to the doctor, who'd informed them that she was likely already a couple of months along. "Does that make sense?" the doctor had wanted to know. It had. All she'd had to do was count backward.

Piper had watched Max intently as he'd inched toward her wearing a somber expression. She'd slid her legs off to one side of the leather ottoman in front of her chair so that he could sit down. But he hadn't. He'd just stood there, unable to look her in the eyes. What a coward. Why hadn't she seen it? Then he'd spoken the words that would haunt her for what felt like a lifetime. The words she would replay over and over on repeat, until they barely made sense anymore. "I'm leaving tomorrow. I need time to find myself."

It seemed so puerile, looking back. What did that even mean? To find oneself. Wasn't it a luxury reserved for recent college graduates who were either too lazy or too childish to immerse themselves in the real world of having a job, paying bills, living on their own without the financial support of their parents? Wasn't it an extravagance earmarked for people who didn't have or desire responsibility? For people who hadn't just gotten their steady girlfriend pregnant. Yet, for whatever reason — perhaps because she too was immature — it had sounded plausible. *He is shocked,* she'd rationalized. *He didn't see it coming,* she'd convinced herself. A funny thing, since he'd been the one to suggest unprotected sex. Still, in fairness, she'd been equally surprised and a willing participant. It would be okay, though. Eventually, it would all be okay. He'd take a little trip. Maybe visit his grandmother in Florida. He'd clear his head, and then he'd come home to her. She'd be fine without him for a few weeks, even a month. As long as he returned eventually.

Had he known then, in that moment, that he would not, in fact, come home to her? That was another question that had plagued her for too long. Did he know? Whether he'd known or not what his intentions had been, history told the tale, and that was precisely what had happened.

When he'd hugged her close to him. Kissed her delicately on the mouth, the way he had so many times before. When she'd traced his pink lips with her finger. Seized his boyish face in her hands. She'd had no idea it would be the last time. The last time she'd see him.

Until now. Of course, at some point she'd come to the conclusion that he wasn't coming back. But that realization hadn't been immediate. It had taken her at least a year to fully grasp it.

Piper got out of her car, allowing reluctant impetus to force her along the cobblestone path and up the cement steps to the entrance to the diner. An old man hunched over his walker pushed the door open with his apparatus and offered her a grin as she held it for him to pass through. She scanned the restaurant, but Max wasn't there. Maybe he wouldn't show. Maybe he'd skipped town again. Piper checked her watch and noticed she was about ten minutes early.

"Would you like to be seated, miss?" the hostess asked, standing at attention with a stack of menus.

"Um, sure. Yes, thank you."

"How many are in your party?"

"It'll just be two of us." Piper nodded, noting the paradox of the word *party*. This encounter was sure to be anything but joyous.

"Excellent. Right this way." She led Piper to a booth in the far corner of the restaurant, by the bathroom. If Annabel had been with her, she would have protested. But Piper didn't care. She wasn't planning on eating anyway. Her stomach was in no shape to hold down food, given the knots it was tied in. "Your waiter will be right with you."

The hostess smiled distractedly, placing the menus on the table, as Piper hung her coat on the rack beside her and slid into one side of the booth.

"Thank you." She smiled back at her politely.

If she was being honest, the whole thing felt surreal, like she was living someone else's experience. Why had she even bothered to dress up, blow out her hair, and carefully apply the most subtle makeup she could manage without appearing as if she'd tried too hard?

If Todd had noticed, he hadn't said anything. Of course she'd told him she was going to meet Max. There were certain things that were inappropriate not to share. She'd even asked his opinion, said she wouldn't do it if he felt uncomfortable with it. But, to the contrary, he'd told her to go. He'd said he thought it was the right thing to do, if not for her, then for Fern. Strangely, Fern hadn't directed any of her anger at Todd. Rather she'd lobbied to get him on her side, which Piper had encouraged. If she was going to be cast as the bad guy, the very least she could do was let Todd play the role of savior. "What if he wants to see Fern again?" she'd asked, stricken with panic.

"We'll cross that bridge," he'd assured her.

"If he thinks he's just going to waltz back into her life, into *our* lives, after all these years . . ." She'd clenched her fists into taut balls of rage.

"Let's take it one step at a time," he'd suggested in a calming tone, and then wrapped his arms around her. "Try to relax."

Relax. As if that was even a remote possibility. She hadn't said as much to Todd, though, since this couldn't be easy for him either. Clearly, it wasn't the same, but still. How would she feel if the mother of his nonexistent child plunged into their lives by showing up at the front door of their home on Christmas night? Probably not entirely thrilled, to say the least. Piper stared out the window. Her mind was too crowded with random thoughts to actually concentrate on one particular thing.

"Hey, Piper." She jumped at the sound of his voice.

"Hello." She pursed her lips as he sat down across from her.

"Thank you for agreeing to meet with me." He sounded earnest.

"You didn't leave me much choice." She examined him closely now, more so than she had two days earlier, when the sheer force of shock had disoriented her. He looked older, as was to be expected. But, to her annoyance, age suited him. The same way it did Todd. Sure, Max's once-bushy brown hair had thinned out a bit, even receded slightly. But his captivating blue eyes and mischievous grin had remained intact. He'd even grown a sleek beard, which he wore well. Very well. The smallest part of her felt an urge to jump across the table and kiss him. Just to prove to herself that the intensity of their attraction had dulled. More like vanished. She hoped.

"You could have said no."

"I suppose."

"Although you always had a hard time saying no to me." He smiled his charming smile.

"It seems that's how we got in this situation in the first place." Piper bristled. How *dared* he make light of this?

"I know you're angry with me. And you have every right to be," he started.

"Max. I'm not here to talk about us. It's ancient history. *We're* ancient history." She paused to take a breath. Piper had promised herself, Todd, Annabel, and Mackenzie that she wouldn't let him rile her. "The only reason I came today is to see why you're here. What you want. And because I love Fern. You know, my daughter."

"She's our daughter, P."

"Don't call me that." She wagged her finger. "You don't get to call me that. In the same way you don't get to call Fern your daughter. A father is someone who's there. To help raise their child. You are nothing more than a sperm donor." Piper's austerity startled even her.

"That's kind of harsh, don't you think?" He ducked his head and, for a quick second, she felt bad. But only for a quick second.

"You tell me."

"Listen, P. — Piper. I'm not just here to waste your time."

"That's a relief, because I don't have a lot to spare."

"I know I've been a deadbeat dad." He hesitated, purportedly waiting for her to object. She didn't. "I know this isn't going to be a simple fix."

"Simple fix?" She narrowed her eyes. "What, exactly, are you looking to fix?"

"My relationship with Fern," he blurted, as if it were a foregone conclusion. "And, eventually, my relationship with you."

"If you haven't noticed, I'm in a serious relationship."

"Fern told me. When she wrote to me. I just meant, you know, if I'm going to get to know my daughter, it would be a bonus to get along with her mom."

"Well, I'm sorry. Forgive me if I'm not comfortable with you showing up unannounced after over a decade and getting to know your daughter, as you put it. If you'd wanted to know your daughter on any level, you wouldn't have left or remained MIA for eleven years."

"I've made mistakes." He nodded pensively.

"*Mistakes?* A mistake is when you forget to call a friend back. Or when you send an e-mail to the wrong person. Running out on your family and staying gone isn't a mistake. It's a decision. One that has consequences."

"Fern wants to know me. She wants to know her father."

"Fern is a ten-year-old little girl with a vivid imagination. She's created this inflated idea of you in her head. An idea that likens you to some sort of superhero and is, clearly, far from the truth."

"I have the right to at least see her, Piper."

"Do you? By whose estimation?"

"I don't know." He shook his head. "This isn't how I thought this would go."

"Really?" She balked. "What, exactly, did you expect? That I'd welcome you with open arms? Invite you over for poker night?"

"You play poker?"

"No. But that's not the point."

"Piper, I'm not going anywhere."

"Don't threaten me." Her voice was shrill. "And, by the way, that's a bit hard to believe coming from you."

"*Please,* Piper."

"Please what? Stay. Go. Join the circus, for all I care. Just leave me and Fern alone. We've done just fine without you."

"I meant I'm not going anywhere until I can see Fern again. Tell her my side of things." He exhaled. "Please give me that chance."

Piper sat silently, unsure of what to do. What to say. Until finally she stood up, grabbed her coat and purse, and stomped out of the diner without looking back.

FIFTEEN

The holidays had come and gone too quickly this year, at least for Mackenzie's taste. Unlike so many other women she spoke to, she'd never viewed Thanksgiving and Christmas as burdens to be endured until visiting family members returned home, stringent diet regimens could be resumed, and children were back in school, where they belonged. In fact, it had come as quite a surprise to Mackenzie, when she'd first gotten married and moved to the suburbs, to hear people griping about being saddled by seemingly endless to-do lists relating to a season that was meant to be synonymous with unadulterated joy.

There were catering orders to be outlined and then placed, because God forbid anyone should crack open their stove or light a burner. There were gifts to buy for significant others, parents, children, and even pets. That had been another culture shock for Mackenzie — the concept that people invested a great deal of time and energy into considering what their cats and dogs might like to find under the tree. Rarely was it a chew toy or a meaty bone for the Busters of Eastport to gnaw on, but rather some sort of fur coat to keep them warm. Weren't they born with those? Or perhaps a pair of rhinestone-studded rain boots, for fear that their paws might go unembellished, or, worse, that they could get damp in inclement weather and subsequently track muddy footprints onto their owners' antique Tibetan rugs.

Mackenzie felt especially grateful to have avoided all of that nonsense this year. To have eschewed dressing in her finest and being forced to sit at CeCe's elaborately decorated dining room table, with waitstaff swirling around them in a frenzy, as CeCe barked orders and clenched her jaw at each and every misstep. Inevitably, there would be one scapegoat: the one who had revealed himself to be the weak link from the onset, unaware that exposing vulnerability was tantamount to jockeying for abuse in the Mead household. The poor soul would be railed on by CeCe without relenting. And there was nothing discreet about it. In front of family, CeCe's true colors were vibrant and often blinding. In her mind, there was no one to impress or put on a show for. The two faces of CeCe. Unfortunately, neither of them was particularly pretty.

Mackenzie had often wondered if CeCe had been different when Trevor's father was alive. If perhaps his death had changed her fundamentally, hardened her into the woman she'd become. CeCe never spoke of him, nor did she appreciate being asked. How many reporters had committed that interview-ending mistake? For Trevor's part, he rarely mentioned him either. He'd been on the young side, age nine, when his dad had died due to complications from a lifelong issue with his heart. Still, by nine you knew who your father was. Most likely you worshipped him. Wanted to walk in his footsteps until you could wear his shoes.

Jonathan Mead had run his namesake publishing company until the day before he'd passed away. A week after he'd been buried, CeCe had glided into his position, as it had been told, with the ease of a professional ice skater. She'd sharpened her blades by changing the name from Jonathan Mead Publishing to Mead Media, and had swiftly purchased a dozen regional magazines and journals, amassing them all under one large umbrella, no doubt preparing herself for her impending rainmaking.

Mackenzie had asked Trevor only a few times what he remembered most about his father, what lasting impression he'd left. For whatever reason, she'd expected to hear adjectives like *menacing, powerful, strict,* maybe even a little bit scary. She'd figured that anyone who'd been married to CeCe, anyone who'd *remained* married to CeCe, had to be a worthy opponent. Because, by Mackenzie's estimation, every relationship CeCe engaged in was another game of Russian roulette, and she'd never witnessed anything different. As irony would have it, Trevor had not used those adjectives. Quite the opposite, in fact. He'd admitted that his memory of his dad was somewhat foggy, given that he was a workaholic and his hours spent at home were limited. However, during what little quality time they did have together on the weekends or on family vacations, Trevor said he recalled a man who was kind and generous. A man who was impervious to his mother's absolute way of thinking and her fluctuating moods, which — if his memory served him correctly — did not have the vast range of volatile emotions they did today. He was also a man who loved his wife deeply, but still knew how and when to put her in her place. Mackenzie had relished this particular piece of information. She couldn't help herself. In all of the years she'd known CeCe, she'd never seen anyone — not one single individual — even attempt to put CeCe in her place.

Lately, Mackenzie had been thinking about Trevor's father and wanting more than ever to give Trevor a child of his own. Though, truth be told, nature hadn't been altogether reliable on the baby-making front, and Mackenzie was beginning to think that CeCe might be right; maybe they should see someone. Get to the bottom of why things weren't going the way they'd hoped or planned. She opened her desk drawer to find the card CeCe had given her with the name of the physician she'd met at the American Cancer Society gala. Dr. Stanley Billingsly. The *top* fertility specialist in New York City, according to CeCe and her "sources." It was impossible to tell who CeCe's "sources" actually were, whether they were real, live people or fabrications of her imagination, but, either way, she always referenced them when there was a point to be made. "My *sources* said it's indisputably the best Italian restaurant west of Florence." "My *sources* insist that red no longer looks good on magazine covers." "My *sources* told me dogs who accompany their owners to work live longer, happier lives." Apparently, Aspen agreed. He may have been her "source" on that one.

Just as Mackenzie was about to dial Dr. Billingsly's number, there was a knock on her office door.

"Come in," she called, guessing it was Trevor; otherwise her assistant, Rose, would have buzzed her over the intercom first.

"Hey." Trevor let himself in.

"Hey, honey." She stood up and walked around her desk to give him a kiss. He'd returned late the night before from a business trip and had been up and out of the house before her alarm had buzzed this morning. "You look stressed."

"Janet completely screwed up the press release for the new journal we just acquired, and I need you to deal with it." He slumped into the chair across from hers, frowning, as she returned to her seat.

"Sure, of course. Have her e-mail it to me before she sends it out."

"She already sent it out. That's the problem. Not only did she get the name of the journal wrong, but she misspelled the editor's first and last names too. I mean, for Christ's sake. Is it that hard to spell Laurie Barker properly? My mother doesn't even know yet, and I need to fix things before she gets wind of it. She'll be here in two hours, after her hair appointment."

"Shit, okay." Mackenzie's job was in large part about dousing fires, but public relations wasn't really her department. While there were certainly a number of overlaps between PR and marketing, what many people didn't understand was that they were not one and the same. Not to mention that there were completely separate departments of people devoted to running and overseeing each of them. "Obviously, I'm happy to take this on, but can I ask where Andy and Mike are? Aren't they Janet's bosses?"

"My mom fired Mike, and I think Andy is in way over his head, for obvious reasons. You know, until we find a replacement."

"Mike is *gone*?"

"Yup. Effective three o'clock yesterday, when my mother reprimanded him for something and he told her to lay off him."

"No." Mackenzie widened her eyes in horror.

"Yes."

"Poor Mike." Mackenzie had always liked him. The best word to describe Mike Harrington was *mensch.* He was a guy whose office was littered with photos of his wife and four kids. A guy who never left said of-

221

fice past six o'clock, so he could make it home in time to have dinner with his family. But also a guy who could be counted on to work from home once his two daughters and two sons were safely tucked into their beds. Mike Harrington was a faithful husband, father, and employee. He was also an idiot for having talked back to CeCe. Or maybe he was the smart one.

"Yeah." Trevor sighed. It was hard to tell whether he actually cared about Mike being let go or whether he was beleaguered solely by the burden he was left to bear in his absence. The burden he was now transferring to her. "So anyway, I can trust that you'll make this right?"

"Absolutely." Mackenzie checked the clock. She'd promised Piper she'd meet her for lunch at one. More precisely, that she'd meet her at the restaurant where Henry Ford was dining with an as-yet-unidentified companion.

"Excellent. This is really helpful." He got up, readying to leave.

"Actually, I was hoping to talk to you about something else. If you have a quick minute."

"Can it wait until later? I have papers piling up, and my in-box is chiming like a pinball machine." He ran his fingers through his shock of bushy brown hair.

"Tonight?"

"I have a dinner after work."

"Tomorrow night?"

"We have that thing. The . . ." He crumpled his face in thought.

"Juvenile Diabetes Gala at the Landmark Club."

"Yes, thank you." He pointed his finger in the air.

"I think we should see a fertility specialist," Mackenzie blurted. Suddenly it felt urgent and like waiting until the day after next could make a difference, if another must-attend event didn't crop up.

"Oh, um, okay. That was a little out of the blue." He sat back down.

"Sorry. Your mom gave me this guy's card." She slid it across the desk toward him, as CeCe had done to her.

"Do you really think it's necessary?"

"I don't know. I didn't. But now I'm wondering. It couldn't hurt to call, right?"

"I guess not." He shrugged, and she could tell his mind was elsewhere, most likely on righting Janet's gaffe before CeCe volcanically combusted.

"So I'll call and make an appointment?" It wasn't meant to be a question. They were in this together, weren't they?

"Maybe we're getting ahead of ourselves." Trevor's cell buzzed. "I have to take this. Can we table this conversation?"

"Yeah, sure. That's fine. Go ahead." She smiled faintly.

"Trevor Mead," he answered in his business voice, and then mouthed, "I'll call you later," before turning to leave her office.

Once he'd shut the door behind him, she looked down at the card again. Then she picked up the phone and dialed the number before she had a chance to change her mind. "Hello. This is Mackenzie Mead. I'd like to schedule an appointment with Dr. Billingsly." She cleared her throat. "The sooner, the better."

Righting Janet's wrong had been a far more arduous task than Mackenzie had anticipated, which had rendered her fifteen minutes late for lunch with Piper, whom she'd been unable to reach on the phone to tell her as much. She'd run the three blocks from the parking lot down the street and, now, as she burst through the front door of the restaurant breathlessly, she scanned the room for Piper. This was not how she'd expected her very first stakeout to go.

Zuckerman's Grill was considered one of the chicer lunch spots in town, all the way on the opposite side of Eastport from Mead Media, so Mackenzie had been there a only few times, though those few times had been memorable. She'd been longing for their tomato soup and crispy sweet potato fries since breakfast. Skimming the well-heeled crowd once more for Piper's smiling face and wildly curly hair, she landed on her assistant, Lucy, instead, sitting at a table in the corner by herself.

"Fancy meeting you here." Mackenzie approached the table and stood across from Lucy, who was obliviously tapping out a text on her cell phone.

"Oh, um, hey." Lucy looked up, fidgeting in her chair. "Sorry you got me instead. Piper had a last-minute work assignment. I tried you at the office, but Rose said you were already gone." She seemed nervous.

"Not to worry," Mackenzie reassured her, then hung her leather jacket and purse over the back of her chair and sat down. "Is he here?" she whispered, because it felt like the appropriate thing to do, given the circumstances.

"Yup. Behind you to your right. Three tables down. It's safe to look," Lucy whispered back, and a jolt of excitement passed through Mackenzie's body. Of course, she didn't want to actually catch Henry doing

225

something wrong, because that would hurt Annabel immeasurably. But she'd be damned if she wouldn't have fun trying to prove Annabel wrong.

"Shit. He's with a woman," Mackenzie said, and craned her neck around her right shoulder, then turned back to face Lucy.

"I know." Lucy twisted her mouth.

"Is it Slutty Red Suit Woman?"

"Huh?"

"Sorry. That's what Annabel has taken to calling her. What I meant is, do you know if it's the same woman he had dinner with at Nellie's Tavern?" Mackenzie stole another quick peek.

"Right. No, I don't. Piper wasn't able to get a picture last time." Lucy held up her phone. "But I was! And I just texted it to Piper. I'm sure she'll get back to me as soon as she can."

"She certainly fits the description."

"I know."

"Anything romantic? Hand holding? *Kissing?*"

"Nothing that obvious. But she keeps throwing her head back to laugh really loudly at everything he says. And she's touched his arm a few times."

"Great," Mackenzie mumbled. "Annabel is going to be apoplectic."

"About an arm touch?" Lucy didn't seem to entirely get it. Why would she? She'd never been married. According to Piper, she'd never even had a serious boyfriend.

"Oh yeah. Clearly you don't know Annabel."

"Can't say that I do. But aren't they getting divorced?"

"Yup. Doesn't matter, though. He's still her husband."

"Shit." Lucy stared down at her phone.

"What?"

"Piper just texted me back. Same woman."

"Crap." Mackenzie exhaled. "I had a feeling."

"And she needs me to leave now and come help her on location."

"Oh, okay. That's no problem. I can stay here and eat something until they leave."

"Are you sure?" Lucy asked, already standing to put on her coat.

"Of course! Far be it from me to get in the way of Mead Media business." Mackenzie smirked. "Go on. I'll take your seat so I have a better view."

"Okay, thanks. Well, it was, um, nice to see you."

"Nice to see you too." Mackenzie nodded and smiled kindly as Lucy hurried off. She could tell Lucy felt awkward around her, and she realized then that Lucy was probably around the same age as she was, if not a couple of years younger. In an alternate universe, they could have been friends. Lucy could have been her college roommate or her equal colleague. It was amazing to think how one chance meeting with Trevor all those years ago had set her on such a divergent path from most women her age.

Ten minutes later, Mackenzie was sitting contentedly in front of a bowl of tomato soup with a heaping side of sweet potato fries, willing herself not to grunt every time Red Suit Lady — who today was wearing a figure-hugging navy blue suit instead — threw back her head in laughter. As Mackenzie lifted a spoonful of piping-hot soup to her lips, she noticed a familiar-looking man walking directly toward her.

"Mackenzie Mead, right?" He stopped in front of her. She couldn't place his face, but she definitely remembered his swoon-worthy dimples, smooth olive skin, and pale gray eyes. *Comforting* eyes.

"That's me." She grinned. It wasn't the first time someone had come up to her in a public place. It was rare, but occasionally people recognized her from a photo they'd seen of her with Trevor or CeCe in the society pages of a local magazine.

"You probably don't remember me," he started. "I hope you don't mind me saying hello. I was the doctor in the emergency room when your friend brought you in a couple of months ago."

"Yes! I'm so sorry. It took me a minute. And I forgot the hospital is just around the corner. I was a little out of sorts that day."

"Of course. Understandably so." He extended his arm to shake her hand. "I'm Dr. Blake. James Blake."

"It's all coming back to me now." She glanced around the packed restaurant. "Are you here with someone?"

"Nope. Just a short break between shifts." He noticed what she was eating. "Looks like you've got it right. Their tomato soup is killer, as are those fries."

"You're telling me." She motioned to the seat across from her, still keeping one eye focused on Henry and his lunch companion. "Why don't you join me? I couldn't possibly finish all of these fries," she lied. She very well could finish each and every one herself. And had planned to. But she didn't want to be rude.

"Are you alone too? I don't want to impose."

"All by myself. My friend had to skip out

for work at the last minute."

"Okay, then." He sat down just as Henry and his date stood to leave. Should she follow them? It felt impolite to leave James as soon as he'd sat down, but at the same time, she'd come here on a mission.

"Would you excuse me for just one minute? I have to run to the ladies' room."

"Sure." He stood when she did, like a proper gentleman.

"I'll be right back." She trailed slowly behind Henry, so as not to alert him to her presence. She watched them walk out the front door. And then she watched the woman lean in and place a lingering kiss on Henry's cheek, just a bit too close to his mouth for her liking. "Shit." Mackenzie sighed, returning to the table and James moments later.

"Everything okay?"

"Yup, all good." She tried to eradicate the grimace from her face. Annabel was not going to be happy if she told her everything she'd seen.

"I'm glad I bumped into you today, Mackenzie." James pilfered a French fry from her plate. She could feel his eyes on her. Those *comforting* eyes.

"Thank you." She smiled and met his gaze. "I'm glad you did too."

"So, what brings you over to this side of town?" He motioned to the waitress for a fresh glass of water.

"A little business, a little pleasure." It wasn't her intention to come off as elusive, but, really, what choice did she have? She couldn't very well divulge the real reason she'd selected this particular restaurant. How absurd would that sound? "Then it's back to the office for me."

"Me too." His lips curled into a grin. "And then the opera tonight."

"You like the opera?" Mackenzie had yet to meet a man her age who appreciated either a new production or a classic revival. She'd brought Trevor once and only once, to see Gioachino Rossini's *The Barber of Seville,* and he'd slept from the moment the curtain opened all the way through to the final bow.

"I don't think anyone likes the opera. You either love it or you hate it. The former is true in my case. It's a bit of an obsession, if I'm being honest. My grandmother used to take me as a child and it sort of became part of the fabric of my being."

"For me too!" Mackenzie nearly shrieked with excitement. "I grew up in a rural city in Georgia, so, as you can imagine, no opera house there. But when I moved to New York

City, a friend brought me for the first time. It was life changing. *Life changing.* I went through two packs of tissues." She felt herself chattering. "Where do you go?"

"The Met." He nodded, as if it was the only answer.

"Of *course.* Amazing." She took a deep breath. "What are you seeing?"

"Tonight? *La Bohème.*"

"Ah, Puccini." She released a sigh. "I'm so jealous."

"You're welcome to join me some time. I have season tickets."

"I would absolutely love that. If you're serious."

"I never joke about the opera." He laughed softly. "And I usually go alone, so I'd appreciate the company. That is, if your husband is okay with it."

"Oh, Trevor wouldn't mind at all. He hates the opera."

"Excellent." James cleared his throat. "I'm sorry I have to run, but work is calling."

"Absolutely. It was such a pleasure to chat with you."

"The pleasure was all mine."

Sixteen

The thing about grief is there is no way to control it. No way to prevent it from whistling toward you like a freight train and flattening you to the track like a ribbon of fettuccine. There were days when Annabel had been able to keep it safely at bay, hold it at arm's length, engaging in whatever means of distraction she could find. Sometimes it was an exercise class. Sometimes it was lunch with an old friend, ideally an old friend she hadn't seen in a while, thereby allowing her to immerse herself in everything new that was going on in her life, rather than dwelling on her own. Sometimes all she needed was an inane television show and a chilled glass of Pinot Grigio to scare off the demons, even though in her gut she knew they were skulking just around the corner, waiting to pounce on her when the first opportunity presented itself. The very second she let down her guard down and let her mind wander.

Those were the other days. When something — anything, really — could send her into a vicious downward spiral about the state of things in her household. Last week it had been driving by Henry's office that had nudged her off the ledge. She hadn't even realized she was in his neighborhood until she was. Apparently, her car had steered its way there on autopilot. Annabel had taken a long, deep breath before approaching his block. She'd told herself she was fine. That she'd barely ever come to his office when they'd been married. Or not divorced. Whatever they were to each other in the awkward limbo they'd been existing in for the past few months, as their lawyers negotiated a settlement they would both deem fair. She'd tried to convince herself she could get through it. She didn't even have to look at his building. Only she had. And that had been all it took. Her eyes had sprouted fresh tears, and her heart had cinched in her chest. She'd gone directly home and cried the afternoon away, unwilling to burden anyone with what she reckoned to be self-imposed misery.

After all, people got divorced all the time. Every day. Probably every minute. It was the same as everything else you speculated about along those lines. Like when you were brushing your teeth and you thought, *I wonder if anyone else is brushing their teeth at this very moment.* Yes, they were. Or when you were having a dance party with your kids and evoking throwback moves like the Running Man and the Roger Rabbit from the 1980s, and you thought, *There's no way anyone else is having a dance party with their kids and evoking dance moves from the 1980s at this very moment.* Sorry, but they were. As Henry had once explained to her, there are simply too many people in the world, too many like-minded people, that nothing, absolutely nothing we're doing at any given moment isn't being done by someone else — whether that person is down the street or across the country. She'd never really believed it until now. Yet every time she told another person that she and Henry were going through a divorce, they always and immediately said they had at least a half dozen other friends who were also splitting up. Annabel was never sure if she should feel relieved or appalled that she was in such vast company.

And why was it that people just threw in the towel so easily these days? One of the recently divorced moms at Harper and Hudson's school had confided in her that it was her husband's loud chewing that had sealed the deal. "I couldn't bear to listen to him crunching and munching for another minute. And the way he inhaled his food like someone was going to steal it out from in front of him if he didn't finish every last morsel in record time. I couldn't even hear myself think, much less enjoy my own meal," she'd lamented. It had seemed petty to Annabel. Who gave up on twelve years of marriage because their significant other couldn't manage to eat quietly enough?

She'd read an article online written by another woman who'd admitted that her husband had never cheated on her, never yelled at her, never so much as looked at her the wrong way, but that he'd been a lifelong, avid fisher and she could no longer take the way he smelled when he came back from his regular fishing trips. "The scent lingered for what felt like forever. I'd wash our bedsheets six or seven times and they still stank!" Granted, it didn't sound pleasant, but a divorce over Dover sole?

Of course, Annabel wasn't stupid. She knew that the chewing and the fishing trips were merely the straws that had broken the proverbial camels' backs. That there must have been weightier issues in those marriages — ones that had been ignored, not identified, or kept close to the vest for fear of humiliation. Still, she couldn't help but feel that Henry's reasoning hadn't been that much more concrete. Perhaps not as trifling as wayward munching or a pungent odor, but incomplete nonetheless. And shocking all the same.

If she was being honest with herself, there were instances when she'd sensed his frustration. When she'd realized that he'd felt stifled by her need to have everything just so. Still, she couldn't understand what was so wrong with that. He went to work all day, every day, often late into the evening. He wasn't the one who dealt with everything for the house, for the kids, for himself. So why was it, then, that he resisted letting her run things the way she wanted to? Wasn't she sort of the CEO of their life? She certainly would never have waltzed into his office and started spouting directives or tried to demonstrate how he could do things more efficiently. How many times had he paused before doling out constructive criticism, as he'd called it, or thanked her for putting dinner on the table every night, even if she hadn't necessarily cooked it from scratch? Never. How many times had he offered a note of gratitude for the fact that, no matter what was going on for her on any given day — whether she was sick with a stomach bug or physically exhausted from a sleepless night — she still drove the kids to school and picked them up when they didn't want to take the bus, and she carted them to every extracurricular activity, made sure they were fed, bathed, and loved, all while ensuring that Henry's dry cleaning was collected punctually, stripped of its plastic covering and wire hangers, and hung neatly on polished wooden hangers in his closet? The wooden hangers she'd purchased so that everything appeared uniform, which he never would have cared about if she hadn't made it look so nice in the first place. Sometimes she wondered if all of her wheel spinning had ended up coming back to bite her in the ass.

Apparently it had, according to Mackenzie, who'd called her the previous afternoon to convey the details of her lunch "with" Henry, who'd clearly been distracted by a female companion of his own. Annabel had said she was fine with it. That she'd expected the worst and it didn't sound quite that bad. Yet. Mackenzie had been dubious, but Annabel had held her ground. Keeping the grief at bay. She'd even managed to keep it there all evening, distracting herself with her regular duties — bath time for the boys, followed by dinner and then snuggles in her bed. Henry had never allowed them to snuggle in their bed at night. He'd felt strongly that it created bad habits. But now that he was no longer around, she could do what she wanted, and she delighted in taking those liberties, as did Harper and Hudson. Anyway, the bed was far too big for one person.

Only once they'd been tucked away in their rooms and Annabel had retreated to her own, she'd no longer been able to distance herself from her anguish. It came charging at her like a stampede of bulls. And she'd been crushed. Physically and emotionally. She'd wept ferociously until she'd fallen asleep against a damp pillow, and awakened with eyes so puffy she could barely pry them open with her fingers. That was when she'd called Mackenzie and Piper. She must have sounded distraught, because they'd both rushed over immediately with rations of junk food, trashy magazines, and effusive affection.

"Let's keep this in perspective." Mackenzie opened a bag of Cool Ranch Doritos and tilted them toward Annabel, who was curled into a ball under a large, fuzzy blanket on the couch in her family room, gripping a box of tissues like her life depended on it. Mackenzie and Piper were seated on either side of her like bookends, trying to keep her emotionally balanced. "We don't actually *know* that anything is going on between them."

"We know he's fucking her." Annabel spit out the words, as if their bitterness left a bad taste in her mouth.

"We absolutely do not know that!" Mackenzie shook her head.

"I do," Annabel grumbled and plunged her hand into the bag of chips.

"It was just a kiss on the cheek, sweetie. Isn't that right?" Piper looked to Mackenzie for confirmation.

"That's right." She nodded.

"Still, it was a kiss. Another woman *kissed* my husband." Annabel shoveled a small handful of Doritos into her mouth and continued to speak while she chewed. "How would you guys feel if Trevor or Todd were going around having lunches and dinners with some other chick and then *kissing* her?"

"Obviously, we would be upset too." Piper tried to pacify her. "But I think Mackenzie's correct on this one. We need more evidence before we convict him. Innocent until proven guilty, remember?"

"You mean like O. J. Simpson? I highly

doubt Nicole Brown Simpson or Ron Goldman would agree with that."

"Henry isn't a murderer." Mackenzie tore into a pouch of Peanut M&M's and spilled some into Piper's palm.

"He murdered our life." Annabel sniffed.

"And there goes the perspective."

"I'm sorry, but I don't want to have perspective right now. I just want to be pissed. And angry. And all of the other adjectives like those. It's so embarrassing. I mean, how long do you think this has been going on? For all I know, it's been months. Years!"

"I highly doubt she'd still be kissing him on the cheek if it had been years," Mackenzie reasoned.

"Oh, my God." Annabel started to cry without warning. "Do you think he's *in love* with her?"

"No!" Mackenzie and Piper answered at the same time.

"Honestly, she looked way more interested in him than the other way around."

"So she did look really interested in him." Annabel released a sob. "I knew it."

"That was not meant to be the takeaway." Mackenzie exhaled. "The point is that we have no reason to believe that he loves her or is in love with her or even that something

241

is going on."

"Then why do they keep going out together?" Annabel blew her nose loudly into a tissue.

"It's only been twice," Piper added, and placed her hand on Annabel's arm.

"That we know of," Annabel snapped, and then immediately apologized. "Sorry. It's not you I'm upset with."

"It's okay. I understand." Piper smiled supportively.

"The thing is, for all we know, she could be shacking up at his apartment every night."

"I don't suppose the kids have mentioned anything?" Mackenzie treaded carefully.

"No, I don't think he'd do that." Annabel sat up straight and tucked her hair behind her ears. "Let's not talk about this anymore. I need a break."

"That sounds like a great idea," Mackenzie agreed, exchanging a knowing glance with Piper.

"What's going on with you guys?" Annabel asked, ready to invest herself in someone else's issues. Anyone's issues other than her own.

"Well, let's see," said Piper. "Max has been harassing me via text messages to see Fern. And it's like, dude, you disappear for a decade and *now* you're in touch three times a day?"

"And?" Annabel raised an eyebrow.

"And I'm not prepared to discuss anything with him yet. It's too late for any of his explanations to make any difference to me. Of course, Fern is still fuming at me. In an ironic turn of events, she'll communicate with me solely through Todd, who, if I wasn't so miserable about the whole thing, might actually be able to derive some pleasure from their newfound bond. Also, have I mentioned that Todd seems to be a little out of sorts ever since Max reappeared on the scene?"

"Can you blame him?" Mackenzie crunched down on an M&M.

"Of course not! I just don't know what to do. I mean, I kind of assumed Max would be gone by now. All of a sudden he wants to be father of the year? What the hell is that all about?"

"Have you asked him?" Annabel leaned forward, relieved to be fully engaged in Piper's predicament. "Maybe it wouldn't be the end of the world to let him see her. That might be enough to satisfy him and send him on his way."

"That's true," Mackenzie concurred. "I say set up a lunch in a public place for the three of you to talk. And remember to keep Todd in the loop on everything and continue to bolster his confidence in your relationship. Men need that."

"How did you get so wise?" Piper took a large gulp from a bottle of Diet Coke.

"You mean because she's barely a day over fifteen?" Annabel smirked.

"Very funny." Mackenzie stuck her tongue out. "It must be from watching all those episodes of *Dr. Phil.*"

"Speaking of doctors. How's the baby making going?" Annabel softened her expression to one of concern.

"Um, nice transition there." Mackenzie cocked her head to one side and rolled her eyes good-humoredly. "Actually, it's not going. I suggested seeing a fertility specialist to Trevor, but he's not convinced we need it."

"That's surprising." Piper lifted a piece of red licorice from the junk-food stash on the coffee table. "Wasn't CeCe the one who originally suggested it?"

"Yup."

"And doesn't Trevor agree with his mother most of the time?"

"He sure does. Wait — you must work at Mead!" Mackenzie laughed. "I'm not sure what's going on. But I made an appointment anyway."

"Without telling him?" Annabel pointed to the bottle of Diet Coke on Piper's side of the coffee table, and she passed it to her.

"Yeah. And I know. I'm planning to tell him and ask him to come with me. I couldn't get in for a couple more weeks, so I've got time."

"Why didn't you just drop CeCe's name?" Piper asked.

"I don't know. I felt weird about it. There are all these women just as desperate to get pregnant as I am, probably more so, since many of them are older. It just didn't seem right to get ahead of them because my mother-in-law met the doctor at some fancy charity gala."

"That's awfully nice of you," Annabel interjected. "I'm not sure I would have been that considerate."

"Thanks. Truth be told, I'm also happy for the extra time to convince Trevor."

"It's pretty amazing . . ." Annabel started, without finishing her thought. And then sat silently, as did the other women.

"What is?" Mackenzie prompted, as she and Piper shared another look. Another look that Annabel witnessed.

"Don't worry; I'm not going to fall apart again. At least not this minute." She smiled and then frowned. "It's amazing that here we sit. Three fabulous ladies, at least in my estimation. And yet there's something missing from all of our lives — or, in Piper's case, one person too many. Why is that? Why can't we all just be happy and whole?"

"We will be." Mackenzie leaned in to hug Annabel, and Piper did the same.

"How do you know?"

"I guess I don't." She shrugged. "But I have a feeling everything will work itself out."

"I want to see her photo," Annabel announced suddenly.

"Who's photo?" Piper asked instinctively, even though they all knew whose photo she meant.

"I don't think that's a good idea," Mackenzie declared emphatically.

"Neither do I," Piper echoed with similar force.

"I need to see it. I need to know what she looks like," Annabel insisted.

"You're a glutton for punishment," Mackenzie mumbled disapprovingly.

"It's my decision — for better or for worse. Let's have it."

Piper dug through her purse for her cell and, once she'd found it, scrolled through her text messages for the picture of Henry's *friend.* "Are you sure about this?" She held the phone to her chest.

"As sure as I'll ever be." Annabel inhaled a deep breath and then exhaled before taking the phone from Piper's steady grasp. She stared at the photo for a split second and then, without hesitation, looked up at both of them. "Holy shit. I know this woman." She nearly choked on her own words.

"Who is she?" Mackenzie and Piper shared an anxious glance.

"Her name is Lillian Duffy." Annabel closed her eyes. "And she used to work for my husband."

Seventeen

Had she known this day would arrive eventually? If you'd asked Piper prior to Christmas, she'd have balked at the implausibility of ever having Max back in her life in any way. Although she'd certainly spent weeks, months, even a year or two, if she was being honest, expecting him to return — if not praying that he would. At first she'd conjured excuses for him. Anything she could think of — even the truly outlandish. Perhaps he'd been kidnapped on his way home to her and had been entombed in some psychopath's basement, with only bread and water to consume and the same dirty jeans and tie-dyed Grateful Dead T-shirt with the dancing bears he'd been wearing when he left. Or maybe he'd fallen on the pavement while jogging and hit his head, rendering him unable to remember where he'd come from or anyone he knew. How else could he

have disappeared so quickly and so perma-
nently?

She'd never called his parents. Why?
Because she'd felt faithful to him, despite
the fact that he'd walked out on her. Because she'd known that he hadn't told them
about her baby. *Their* baby. Because then
they would have forced him to stay. Piper
hadn't seen or heard from anyone in Max's
family since that fateful day. Sometimes,
when she'd allowed herself a moment to
think about him and the circumstances of
all those years ago, she'd wondered if he'd
ever shared the news of Fern with his
mother or father. Max's mother, Delilah,
would have loved being a grandparent.
She'd never had a daughter of her own; Max
was one of four brothers. She'd once confided in Piper that she would have stopped
at two kids if she hadn't been so hell-bent
on conceiving a sweet little girl to dote on.

Piper and Delilah had hit it off from the
first moment Max had introduced them.
Delilah had ushered her into their home,
and they'd sat at the kitchen table for hours,
gabbing about everything from their favorite
television shows to the clothing brands they
preferred to wear — even though neither of
them was particularly fashionable. In fact,
most every time Max had brought Piper to

his house, Delilah had stolen her away for girl time, as she'd called it, while Max and his father had tinkered with their cars in the garage. Before long, Delilah had divulged to Piper that she felt like her surrogate mother and that she'd hoped that she and Max would marry someday — sooner rather than later, please. In the end, Delilah's testimony had forged a false sense of security in Piper. A false sense of security in her relationship with Max, a point Piper would later come to resent.

Of course she'd thought about what might have happened if she'd never gotten pregnant. If her relationship with Max had been given the breathing room to develop at its own pace, would he have stuck around? Would he have proposed? Would they have spawned a brood of kids a few years into being married? Piper had always imagined herself with three children. Two boys and a girl. She relished the idea of older brothers adoring their younger sister and protecting her from the angst that growing up so often dispensed. But none of those children would have been Fern, and that was the piece she could never seem to get past. Life without Fern. It felt unequivocally impossible.

Yet here she was, sitting across the lunch

table from the man she loved — the man who had persevered by her side in the face of this unexpected obstacle — waiting for her tenacious ten-year-old to grace them with her presence so that they could go meet the man who had disappointed and failed them both in every comprehensible way.

"Let me make you something to eat. A chef's salad? A turkey sandwich? I picked up that challah you like from the Jewish deli. And some matzo-ball soup." Todd stood up and walked toward the refrigerator. "You need sustenance."

"I'm not hungry." Piper rubbed her eyes. She'd been awake most of the night, tossing and turning, unable to stop choreographing the events of the following day in her head. Would she walk ahead of Fern, acting as a barrier, so he didn't rush in and hug her? Would she let Fern sit next to him in the booth at the diner? Would she try to get there first or intentionally arrive a few minutes late, in order to let him squirm? Would she and Fern map out what they were going to talk about on the car ride there? Would she tell Fern ahead of time that she hoped their meeting would scare him off and send him packing for the foreseeable future? And that this desire was the only reason she'd agreed to have coffee with the three of them together to begin with? Definitely not.

"Oh, babe. I know this is hard on you." Todd came up behind her and started rubbing her shoulders. "But I'm here to support you. Whatever you need."

"I know. And I love you desperately for that and so many other things." She turned toward him, and he bent down to kiss her on the forehead.

"Are you nervous?"

"Yup." Piper nodded. "Why do you ask?"

"Your forehead is a little clammy."

"Great." She sighed theatrically. "For the record, I'm also angry and beginning to regret this altogether." Todd pulled his chair closer to hers and sat back down, facing her. "I really don't want to go. Maybe I'll text Max and say I'm not feeling well."

"Listen." Todd took Piper's hands in his. "As I'm sure you can imagine, this is not my top choice of ways for you to spend your Saturday either. However, you have a little girl upstairs who's currently weeding through every piece of clothing in her closet to find the ones best suited for her first real meeting with her dad. A little girl who's barely muttered two words to you since the holiday. I don't think you can put it off any longer."

"Are you sure you don't want to come with us?" Piper looked up at him pleadingly, even though she knew it wouldn't be the responsible decision. Nor would it be fair to Todd or Fern.

"You know I would do anything for you, Piper, including come with you if I thought it was the right thing to do. That said, for your sake and Fern's, you're going to have to go it alone on this one." He smiled. "I will, however, promise to make you ladies all of your favorites for dinner tonight. Some mashed potatoes, creamed spinach, three cuts of filet mignon grilled to medium-rare perfection. How does that sound?"

"If I actually had an appetite, it would sound amazing." She watched Todd's smile droop. "Although I'm sure once this is behind me, I'll be ravenous."

"I have a feeling. I'll do the grocery shopping while you guys are out."

"What would I do without you?"

"Eat a lot of takeout, like you used to." They laughed together, just as Fern entered the kitchen.

"I'm ready." She stood before them, resplendent in her second-favorite party dress — all white with small yellow flowers around the cuffs, neckline, and waist. Second only to the pink one she'd donned on Christmas.

"Don't you think you're a tad fancy for the diner?" Piper questioned. She was still stung by the way Fern had been treating her ever since Max had announced his arrival.

"I think she looks absolutely beautiful," Todd asserted, squeezing Piper's thigh under the table.

"I suppose," Piper grumbled.

"She's just jealous." Fern sniffed, pointing her nose in the air.

"Excuse me, young lady?"

"Let's all relax." Todd had been playing the role of impartial referee for weeks now, a position Piper did not appreciate having to put him in. "Your mother isn't jealous. She —"

"Sure she is," Fern said, cutting him off. "She's afraid my dad is going to love me more than he loved her."

"That's quite enough." Piper slammed her fist on the table, and both Todd and Fern jumped. "You know what? I don't have to do this. I can just call your father and tell him to go back to wherever he came from. Wherever he's been for the past decade while I've been raising you."

"You wouldn't." Fern's eyes narrowed and then quickly brimmed with tears.

"Stop it." Todd's tone was steady but firm. "I don't want to hear any more. You two love each other, and instead of banding together, you're letting this come between you." He exhaled, visibly exasperated by their juvenile behavior. "Fern, your mother is doing something very nice here for you. And, Piper, you know how important this is to Fern. So if neither of you has anything nice to say to the other one, then don't talk at all. Just ride there in silence."

"I'm sorry. You're right." Piper spoke softly. She was not typically the sort of person who slammed her fist on tables. Or who harbored any hostile feelings toward her child. It was all Max's fault. If he'd just stayed away, none of this would be happening. How ironic it was that she'd spent all those years frantic for him to return, and now that he had, she couldn't get rid of him fast enough. "Are you ready to go?"

"Yes," Fern murmured, looking down at her black patent-leather Mary Janes. The ones Piper had spent far too much money on, because there was always single-parent guilt hovering over her like a murky storm cloud. "I'll be in the car."

"Okay, then." Piper stood up as Fern

walked toward the front door.

"You can do this." Todd hugged her to him. "Stay strong. Try to keep some perspective if you can. And remember that I love you more than anything."

"I love you too." Piper nuzzled her head into his chest. "I'm just so scared."

"I know," he said as he squeezed her tighter. "I know."

They'd done just as Todd had suggested: driven to the diner in excruciating silence. By the time Piper had pulled her car out of the garage and onto the street, the tension in the air had already clotted into a heavy molasses, forming an impenetrable barrier between them. Fern had gazed out the window wordlessly. Piper had stared straight ahead of her, eyes on the road, clutching the steering wheel as if the car might suddenly swerve off course, save for her death grip. If this had been any other day, any other circumstance, she would have turned to her daughter and said, *A penny for your thoughts.* But it didn't feel right. And she knew Fern wouldn't take the bait. Piper could tell that she was confined by her own way of thinking. She was stubborn, like her father. And, apparently, unforgiving, like her mother. Except how, then, could she have absolved Max so easily? Didn't she feel as though he'd wronged her too? After all, he had, in fact, walked out on the two of them.

Piper screeched into a space in the parking lot, jerking the car to a halt. Not a second after she'd stopped the car, Fern unbuckled her seat belt and flung the passenger's-side door open, let herself out, and slammed it behind her. Piper shook her head. Why hadn't she anticipated that? Instead, she'd hoped to take a minute or two to say something reassuring to her daughter. She wasn't even entirely sure what it would be. But something had to be said.

She'd wanted to tell her that she loved her no matter what and she understood that Fern was upset with her at the moment. She'd wanted to convey to her that her feelings were her own and that just because Piper did not feel kindly toward Max, it didn't mean that Fern shouldn't. She'd wanted to hug her close, which she hadn't been able to do since before Max's Christmas appearance. Yet now here she was, trailing behind Fern, who'd dashed toward the entrance to the diner with an enthusiasm that reminded her mother of her very first day of school. Her very first day of school that Max had most definitely not been there to witness. It was one among countless milestones he'd missed out on.

By the time Piper was able to catch up with Fern, who was already inside and had snaked her way in and around all of the crowded tables, she'd found the two of them together — father and daughter — in a snug embrace. A volatile cocktail of emotions rose in her chest and then infiltrated her entire body. Her first thought was that he didn't deserve Fern's affection. That he'd stolen the hug that had been meant for her. Only it hadn't been. Fern had chosen a new recipient for her affection.

Very quickly, though, her indignation vanished and was replaced by a sensation she hadn't expected to experience, especially not so suddenly and completely. It was happiness. And it had crept up on her without warning. There was a part of her, a part she'd previously denied, that wanted this for Fern. Sure, Todd was an ideal father figure, but he wasn't a father. More to the point, he wasn't Fern's father. And somewhere beneath the anguish, the resentment, and the fear, somewhere repressed in the depths of her soul, was the buried realization that Fern needed Max — a revelation that was both alarming and strangely comforting all at once. It was a gift she'd never thought she'd be able to give her, and now here it was. Now here *he* was, standing directly in front of her as if he had a pretty red bow tied around him.

"Piper." He nodded once when he greeted her. "It's good to see you. Thank you for agreeing to this." He slid into the booth and patted the seat next to him for Fern to do the same. As if it could have gone any other way.

"It's fine." She smiled weakly. She still hadn't received an explanation, if there actually was one, for his ten-year-long disappearing act. Clearly, this wasn't a fitting occasion or the appropriate company with which to hash things out with him, but it certainly didn't help bolster his case from Piper's perspective.

"I'm so glad to finally be able to spend some time with you." When Max turned toward Fern, her entire face illuminated like a fireworks display on the Fourth of July.

"Me too." She blushed.

"Let's see here." He looked at the menu. "I know we were supposed to meet for a coffee — maybe a milk shake for you — and that it's on the late side, but I haven't had lunch yet."

"Neither have I," Fern answered immediately, quite obviously imbued with joy at the suggestion of more time with her father.

"Piper?" His blue eyes landed on her and remained there, as his lips curled into an expectant grin.

"I'm not hungry, but it's fine if you guys want something," she relented, silently reminding herself that this may be all Max needed before heading out of town again.

"Excellent. I'm going to have the pancakes."

"Me too!" Fern almost shrieked. "They're my favorite. At the place we usually go, I get them with chocolate chips and strawberries. Do you think they'll have that here?" She scrunched her perfect nose, with its constellation of freckles.

"I'm sure we can arrange that." Max patted her on the head like a real father would.

"I like mine with lots of syrup. What about you?"

"It's the only way to eat them!"

For the next forty-five minutes or so, Piper sat in relative silence as Max and Fern's conversation bounced back and forth like a tennis ball at the U.S. Open. She was a fifth wheel, which — as it happened — didn't really bother her. She had little, at least nothing nice, to say to Max. And wasn't this the purpose of the meeting anyway — so

Fern could satisfy her enduring curiosity and Max could . . . What? Ease his guilt? Did he even feel guilty? If so, he certainly hadn't displayed many signs of it.

By the time the waitress finally brought the check — two stacks of pancakes, two chocolate milk shakes, and a shared apple pie with vanilla ice cream later — it was already well after three o'clock.

"Mom, can you believe Max knows how to ice-skate, just like I do?"

"Imagine that!" Piper feigned excitement, mainly relieved that Fern hadn't called him Dad.

"Can we go together? Please, Mom?"

"We'll have to see about that. Max and I can discuss it at another time." Piper scooted out of the booth and reached for her coat and Fern's, which were hanging on the hook beside her.

"I meant now." Fern didn't move. "I want to go skating now."

"Well, that's not possible. You don't even have your ice skates with you."

"I can rent them. Ali Donner does it all the time when she comes with me and . . ." She paused. "Todd." His name was barely audible.

"Good for Ali."

"This is so unfair." Fern balled her hands

into fists. "I knew you were going to be like this."

"Fern." Piper's voice was laced with irritation. Max looked away as she shot her daughter a stern look with widened eyes, to indicate that she wasn't messing around.

Fern bowed her head, and suddenly Piper felt shameful to be depriving her of such a simple pleasure. Furthermore, she was sick of being the bad guy. "Fine."

"What?" Fern's head popped up in surprise. "We can go?"

"We can go. *You* can go. I'll stand on the sidelines."

"Yes! You're the best mom ever. Did you hear that, Max? She said we could go!"

"Thank you." He smiled appreciatively at Piper. "This means a lot to me."

Five hours later, Piper and Fern finally arrived back at their house. In Fern's words, it had been the best day of her life. So there was that. Max and Fern must have circled the rink a hundred times, until Fern had begged to sit at the crappy snack bar and partake in a greasy dinner of corn dogs and soggy French fries washed down with an alarmingly red strawberry Slurpee. As they walked through the front door, Fern was still chattering a mile a minute. She had

262

done so the whole way home — a welcome change from their muted ride to the diner earlier that afternoon. Todd was sitting in the living room in the dark, with the lights from the television flickering around him. He didn't get up to greet them, nor did he say anything at all. That was when it hit her. She'd promised him they'd be home for dinner.

"Why don't you go shower and get ready for bed?" She nudged Fern toward the stairs.

"Okay, Mom." Apparently they were on good terms again.

"I'll come up and tuck you in soon," Piper called after her, before walking into the living room and sitting down on the sofa next to Todd. "Hey. I'm so sorry I didn't think to call."

"Hey." He didn't look at her.

"I'm sorry we're late." She reached out to stroke his arm, but he recoiled as her hand came near. He'd never done that before. Sure, she'd sensed that there'd been a strain between them since Max's arrival, but he'd always maintained that he understood her predicament. And that he supported her unconditionally, no matter what happened.

"I am too."

"Fern just got so carried away, and I felt

like . . ." He put his hand up to stop her from speaking.

"I don't want an excuse, Piper."

"Then what do you want? Anything." Her voice had taken on a slight pleading note.

"I don't know." He shook his head. "I'm going to bed."

"I'll come with you." She stood too.

"Do what you want. I don't feel like talking right now, though."

"Okay." He turned to walk away. "I'm so sorry," she whispered.

But he was already gone.

EIGHTEEN

"You lie back and relax," Dr. Ho instructed, as Mackenzie squirmed on the abrasive medical-exam paper in her struggle to find a comfortable position.

When Annabel had suggested acupuncture as a possible fertility treatment, Mackenzie had envisioned more of a spa-type experience, *not* the dingy home office of a five-foot-four, elderly Asian man. "He was a renowned physician in China, and then when he immigrated to the United States, he became an acupuncturist. Three women I know who tried everything from Clomid to intrauterine insemination to in vitro fertilization were pregnant within four months of seeing Dr. Ho," Annabel had insisted. And then added, "What do you have to lose?"

Nothing was the answer. Except, perhaps, the remaining dregs of her sanity. And whether that was still intact was already debatable. The thing was, Mackenzie did not like needles. At all. But when Annabel had furthered her point by declaring that her friend's thirteen-year-old daughter Rebecca's asthma had also been cured by Dr. Ho's magical pricks, Mackenzie had given in. If a mere teenager could do it, so could she. She hoped. Especially since her conversation with Trevor about seeing a fertility specialist had not achieved the result she'd desired or expected, and she'd been forced to cancel their appointment with Dr. Billingsly. It was uncharacteristic of him to deny her anything, much less dig his heels in about something she'd thought they both wanted, but what could she do? It took two to tango.

In a fit of desperation, Mackenzie had mentioned her frustration to her mother-in-law. Against her better judgment, but she hadn't been in the most lucid state of mind. Rationally, the last thing she wanted was for Trevor to feel like he couldn't trust her or that when she didn't get her way, she went running to his mother behind his back. Still, this felt different. If CeCe was pushing her, she was surely pushing Trevor even harder, which was typically all it took. As anticipated, CeCe had been both surprised and troubled by her son's unwillingness to do whatever it took to produce a grandchild for her. And she'd promised Mackenzie that she'd work on him, even if it took a little time and some clever maneuvering. Translation: *manipulating.*

In the interest of full disclosure — *Okay, well, maybe not* full *disclosure* — she had shared with Trevor her plans to see Dr. Ho. He'd scoffed at the idea, which had riled her. She'd told him he was obviously far too close-minded to acknowledge the legitimacy of alternative medicine. Of course, she'd failed to admit that she wasn't exactly a fervent believer either. They'd bickered, not heatedly, but bickered nonetheless — which they never did — and Mackenzie had been left feeling alone in her pursuit to bear his child. *Their* child. She'd even started to question if something had changed between them.

There'd always been a certain formality to their relationship, though lately Trevor had seemed even more aloof than usual. She knew he was distracted by issues at work; he was, in fact, the one who had to tidy up the shrapnel after every one of CeCe's famous firing storms. Still, she couldn't dispose of her hunch that something wasn't right. Yet when she'd made mention of it to him, Trevor had said she was crazy to think anything was wrong between them and that he was merely stressed out, maybe more so than usual. Then CeCe had taken it one step further in communicating her belief that perhaps the idea of going to a fertility specialist was making Trevor feel like less of a man, and that it was Mackenzie's responsibility to offset that emotion by paying him extra attention and bolstering his frail ego.

Ultimately, Trevor had told her to do whatever she felt was best in the way of acupuncture, and that he'd support her no matter what, even if she thought covering her body in glue, diving into a pit of feathers, and skipping across their lawn while tweeting like a bird would do the trick. That had gone a long way toward lightening the mood.

"When you start trying for pregnant?" Dr. Ho focused his beady brown eyes on Mackenzie's exposed belly, as if steep concentration alone might make it swell. She wondered exactly how long he'd lived in America.

"About three years."

"I see." He nodded sagely, as if the number held some philosophical truth. "You move bowels often?"

"Excuse me?"

"You go to bathroom regular? Number

268

two?" Dr. Ho scurried around the cramped space like a squirrel gathering nuts — all ninety pounds of him. Only his nuts came in the form of shiny, sharp pins.

Why on earth hadn't she taken Annabel up on her offer to accompany her, rather than agreeing to meet her for lunch afterward? She could really use someone's hand to death-grip at the moment.

"Um, yeah. I guess so." Mackenzie flinched as Dr. Ho yanked one of his needles from its plastic tube. The waxy white paper beneath her shifted, leaving the bottom half of each of her legs affixed to the cheap synthetic exam table.

"You have any allergies? Any medical conditions?" Dr. Ho cross-examined her as he darted around, dotting strategic spots on her body with iodine. At one point he even produced a tiny tape measure for optimal precision.

"Not that I know of." Mackenzie's voice splintered as one lone tear trickled down the right side of her face until it met a loose blond tendril that had freed itself from her ponytail. Why was she doing this? Why was she in this little office with this little doctor, getting punctured like a pincushion? Was this really necessary when they had the means to employ a real physician with the

269

support of traditional scientific techniques to his credit? It was impossible to say until you came to the realization that you were willing to try just about anything.

Mackenzie's heart began to throb and the tears started rolling faster and harder from the corners of her eyes, dripping down into her ears. She took a deep breath as the first needle pierced her lower abdomen. And then she exhaled, relieved to have survived it without writhing in pain.

"That's it?" She sniffed, tilting her head upward to make sure the needle had gone in. Sure enough, there it was, sticking up like a flagpole directly under her belly button. Dr. Ho offered a brisk nod but said nothing, and he remained silent as he continued to stick her like a live voodoo doll.

Even though the needles didn't really hurt, the mere fact that she resembled a porcupine made her vaguely queasy, and she thought it better not to watch him in action. Instead, Mackenzie scanned the room, in search of something else to focus on. *Anything else* to focus on. Unfortunately, the stark white walls of Dr. Ho's cubiclelike office were as suffocating as a Jewish mother on her daughter's wedding day. Mackenzie coached herself to ignore the mild claustrophobia she'd been subject to since one very misguided visit to the tanning salon in college, when her friend Gigi had convinced her that bronzing her porcelain skin would make her glow. Unfortunately, the only glow she'd experienced had been from the torrential perspiration that had commenced the moment she'd closed the top of the tanning bed over her body.

Find something to zone in on, she implored herself, and spotted a vibrant Chinese calendar on the wall in front of her, sandwiched between an anatomical poster and three white lab coats hanging on a succession of metal hooks. Did Dr. Ho have a different coat for each kind of acupuncture? *Ah, you have back problem. Let me wear coat number two today.*

"I apply heat now." Dr. Ho scuttled to the corner of the room, and Mackenzie craned her neck to observe him until he turned back toward her with a small hot stone clasped by silver tongs, and proceeded to hover it over each needle. She welcomed the warmth, unaware until that moment that she'd broken a cold sweat and was shivering.

"Okay. That's all. We done." Dr. Ho spoke in a clipped tone while offering Mackenzie the first smile she'd seen from him thus far. He proceeded to pluck out each needle like the expert he apparently was.

"So, what's wrong with me?" She released her long hair from the ponytail holder, allowing the strands to dangle off the side of the table like an assemblage of party streamers.

"Low kidney energy. You need come back." Dr. Ho nodded conclusively.

"Low kidney energy?" Mackenzie shot upright. "Oh, my God! Am I'm going to need *dialysis*?"

"No. Kidneys are fine," Dr. Ho replied pragmatically, signaling Mackenzie to get off the table. Clearly, there were other patients to prick.

"What does that mean, *kidneys are fine*? You just said they were low on energy." She slid off the table, with the exam paper adhering to her left butt cheek. "Do I need to go to the hospital and have tests?"

Mackenzie felt suddenly short of breath. She didn't drink alcohol excessively. She didn't have diabetes or high blood pressure — not even a history of either in her family. She had lost a few pounds lately, quite unintentionally, probably due to the residual stress from not being able to conceive. But she certainly wasn't one of those women who followed a strict diet. Unlike Annabel.

"No hospital." He laughed nervously. Did

he find this funny? "Low kidney energy not to do with kidneys. You come back next week." It wasn't a question.

"Um, okay. I guess." Mackenzie peeled the wax paper from her moist flesh. "What do I owe you?"

"One hundred thirty dollars. Cash."

She nodded obediently, rifling through her purse to find her wallet, before handing over three crisp bills. She would have expected the loss of her dignity to cost more.

NINETEEN

"I can't believe you're going to eat all of those."

Annabel's eyes were fixed on the brimming plate of onion rings the waitress had just placed in front of Mackenzie. She was determined to lose ten more pounds by March if it killed her, which it might. There was no one that reviled food deprivation more than Annabel did, which was precisely why she permitted herself one cheat day every week and, therefore, spent Monday through Saturday fantasizing about what she'd allow herself on Sunday. Though she'd never admit it to anyone, sometimes she'd even make a list of all the trigger foods she'd been craving, so as not to be remorseful the following Monday when she realized she'd meant to have a glazed doughnut. Or three.

"By now you better believe it." Mackenzie shoved a whole onion ring into her mouth to further her point. "I've lost a few pounds in the past couple of weeks, unintentionally, so I'm trying to reverse that."

"Poor you," Annabel teased, before staring down at her pitifully sparse bowl of mixed greens with vinegar only. She'd been told that olive oil contained good fat, but since Annabel had never met a fat that seemed good in any way, she chose to ignore that particular morsel of information.

"I knew you'd say that." She slid her plate toward Annabel. "Go ahead. What's the worst that could happen?"

"Well, let's see. My ass could get bigger than it already is. Or the bulging muffin top that spills over the top of my jeans could bulge a little more. That would be awesome, don't you think?"

"Would you quit your moaning? I've told you a thousand times you look great, and you know I wouldn't bullshit you."

"Yes, but would I look better fifteen pounds thinner?"

"Is it worth being miserable in order to make that happen?"

"You didn't answer the question."

"Neither did you."

"Fine, I'll let you off the hook." Annabel pierced a cherry tomato with her fork and lifted it to her mouth. "So, what happened with the acupuncture?"

"It was fine, I guess. It definitely didn't hurt the way I thought it would, which is so odd, considering you just lie there, stiff as an erection, while someone jabs you with needles. Still, it was a little weird. He said I have low kidney energy."

"What the hell does that mean? And, by the way, I'm totally stealing that line. *Stiff as an erection.*" She giggled girlishly.

"Steal away." Mackenzie took a sip of her water. "That's what I asked. Apparently, it has nothing to do with my kidneys, but everything to do with why I haven't been able to conceive."

"Really? Dr. Ho said that?"

"Not in so many words. But that seemed to be the gist of it. He wants me to come back every week."

"Until what?" Annabel could tell Mackenzie was incredulous. If she was being honest, so was she, even though she was the one who'd originally suggested it.

"Your guess is as good as mine. I suppose until my kidneys get their energy back."

"And then he thinks you'll get pregnant?"

"Unclear. Although I believe that's the idea."

"Interesting." Annabel thought about this. "I'll go with you next time. You know, if

Trevor doesn't want to."

"I don't think Trevor has any plans on coming anytime soon." Mackenzie looked down.

"What's going on there? I thought he was so gung ho about knocking you up."

"So did I." Mackenzie sighed, visibly dejected. Annabel had never seen her this way before. Not in the nearly five months they'd known each other. Well, she'd been beside herself when she'd lost the baby, but that was an extenuating circumstance. Normally, Mackenzie could be counted on for her chipper demeanor, which, in turn, boosted the spirits of those around her. She was typically the one lifting her friends up, not the other way around. It was disturbing and, surprisingly, somewhat of a relief at the same time, confirming to Annabel that everyone had their personal struggles and no one's life was as rosy as it appeared from the outside looking in. "He's been distant lately. Something is off."

"Did you ask him about it?"

"Yup. He said it's nothing. All in my mind."

"I love when men say shit like that. As if we're looking for there to be a problem."

"Speaking of problems . . . Did you say anything to Henry about Lillian Duffy?"

"No, I didn't." Annabel shook her head.

Annabel's realization that she actually knew the woman Henry had been dining out with for the past few months had paralyzed her. Why hadn't she expected that? It was entirely unlike Henry to go out and pursue meeting someone new, much less allow a friend to set him up on a blind date — if he had any friends whose wives weren't close with Annabel and would permit their husbands to do that to her.

And even if she had considered the possibility that the mystery woman had been someone she was familiar with, Lillian Duffy would have been the last person on her radar. Sure, she was tall and slender with willowy limbs. Sure, she was attractive — beyond attractive, really. Some might even say beautiful. But she was also cold and calculating, if Annabel remembered correctly how she'd savagely manipulated a situation on Henry's behalf. He'd hired her as a consultant three years ago when he'd decided to acquire yet another in a long line of smaller technology companies in order to strengthen his position in the fiercely competitive digital marketplace. Henry had dubbed Lillian a tiger — or maybe it was a piranha, those infamous predators known for their razor-sharp teeth, their taste for blood, and their penchant for consuming most anything they could find. He'd said she was the ace in his pocket. Or something like that. And he'd been right. Lillian had vetted the competition and demolished them within a week's time, paving the way for Henry to move full speed ahead. Annabel had met her on only two occasions, neither of which had been especially memorable. After that, to the best of Annabel's knowledge, Lillian had moved on to act as someone else's hired gun, at which point Annabel had erased the thought of her from her mind.

"Good girl."

"You told me not to," she reminded Mackenzie, who continued to urge her to stay out of it until there was something worthy of her involvement.

"I know, but I didn't think you'd listen."

"Thanks for the vote of confidence."

"I hope you don't feel like I'm trying to work against you. I want you to be happy, and I think for now that means letting me and Piper get to the bottom of it."

"Yeah, yeah." Annabel waved her hand in the air. She'd heard Mackenzie's spiel before. "He's coming by to pick up the kids tonight. Don't worry — I'll be on my best behavior."

"I have faith." Mackenzie smiled.

"Oh, sure. Now you do!" Annabel laughed playfully.

"Remember: think demure. Relaxed. Calm."

"But I'm not any of those things."

"You've come a long way — trust me."

"How so?" Annabel was skeptical, fairly certain that no one had ever called her demure.

"Are you kidding? You're *way* less uptight than you were a few months ago," Mackenzie avowed.

"You think?" Annabel considered this. She had felt lighter lately, less encumbered by the daily minutiae. She was no longer checking and double-checking her to-do list every five minutes. In fact, come to think of it, she'd forgotten to make her monthly list altogether, and it was already midway through February.

"I don't think; I know. Piper commented on it too, and she's known you for longer."

"Really?" Unpredictably, this instilled Annabel with confidence and the desire to let up on her stringent way of doing things even more. What would happen if the laundry didn't get done until one day later than it normally did? Or if she was three minutes late to drop the boys at school? Would the world come to a screeching halt if the kids left their toys littering the family-room floor at night before going to sleep? Certainly they wouldn't burn holes in the ground. It wasn't that she was necessarily willing to change her entire personality, but she was beginning to see, with Mackenzie and Piper's help, that there was a distinct line between being type A and being type C — the C standing for *crazy.*

"Really." Mackenzie bit into another onion ring, leaving only two. "My mother used to tell me that if you want to live and act a specific way, you should just do it, whether it feels right at first or not. Either it never will or quite the opposite will happen and you'll start to become the person you want to be without having to put forth a huge effort. I'm pretty sure the latter is the case with you."

"So, in other words, if I push myself to appear relaxed, I'll become a naturally relaxed person?"

"Exactly. I mean, it's obviously not so cut-and-dried, but you have the basic concept." Mackenzie placed her hand on top of Anna-bel's. "You may not have realized it, but I think you were miserable before. Not a miserable person, as Henry suggested. Just miserable in how you felt about things at home."

"Before Henry left?"

"Yes, before Henry left. And I'm not saying he was the reason why. But he was tangled up in it somehow. By stepping away from the relationship, in a sense, he's allowed you to find out who you are again, beyond being a mother and a wife. I have a hunch you're going to like this version of yourself much more."

"I think I already do." Annabel grinned. "Are you going to eat that last onion ring?"

"I wouldn't dare." Mackenzie grinned back. "It's all yours."

"You are so very handsome, you know that?" Annabel knelt down on the cold Neptune blue pebble mosaic floor tiling in her bathroom and ran a comb through Hudson's stubborn blond curls. "And I'm going to miss you while you're at Daddy's."

"I'm going to miss you too, Mama." He hugged her spontaneously, which caught Annabel off guard, sending both of them tumbling to the ground. "I knocked you over!" Hudson laughed raucously, as Harper swept into the room to find out what all the commotion was about. Harper, her angel, had, postbath, gone straight to his room to dress himself in his favorite pair of fireman-themed pajamas. Hudson, on the other hand, while passionately independent in many ways, typically more so than his brother, still insisted that Annabel attend to him whenever humanly possible. There was nothing he relished more than his mother's exclusive attention, which, these days, there was more of to go around. Now that she didn't have to address Henry's needs anymore.

"My two gorgeous, sweet boys." Annabel got to her feet and opened her arms wide for both of them to hug her around the middle, affixing their warm, still somewhat damp cheeks to either side of her body. "Are you hungry? Would you like to have some dinner before Daddy gets here? He seems to be running a little late."

"Daddy's always running late," Hudson lamented. Until recently, Henry and Hudson had butted heads in the worst way, probably because they were the same person. Dogged. Inflexible. Entitled.

Henry had once spent an hour at the dinner table with Hudson, both of their arms folded across their chests, until Hudson had consumed every last bite of food on his plate. Annabel, for her part, would have given in after ten minutes, allowing him to leave three-quarters of everything uneaten — a point she knew Henry resented. And he wasn't actually wrong. "They're going to walk all over you if you don't put your foot down," he'd impressed on her countless times. She'd ignored his overtures, insisting that they were too young to be held accountable for every little thing. Of course she'd regretted this assertion about six months later when the boys had, in fact, come to the conclusion that Mommy was the pushover. The one who would make threats she'd never follow through on, such as, "If you don't clean up all of your toys right now, there will be no television for two days!" As if. The truth was that plopping them in front of *Yo Gabba Gabba!* for half an hour was probably more valuable to her than it was thrilling for them. Thirty minutes of peace. Thirty minutes during which she could check her Facebook page, pour a glass of wine, and maybe even return a few e-mails before the pitter-patter of four little feet came in search of her.

"And he's always on the phone when we're at his house," Harper added. "Doing work stuff."

"He never plays with us," Hudson chimed in again. Annabel was neither astonished nor alarmed by their assertions. Henry had never been one to set aside work once he walked through the front door at the end of a long day. He lived and breathed it. It was part of who he was, which was one of the things that had drawn her to him. She appreciated a man with a burning fire in his gut, even if she didn't appreciate the size of his actual gut. And Henry was a good father, despite the limited time he had available to spend with his kids. When he did engage, he was there completely, unlike Annabel, who was always available but not always present in the moment. It was something she'd been working on now that she was, effectively, a single mom.

To Henry's credit, she had noticed — now that he had the kids two weekends a month on his own — that he was pitching in much more than he had when they were all under the same roof. Perhaps not in a way that was identifiable to the kids — as in getting down on the ground and constructing LEGOs with them — but he was doing their laundry and filling their bellies. So that was a step in the right direction.

"Well, your daddy is a very busy man. But he still loves you more than anyone in the whole wide world. I know that. Because I feel the same way." She dotted each of their foreheads with a kiss. "Let's go downstairs and talk about what you might like to have for dinner. Okay?" They both nodded.

"I want chicken nuggets and fries with chocolate milk." This was Hudson.

"I want chocolate milk too," Harper agreed.

"What else?" Hudson asked.

"Peanut butter and jelly."

"Mommy says peanut butter and jelly isn't healthy," Hudson taunted.

"Oh yeah? You're just saying that because you're allergic to peanut butter. And you're jealous." Harper scowled at his brother.

"Boys." Annabel feigned her best stern expression, which was hardly stern. "First of all, I did not say that, Hudson. Although I don't think peanut butter and jelly is the best dinner."

"Please, Mommy?" Harper looked up at her with his doelike green eyes, which was just about all it ever took to get her to relent.

"As I was about to say, I'll make an exception this time."

"Yay! I'm having peanut butter and jelly. And you are no-ot."

"Hey, just a second there, kiddo. Only if you're well behaved."

"Okay, Mama." Once they'd reached the bottom of the steps, Annabel scooped Hudson up into her arms, which prompted Harper to hurl himself at her too. And again Annabel found herself at the bottom of a pile on the ground, this time in the middle of the foyer, where the three of them were tossing, turning, and giggling boisterously just as Henry walked through the front door.

"Hey! What's going on here?" He peered down at them with a wide, genuine smile, as opposed to the awkward ones they'd been exchanging lately.

"Holy crap. You scared me."

"Sorry. I totally forgot to ring the bell. I guess old habits die hard." He frowned, and then his lips curled back into an amused grin.

"It's fine, really. You don't need to announce yourself. It's your house too."

Factually, it was the truth, although they both knew he didn't really live there anymore.

"Thank you. I appreciate that." He nodded earnestly.

"The place is a mess. Watch where you step." Annabel got to her feet and then wound her way through the toys, games, minuscule LEGO pieces, and playing cards scattered across the hardwood floor into the kitchen, which was equally chaotic.

"I don't think I've ever heard you say that before." He looked puzzled but still amused, only in a different way. "The house is in complete disarray." He turned his head left and right, visibly mystified, but seemingly pleased at the same time.

"Sorry about that. I didn't feel like cleaning up. What can I say?"

"Don't apologize. It's actually . . ." He searched for the right word. *"Amazing."*

"You think my pigsty is amazing?"

"Yes. Yes, I do." He nodded emphatically and then studied her closely. "Have you lost weight?"

"Maybe a bit. I'm not sure," she lied. She'd dropped exactly seven and a quarter pounds, not that she was counting.

"You definitely have." His eyes remained fixed on her. "You look good, Annie. Really good."

"Thanks." She smiled appreciatively. And noted his use of her long-abandoned nickname, the one he'd affectionately called her until . . . Come to think of it, when had he stopped? "You're staring at me."

"Yeah, sorry. I just . . ."

"You just what?"

"Nothing. It's nothing." It didn't seem like nothing.

"Okay, then. I was going to feed the kids dinner, but if you have other plans . . ."

"No, that sounds great." He cleared his throat. "I don't want to impose, but do you want to maybe all eat together? We can order Japanese if you want. I know it's your favorite."

"You hate Japanese." Annabel cocked her head.

"Not really. I was just sick of it, since we ate it four times a week."

"We did, didn't we?" She scrunched her nose. Suddenly it felt like another lifetime, even though it had been only a few months ago. "Seriously, whatever you want. Pizza, Chinese — doesn't matter to me." She shrugged. She'd become accustomed to tossing herself a salad for one most nights.

"Really? You were always so particular."

"Well, I guess things have changed."

"I guess so." Henry sat down on a barstool at the counter, and Annabel did the same. He creased his brow. "Do you ever get lonely here when the kids are with me?"

"Sometimes," she admitted to him. No one had ever asked her that before, even though it seemed like such an obvious question for someone who was not only going through a divorce but also splitting custody of her children with her soon-to-be ex-husband. "Do you? In your new place?" *Or is Lillian there to keep you company?* She immediately pushed the thought from her head.

"I do." He sat quietly for a moment.

"Don't get me wrong — sometimes it's nice to have time to myself. To be able to do what I want, when I want."

"I know what you mean. There's a difference between being alone and lonely."

"*Exactly.* I said practically that very same thing to my sister on the phone yesterday. She didn't really get it."

"Probably because she's never been either." For as long as Annabel had known Henry's sister, Lisa, she'd been in a serious relationship either with a boyfriend or her now husband, who never even traveled for work.

"Probably." This was a side of Henry that she hadn't seen in a long time. A softer, more subdued, more pensive Henry. A Henry she felt like she could talk to about anything. Even Lillian. Like, what were her intentions with him? More to the point, what were his intentions with her? But she stopped herself and instead focused on the wise advice Mackenzie had imparted just that afternoon at lunch. "Annie, do you think . . ." He paused.

"That we should order some food?" She finished his sentence, though she suspected that wasn't where he'd been going with it.

"Huh?"

"I'm starving; aren't you?" She was trying

desperately to keep things casual, cool, to ignore the fact that her pulse doubled every time a vision of Lillian and Henry together kidnapped her thoughts.

"Oh yeah, sure." He smiled reluctantly, as if he had more to say but wasn't sure how to say it. Normally she would have tried to draw it out of him, and if that didn't work she probably would have badgered him until he'd say anything to get her off his back. But not anymore. "I'm in the mood for Japanese."

"Sounds good to me."

"Sashimi for two?" He knew it was her first choice, but he'd never liked sharing food, always preferring to order his own dish. "Do you want me to call?" he offered.

"Nah, I got it. I believe there are two delicious boys in the living room who'd love a little playtime with Daddy. Go on."

"Thank you."

"For what?"

"For handling all of this so gracefully."

"You mean the divorce?" she asked, as if there was any question, and he nodded. "You didn't think I would?"

"Honestly? Not really."

"Well, I guess I still have the ability to surprise you, even after all these years."

"I guess you do."

TWENTY

The arctic chill had lifted at long last —
both literally and figuratively. February had
given way to March, stripping the ground
of its thick layer of snow. The jagged icicles
dipping from rooftops had dripped into
slushy mud puddles, until the warmth of
the midday sun had absorbed the final
remaining evidence of an unremittingly
frosty winter season.

And Todd had exonerated Piper for leaving him out in the cold.

It had been no easy task convincing him
to see her side of things. He'd held strong
in his belief that their relationship needed
to come first, not ahead of Piper's and
Fern's, but certainly in advance of any
loyalty she felt toward Max. Not once had
she seen him stick to his guns in quite that
way. He'd always been so nonchalant about
things, so ready to forgive and forget without harboring ill will or resentment. But this

time was different. There'd never been another man in the picture before. Another man whom he knew Piper still had feelings for, whether those feelings were positive in nature or not.

Despite her initial resistance to Max and any bond he was intent on pursuing with either her or Fern, Piper had — to her surprise and everyone else's — let up a bit. She'd started allowing Max to take Fern to dinner without being present to chaperone. She'd even granted him permission to take Fern for the whole day the previous weekend, as long as he checked in every hour or so, fed her three solid meals, kept her safe, and returned her home by eight o'clock and not one minute later. For Max's part, he'd followed Piper's rules in the manner of an obedient minion, most likely out of fear, if not respect.

Piper had sensed, especially over the past few weeks, with Max popping in and out to woo his only child and often lingering longer than was necessary, that Todd was growing increasingly uncomfortable with the current state of affairs. She could tell that he was trying to recapture his place in their lives, now that the father position was no longer vacant. Naturally, he wanted Fern to be happy, and each time she skipped through the front door, beaming, on the heels of another outing with Max, Todd reiterated just how pleased he was to see Fern so full of joy. Still, actions spoke louder than words, and while Piper suspected that Todd wanted to believe what he was saying, it wasn't that simple.

Max had given no indication that he planned to leave Eastport anytime soon, which had compelled Piper to think about what that meant for her, for Todd, and, above all, for Fern. He'd moved from the hotel he'd been staying at into a friend's guest room. A friend who, like Piper, he hadn't seen in more than a decade, but — as luck would have it — had recently split from his girlfriend and was more than happy to have the company of a temporary roommate. She was surprised Max had yet to mention his own parents and whether they were still living in Hastings-on-Hudson, the village they'd grown up in. If so, they weren't that far away, maybe a little more than an hour. Had he called them? Would he want them to meet Fern?

Piper felt like she was occupying a purgatory of sorts, caught between her old life, where Max had been, if anything, an unwelcome memory to this newer, not entirely improved version of her life, where Max was still unwelcome to a certain degree. Only now he was no longer a distant memory. To the contrary, he was a living, breathing reminder of the uncertainty that lay ahead of all of them as they figured out where Max might fit into Fern's life.

She'd promised herself she wasn't going to think about any of that tonight, though, on the second anniversary of the second-happiest day of her life: the first time she'd met Todd. An event subsequent only to Fern's grand entrance into the world.

Todd had made reservations at one of the swankiest restaurants in town, Templeton's. Piper had never been there before, because she'd never had a good enough reason or a hefty enough bank account to do so, but she'd heard from Mackenzie — to whom frequenting such establishments was as routine as brushing her teeth — that they had a sixty-dollar hamburger on the menu. Apparently, it was stuffed with foie gras and topped with a generous ration of black sum-mer truffles, which she'd read were prized for their extraordinary culinary value. In anticipation of such a special evening, Mac-kenzie had been over after work that after-noon to help Piper select an appropriate outfit and, fortunately, had arrived prepared with a trunk full of her own clothing, which had come in handy once she'd declared that Piper had absolutely nothing suitable to wear. Of course, Mackenzie was substantially slimmer than Piper, so they'd been forced to settle on a plain black skirt in Piper's closet that Mackenzie had dubbed passable, as long as Piper ironed it and swore to pair it with Mackenzie's snug gold Calvin Klein sweater, which was certainly snugger on Piper than it was on its owner.

Mackenzie had insisted on wrestling Piper's mop of chaotic curls into a sleek and straight blow-out and then helped her apply just the right amount of makeup to highlight all of her best features. She'd snuck out just before Todd had pulled into the driveway to pick up Piper for dinner. Max had suggested hanging out with Fern for the night until they arrived home, and, in turn, Piper had agreed to let him take her out, not to stay with her in their house. It felt too intimate, too soon. She'd been nervous, as she always was, whenever she handed Fern over to Max, but he hadn't done her wrong yet, at least not this time around. And now, staring at her rakishly handsome boyfriend across the table, it was the furthest concern from her mind.

"I feel like an imposter," Piper whispered, leaning forward so no one could hear her.

"Everyone else here looks so fancy . . . and rich." Suddenly, she wished they were sitting in their sweatpants on the couch, eating Chinese takeout out of the cartons. Or at the casual burger joint around the corner, where the burgers were stuffed with nothing and, if anything, covered with cheese, bacon, and regular, boring old mushrooms.

"We're fancy." Todd smirked, and then gazed at her dotingly, as he was wont to do. Sometimes, and especially in recent months, she wondered what she'd done to deserve such a kind, honest, and — God only knew — patient man. What had he seen in her? A single mom with a consuming and unpredictable job. Wouldn't he have been better off with another dentist or a housewife? Maybe someone younger who wanted to have kids with him, even though Todd maintained that having children of his own wasn't important to him. And that Fern was all he needed.

"Okay, if you say so." She laughed effortlessly. She'd been silly to worry about her relationship with Todd, as it pertained to Max's return. Todd was as solid as ever. *They* were as solid as ever.

"What looks good to you?" He dropped his gaze to study the menu. "Part of me is tempted by the burger, but another part of me says it's a total gimmick."

"I'm with you." Piper scanned the list of entrees. There were Maine sea scallops with Marcona almonds and cipollini onions in some sort of vinaigrette she couldn't decipher the name of. So that was out. There was a blue crab simplissime with creamy potatoes. She had no idea what a simplissime was, so she kept searching until she landed on a dry-aged steak with a handful of accompaniments she could both pronounce and understand. Steak it was. "I'm getting this." She opened the menu to face Todd and pointed at the item. "Because I know what it is."

"We need to get you out more often." He smiled. Coming from anyone else, it might have seemed patronizing. But not Todd. It simply wasn't his style. "I think I'm going to go with the Yorkshire pig with yogurt green curry."

"Pig?" Piper cringed. "You had better not tell Fern, or she'll think you ate Wilbur."

"For the record, Wilbur would have been delicious."

"Gross!"

"Fine. I'll have the salmon," he said, surrendering.

"Good, then I can have a bite."

"Only if you share your steak."

"I'll take it under consideration," she bantered. And they continued back and forth, flirting with each other, which they hadn't done in a long time. The next couple hours passed in a romantic idyll, until they were both properly sated with the most decadent food that had ever passed Piper's lips.

"You're beautiful." Todd took her hands in his across the table.

"Thank you."

"You know how much I love you."

"I do. And I love you too."

"I want to spend the rest of my life with you." His expression turned sober as he let go of her hands and reached into his jacket pocket, causing Piper to remember that she'd left his present on top of her dresser. Silently she hoped he hadn't splurged on something over-the-top, like an expensive piece of jewelry. All she'd been able to manage was a cashmere sweater from his favorite store, and even that had been a stretch with her income.

"I feel the same way."

"I was hoping you would say that." He was smiling again now. "Piper?"

"Yeah?" she answered quickly, before noticing the small velvet ring box he was holding in one hand. And then all at once he was down on bended knee, clasping a sparkling diamond band with an oval-shaped emerald stone as the centerpiece and gazing up at her.

"There's nothing in this world that would make me happier than to have you as my wife. Will you marry me?"

Just as he looked up at her expectantly, her cell phone rang from inside her purse.

A dark cloud of confusion cast across Todd's face as she rummaged in her purse without thinking. "Don't answer that."

"I have to. It's Max's ringtone, and I'm not sure why he's calling."

"Then definitely don't answer it. *Please,*" he implored. But his voice wasn't kind. It was firm, intolerant even.

"It could be Fern." She ignored Todd's plea. "Hello?" She nodded, listening intently to the person on the other end of the line. "Where are you? Is she all right? I'll be right there." Piper stood up hurriedly and reached for Todd's jacket, where it was draped on the back of his chair, to grab his car keys out of his pocket. "Fern's in the hospital! She slipped and fell. It might be a concussion. I need to get there. Can you get a cab? I . . . I have to go." And with that, she was racing out of the restaurant without any time to glance back to make sure Todd was all right on his own.

As she searched the crowded parking lot for his car, feeling frantic and powerless, unable to look beyond her own crippling fear, there was one thing she saw that wouldn't register with her until later.

Henry Ford and Lillian Duffy kissing.

"So, let me get this straight. You just left him there? Down on the ground?" Mackenzie was dubious.

"What was I supposed to do? Clearly, I wasn't thinking straight at the time. Max called and said Fern was in the hospital with a *concussion*. That's pretty much any mother's absolute worst nightmare." Piper turned back toward Fern, who was sleeping peacefully in the sterile bed with a bandage around her head. By the time she'd arrived, Fern had already been examined from top to bottom, and the doctor had informed Max that she was going to be fine. He'd said he wanted her to stay the night for observation and to make sure there was no internal bleeding, but as long as everything remained status quo, they'd be able to take her home the following day.

"I don't know. It just seems . . ." Mackenzie paused, well aware that she was treading on unfamiliar territory, since she had no kids of her own.

"It just seems what?" Piper snapped. The stress of the past few hours had caught up to her and settled in her neck, shoulders, and chest, causing her muscles to throb.

"Sorry. Nothing."

"For the record, I would have done the same thing." This was Annabel. She'd been the first one to get there, even before Piper, who'd called both of them from the car.

"Thank you." Piper nodded her appreciation in Annabel's direction.

"Have you heard from Todd since?" Annabel asked gingerly.

"He texted me to find out how Fern was doing and I texted back. I feel bad that I didn't have a chance to call him before he texted me to check on her." She exhaled. "He said he was going to sleep at his house for the next few nights, so we could have some space."

"He has his own house? Don't you guys live together?" Mackenzie appeared puzzled.

"Yeah. He never stays there. He's been planning to sell it, but I guess he hasn't gotten around to it yet. All of his furniture is still there. It's a process."

"Sure. Of course." Mackenzie smiled softly. "So, Max seems nice."

"I suppose." Piper shrugged. She'd sent

Max to the deli across the street to pick up Fern's favorite treats: Swedish Fish, Reese's Peanut Butter Cups, and Honey Wheat Braided Pretzel Twists — so she'd have them as soon as she woke up. Piper had yet to see Fern alert, and even though, rationally speaking, she knew her daughter was going to be okay, until she witnessed it with her own two eyes, she'd sit by her bedside, fully attentive.

"He's cute too." Annabel glared at Mackenzie. "What? I'm not allowed to notice that Piper's ex is hot?"

"She's right; he is," Piper conceded. "And, frankly, it's really annoying. Why do men always get better-looking with age?"

"It's the same with Henry. He's thirty pounds overweight. Actually, more like fifteen now. He's got half a head of gray hairs. And he's more handsome than he was in his twenties. I, on the other hand, am running to the dermatologist every four months for Botox injections, glycolic peels, and whatever that thing is where they get rid of your dark spots. Yet Henry will be able to grow old gracefully with whomever he chooses to do that with."

"I thought you said things have been going well with you guys." Mackenzie took a swig of the iced tea she'd bought from the vending machine.

"They have. I've really been listening to your advice and I think it's been working. Honestly, we're getting along better now than we did when we were married."

"See? I told you! I'll give the credit to my mom on that one." Mackenzie smiled again, this time more vibrantly. "Who knows? Maybe you guys will get back together."

"I'm not getting my hopes up, but I imagine it's possible. Actually, I admit that I have been thinking about it lately. He's been looking at me differently — like he used to when we first started dating."

"Definitely a good sign, if you ask me." Piper shot Mackenzie a warning look while she thought Annabel wasn't paying attention.

"What?" Annabel was instantly defensive.

"Nothing." Piper tried to dismiss Annabel's concern.

"It's not nothing. I saw that cautionary expression on your face." Annabel turned toward Mackenzie. "So?"

"Don't look at me. I have no idea what's going on." Mackenzie held her hands in the air, palms facing forward.

"I don't know how to say this." Piper dropped her head. She hadn't meant to bring it up tonight. The last thing she needed was the third degree from Annabel, while Fern was lying stiff as a British upper lip in a hospital bed.

"Just say it." A note of urgency crept into Annabel's voice.

"I saw Henry when I was leaving the restaurant tonight."

"Okay, and . . . ?" Annabel was on the edge of her seat, literally.

"And he wasn't alone. He was with Lillian."

"That's nothing new. Been there, done that." Annabel seemed momentarily relieved.

"They were kissing."

"Excuse me?" Annabel's eyes bulged, as did Mackenzie's. "Kissing where?"

"Outside. In the parking lot."

"Not their *location*. *Where was he kissing her? On the cheek? On the forehead? On the hand?*" Her next words caught in her throat and her eyes flooded with tears. "On the lips?" She could barely speak the last part.

"On the lips," Piper murmured, as if not saying it too loud might mean it had never happened. "I'm so sorry."

"No, it's fine. It's fine. I'm a complete idiot. That's what's going on here. I'm a complete fucking idiot. Why would I ever

305

think he was going to come back to me? So stupid. So, so, stupid." She flew out of her chair. "I need to get some air."

"Annabel." Mackenzie stood too, ready to follow her outside.

"Don't. *Please.*" She turned her back on both of them, bowed her head, and walked hurriedly toward the door. "I just need to be alone right now."

TWENTY-ONE

A half hour had passed with no sign of Annabel. Max had returned with snacks and then made himself scarce once again to drive over to Piper's house and to get clothing for her and Fern, so they'd have something fresh to change into. The chemistry between Piper and Max had been palpable, even in the few minutes Mackenzie had seen them interacting. Had Todd noticed the same? It had taken a good deal of Mackenzie's willpower to hold back from mentioning it. Surely Piper was no longer romantically interested in Max. She could barely look at him without a disdain so obvious, it might as well have been written across her forehead with an indelible marker. Still, they had an undeniable connection. A connection that extended beyond their shared child.

"How are you holding up?" Mackenzie was seated next to Piper at the base of

Fern's bed. The nurse had informed them that Fern would likely sleep through the night without waking up. This had alarmed Piper at first, but once the nurse had explained that it was completely normal and that Fern needed her rest, Piper had appeared to take it in stride. *Appeared* being the operative word.

"Well, you know, I've been better." Piper exhaled loudly. Her mood had been erratic, to say the least. It was hard to know what might set her off, so Mackenzie was trying her best to tiptoe around things — to stick to benign areas of conversation — but it wasn't easy, given all that was going on.

"Max seems like he's being helpful," she offered, unaware as to whether the mere mention of his name would rile Piper.

"He has been." She nodded. "Took him long enough, don't you think?"

"I'd say so," Mackenzie agreed, for fear of doing anything but. Not that there was much she could say in Max's defense anyway. "I guess better late than never."

"I'm not sure about that," Piper grumbled. "But I'll take what I can get for now. Especially since Todd isn't here."

"Are you upset about that? I can call him if you'd like, give a little nudge."

"No, it's okay. Honestly, I'm not sure I

308

have any right to be annoyed at him, given how I took off without him, although it would be nice to have him around."

"Does he know Max is with you?" Mackenzie pressed. If she were Todd, she wasn't sure if she'd be racing to Piper's side either. It was a tangled web they'd woven, and one misstep could quite realistically unravel everything.

"He does," Piper replied unapologetically.

"That makes sense, then. He's probably trying to let you guys handle this, since Fern is your daughter." She cleared her throat. "And Max's."

"I know. But still. He's been more of a father to Fern than Max ever was. And . . ." Piper hunched her body and then pressed the tips of her fingers into her eyelids to stop the tears from flowing.

"And what, sweetie? You can talk to me," Mackenzie encouraged, placing her hand gently on Piper's shoulder. "I know it's a lot right now."

"I can't believe I just left him down on the ground on one knee in the restaurant. Midproposal." Piper was crying faintly now. "Of course he doesn't want to be around me! What kind of person does that?"

"The kind of person who's an amazing mother." Mackenzie stroked Piper's back rhythmically. "The kind of person who puts her child ahead of everyone else. That's the kind of mother I hope to be someday. He has to understand that you were focused on your daughter when you got the news that she was injured. It's simply the kind of person you are."

"Come on — even you couldn't believe I'd done that."

"It took me a minute, but as soon as I thought about it, I knew you'd done the right thing. Beyond that, you did what any other concerned parent would have done."

"If the reverse had happened, I'd be mortified. He doesn't deserve this. I don't deserve him." Piper shook her head. "Maybe I should have taken a second to breathe, you know? I could have tried to collect myself. I should have had him drive me to the hospital, rather than running out on him. God, I don't know what to do now."

"Well, I'm telling you, you made an understandable choice in the moment."

"Thank you." Piper smiled for the first time since she'd arrived at the hospital.

"You're very welcome." Mackenzie smiled back. She had so many questions, but yet she kept silent. What would Piper have said if Max's call hadn't interrupted Todd's marriage proposal? What did she think would happen now? Would Todd rescind? Would Max try to stand in the way? It was clear that he still loved Piper as more than the mother of his child. Her mind was spinning, but her mouth remained shut.

"I'm a little worried about Annabel. Do you think she's coming back?"

"I hope so. She left her purse and jacket." Mackenzie motioned to a pile on the counter in the corner of the hospital room.

"Right, sorry. I'm in another world. I can't believe I saw him."

"Henry?"

"Yeah. And, trust me, there was nothing platonic about the kiss."

"Ugh. Poor Annabel. I guess she was the smart one all along. Honestly, I wasn't sure. I was hoping Henry might be one of the good guys."

"I know. Me too."

"It's times like this we should be thankful for Trevor and Todd."

"If Todd still wants to be with me." Piper buried her face in her palms. "What have I done?"

"Don't worry about that for now. You have enough on your mind already. Plus, you don't go from wanting to marry someone to walking away just because life didn't go as planned."

"I'm not so sure about that." Then Fern shifted in her bed, and Piper's head popped up. "Things have been awkward between us ever since Max arrived. If anything, I thought I'd been pushing Todd away by allowing Max to get to know Fern."

"Well, clearly he saw things differently." Mackenzie paused, unsure whether to go there. "You would have said yes, right?"

"Of course!" Piper answered quickly. And then, seemingly thinking better of it, added, "I think so. I mean, I love him. More than anything."

"But?" Mackenzie had suspected there might be a *but*.

"But nothing. I don't know. It's just . . ." She hesitated. "Things are so complicated now with Max in the picture. And Fern thinking she has her father back for good. She was already on edge given that Todd had moved in with us."

"Sure. I understand." Only she didn't. What she wanted to tell Piper was that Max's presence shouldn't matter. That if she wanted to marry Todd, whether it happened next week or next year, she wouldn't be wavering in her reply.

"Well, that makes one of us!" Piper laughed feebly. "Do you think maybe you should go check on Annabel?"

"Only if you promise you'll be okay for a few minutes alone."

"I'm fine." She sniffed. "I swear. Go ahead."

"Can I bring you anything? Some coffee? A bottle of vodka?" She smirked.

"Actually, you could do me a favor."

"Anything," Mackenzie agreed eagerly. In situations like these, she was a doer. She'd never felt comfortable sitting around wallowing, far preferring to take matters into her own hands. To put a plan into action.

"Since I know I'm going to be here all night — and I do not expect you or Annabel to stay with me. *Seriously* — it would be super helpful to have some work to distract me. You know, get my mind off of everything."

"Sure, no problem. You want me to run to the office?" Mackenzie stood up and gathered her coat and handbag.

"I know it's a pain."

"It's no problem at all."

"Thank you." Piper acknowledged the favor gratefully. "I'd ask Lucy, but I'm sure she's long gone for the day."

"It's really no big deal. Trevor has a late dinner tonight anyway. And I'm probably the only one you know who has the key."

"That's true." Piper salvaged a tissue from

the depths of her encumbered purse and blew her nose into it loudly. "Classy, huh?" She sniggered. "Okay, so anyway, when you get to my office, you'll see a thick red folder on my desk. It's the only red folder there, and it'll have a bunch of different case documents in it. If you have any questions, just call me."

"I'm on it." Mackenzie saluted, continuing to endeavor to lighten the mood.

"You're the best. Thank you again. And please tell Annabel I'm so sorry. Go figure: the one time we're not actually spying on Henry is the moment we catch him in the act."

"As they say, when you least expect it . . ." She swiveled on her toes and headed for the door. "I'll see you in about an hour."

Mackenzie made her way along the barren corridor, stopping in front of the elevator to press the Down button. She'd always hated hospitals — the heady scent of urine and illness, the maudlin expressions on each passing face, even the ones whose job it was to appear happy. With Trevor gone for the evening, she'd planned to go directly home after work, slip into a full tub of warm water, and, with a plate of cheese and a glass of white wine, soak her tired body beneath a layer of frothy bath bubbles. Unfortunately, that plot had been thwarted. Still, after a night like Piper and Annabel had endured, Mackenzie knew she didn't have anything to complain about. When the elevator door opened, she stepped inside just before it closed behind her.

"Mackenzie?" She looked up to find James Blake standing in front of her. "What are you doing here? I hope everything is okay."

"Oh, hey!" She smiled, blushing slightly. There was something about a doctor in a lab coat. "Yes, I'm all right — thank you for asking. My friend's daughter had a little accident, but she's going to be completely fine."

"I'm so sorry to hear that. Although I am pleased to hear her diagnosis is positive." The elevator chimed and the doors slid open again. James extended his hand to indicate that she should exit first. "I'm actually in between shifts. Do you have time for a quick bite or just a cup of coffee? I'll regale you with the details of last night's performance of *Rigoletto* at the Met!"

"I wish I did." It was the truth. She liked being around him, even though they'd never spent more than twenty minutes together. There was something calming about his demeanor that comforted her. "I'd give anything to talk Verdi for hours, but my friend asked me to grab a folder from her office, so I'm on my way there now. Will you still be free in an hour or so?"

"Sorry, no. I'll be back on call." He frowned. "Can I take a rain check?"

"You most certainly can." She couldn't help but grin. "It was nice to see you again, even so briefly."

"It was nice to see you too." He paused, watching her intently. "Funny how we keep bumping into each other."

"It must be fate." She laughed.

"It must be."

She hadn't stopped smiling. Not on the short walk to the parking garage. Not during the car ride from the hospital to her office. It had been years since she'd had a friend of the opposite sex. Probably since college. And not because Trevor would have minded. But because she'd never had an occasion to meet one. Rarely were there any men in her exercise classes and, even if there were, they weren't there to socialize. There were a few men at Mead with whom she exchanged the occasional high five or chit-chatted in the hallway for a minute or two between meetings, but that was where it ended. When you worked with your husband and your mother-in-law ran the company, somehow that placed you on a level where other employees didn't feel comfortable shooting the shit with you.

For whatever reason, she was grateful that James had entered her life, and he seemed like someone she wanted to get to know better. She had noticed there was no wedding band on his left hand, and she wondered if he had a girlfriend. He'd never mentioned as much, but they hadn't spent a lot of time together. And when they had, their conversation had remained light and easy. She'd have to remember to ask him next time she bumped into him, which did appear to be happening with curious regularity. If he did, maybe the four of them could go on a double date. If not, maybe she could set him up with Annabel, once she was ready to start dating again. Although she wasn't sure Annabel would be his type. She couldn't put her finger on why exactly; it was just hard to envision them as a couple. Not to mention that she definitely couldn't see Annabel at the opera. She was just a little too uptight to immerse herself in something so cathartic.

Mackenzie rode the elevator up to the second floor of the Mead Media building. She fished around in her purse for the key to the main door before noticing it was already slightly ajar. That was odd. It was already well past ten o'clock. Everyone should have been long gone by now, save for the people who would be at their printing press on the other side of town most of the night, putting the morning issue of the *Journal* to bed. Perhaps it was the cleaning staff? Though, if she recalled correctly from her early days burning the midnight oil, they too had typically packed everything up and headed home by this late hour.

She crept through the space quietly, checking around each corner, just in case. All of the offices were dark except Trevor's and Piper's. She peeked into her husband's office, which was empty. Flipping the lights off and closing the door behind her, she skulked her way to Piper's office. Could that be the faint din of voices she was hearing? The door was closed, but there was unquestionably someone in there. At least one person.

"Lucy?" she whispered. What if it wasn't her? *This is the point,* she thought, *in all of those horror movies where the audience would likely be screaming at the screen for me to get the hell out of here as fast as humanly possible before Freddie or Jason or that guy from* Scream *with the menacing black-and-white mask — mouth agape and jelly-bean eyes — comes chasing after me, wielding a bloody knife.*

No one answered. Mackenzie knocked softly. Still no answer. Judiciously, she turned the knob, allowing the door to release and swing open on its own.

"Oh, my God!" Lucy jumped up from where she was seated on top of Piper's desk. More specifically, on top of Piper's red folder. The one Mackenzie had been sent to retrieve for her. And her lip-lock companion released his embrace from behind her.

"I'm so sorry! So, so sorry." Mackenzie covered her eyes with her hand. She wanted to run, to pretend she was, in fact, one of those doomed women being hunted down by a movie mass murderer, but her feet were pinned to the floor. Because she'd already seen too much. She'd seen the ring on his finger. The ring she'd placed there.

"Mackenzie . . . This . . . It . . . isn't what it looks like," Trevor stammered. Only it was too late for any recovery. The damage had been done.

"I should go." Lucy gathered her things in a hurry.

"No." Mackenzie held up her hand. Her voice was unnervingly even. "Clearly I've interrupted your little rendezvous. I'm the one who needs to leave."

"Mackenzie, wait!" Trevor beckoned, as she started to walk away.

But he most definitely did not follow her.

TWENTY-TWO

It was one thing to suspect your husband was having an affair. And quite another to find out he actually was. Even Annabel had been surprised by her own reaction: out-and-out shock. Until this point it had been largely innocent in her mind. A dinner here. A dinner there. A chaste peck on the cheek, perhaps near the lips, but never a kiss on another woman's mouth. *Never* on the lips. Because that moment, when she'd pressed her mouth to his, had been the turning point in her husband's affair. The moment when the invisible line she'd drawn in her mind had been categorically crossed. And no matter what happened after that, Henry could never cross back.

It was hard to declare that he'd done something wrong, despite the outrage she felt. After all, they were already legally separated and the divorce would be finalized within weeks. Regardless, it felt like a betrayal of the worst kind. Maybe because she hadn't yet come to terms with the fact that her marriage was really over. That the ten years they'd devoted to building a life together no longer mattered to him. The *decade* they'd spent supporting each other's careers, then having babies and ultimately moving into their dream home — all of that would eventually become a faded memory.

Would she look back on that chapter in her life with fondness? She'd heard some women manage it: *My ex and I are the best of friends now! Hard to believe we were ever married!* Or would the open wound in her heart always sting — like someone was grinding salt into it over and over again? So many divorced women she knew had told her that the former would be the case. That for the next few months, her feelings toward Henry would vacillate between hostility and loathing, but that one day she'd wake up and the pain would be dulled. Not gone, but filed down like a jagged nail. And with each passing day, month, and year, it would only get better. *She* would only get better — at distancing herself from a past she'd once been so desperate to hold on to.

Maybe she would meet someone new and eventually get married again. All in due course. Obviously, it hadn't taken Henry long to find a replacement for her. Though she imagined it was different for men. They typically didn't require the same adjustment period that women did. Beyond the basic fear of someone else seeing her naked, there was a requisite comfort factor that couldn't be denied, even when she was fully dressed. Annabel, at least for her part, needed to get to know someone before she opened up to him. She needed to be wooed, courted, and cared for. Was that really so much to ask?

And where would she find this person? Online? In a bar? It seemed preposterous to think about getting all gussied up with the intent of attracting a new mate. What would she say? What would she wear? Surely she wouldn't be interested in any guy who was her age and had yet to find a wife. That was a glaring red flag if she'd ever seen one. But, then, did she want to take on more children to care for? Harper and Hudson were already two times a handful. She couldn't deal with a *Brady Bunch* scenario. Not even half a bunch. It was one thing to expect her to love someone else, but their kids too? It felt impossible, like an affront.

Annabel checked her watch. It was already seven o'clock. Henry was supposed to have dropped the kids off with her by six. Normally, something like this would have aggravated her beyond reason. There was nothing she detested more than a blatant disregard for punctuality. The funny thing was, she just didn't care so much about it anymore. Of course she'd missed the boys terribly over the weekend, but she was getting used to it. She was adapting to her new normal, however that looked. The numbness had officially set in. More than that, she'd finally given up on trying to shape Henry into the man she wanted him to be. Lillian could take on that responsibility now — and good luck to her. It probably all seemed like fun and games at this point. The clandestine dinners. The passionate kisses. *The sex?* She hadn't let her thoughts travel down that particular path. Yet. What she didn't know, she didn't want to know. That was that.

Just as she was about to pour herself a second glass of Chardonnay, the front door burst open.

"Moooooooooom!" Harper called out first.

"Moooooooooom! Are you home?" And then Hudson.

They both raced into the kitchen, where she was perched on a barstool at the center island. She stood up immediately, overjoyed to be on the receiving end of their boisterous hugs.

"Hello, my delicious boys." She squeezed them back, coming down to her knees to dot their warm button noses with kisses. "I missed you so much."

"We missed you too, Mommy." Harper smiled sweetly.

"Guess where Dad took us?" Hudson was breathless. "You'll never guess!"

"The aquarium?" she offered, well aware that Henry thought the aquarium was tedious.

"Nope!" Hudson wore a satisfied expression.

"The museum?"

"Wrong again!"

"I have no idea. Why don't you tell me? I'm so curious."

"To New York City!"

"No way." She'd intended to feign surprise, but she truly hadn't expected to hear that. Henry barely liked driving them twenty minutes from home, much less hauling them and all of their stuff into Manhattan.

"Yup! We went to FAO Schwarz! And there was this big clock that played music. It was huge. Like, up to the sky!"

"That sounds amazing!"

"It was," Harper confirmed. "Dad bought us each a Transformer."

"Well, aren't you the luckiest boys in

town?" They nodded together.

"Can we go upstairs and play with our iPads?" Harper flaunted his most convincing puppy-dog eyes. "Please, Mommy?"

"Okay, go on." They scurried off in a hurry, before she could change her mind, leaving her alone with Henry.

"Thanks for dropping them off." Annabel stood up again as Henry placed two brown bags on the counter.

"I brought Chinese for us; the kids already ate pizza. I got your favorite lemon chicken and steamed broccoli."

"Thanks, but I already had a bowl of cereal." She'd finally stopped dieting. As it turned out, finding out that your husband was, in fact, cheating on you was all the appetite suppressant a girl needed.

"Oh." He looked disappointed. *What? Lillian doesn't like her food drenched in MSG?* "Mind if I stay and eat?"

"It's up to you." She shrugged, busying herself with a stack of dishes and a collection of silverware that had been piling up in the sink. Another discovery she'd made since going through a divorce and finding out her husband was cheating on her was that suddenly the everyday, menial tasks didn't seem at all important. So what if she had to eat on paper plates for the foreseeable future because loading proper ones into the dishwasher just felt like too much effort? There was no one there to appreciate it anymore. Not that Henry had ever appreciated her manic obsession with everything in the house staying clean and organized.

"Okay." He sat down on a barstool and began lifting take-out cartons from the bags. "Are you sure? There's a lot of food here."

"I'm sure." She turned toward him briefly and then back to face the sink.

"Is everything okay?"

"Yup, fine. Why?"

"I don't know. You seem quiet."

"I think I'm just tired." It was the truth. Ever since she'd learned that Henry and Lillian had made out in the parking lot at Templeton's, she hadn't been able to sleep soundly for more than a few hours at a clip.

"I hear you. I feel like I've been a zombie for weeks."

"Being a single parent, even part-time, will do that to you." She placed the last fork in the dishwasher and, for lack of another distraction, took a seat next to Henry at the counter.

"It's actually not that."

"Oh?" *Sorry — must be all the raucous sex you're having with your new girlfriend.*

"You know this big deal I've been working on for months?"

"Yeah." Annabel wasn't aware of the details, but she did know that the outcome could be either a coup or a disaster for Henry's company.

"I think it's in serious jeopardy." He exhaled loudly, hunching his shoulders.

"I'm really sorry to hear that." And she was. Despite her anger toward him, she didn't really wish Henry any ill will. Not to mention the fact that she and the kids were counting on his steady income.

"You have no idea. I mean, I've sunk hundreds of hours into this. Millions of dollars. I'm not sure the company will survive if it goes south."

"That doesn't sound good at all."

"You're not kidding." He sighed. "Do you remember that woman Lillian Duffy I hired a few years ago to consult for me?"

"I think so." Annabel's leg started trembling, and she pressed her palm against her thigh to stop the involuntary motion. How dare her name pass his lips in this house? The lips he'd used to suck face with that tramp.

"Well, I hired her again and . . ." He hesitated.

"And what?"

"Let's just say things aren't going as I'd planned. I thought she was my ace in the hole."

"That's a shame." *Aw, poor Lillian not performing outside the bedroom? Bummer.*

"I honestly don't know what to do."

"What does Don say?" Don was Henry's second in command. The one person he trusted with everything, whereas Annabel used to be that person for him.

"I haven't had the heart to tell him. You're the only one I've spoken to about it."

"I'm flattered. I think."

"Annie?"

"Yeah." She turned toward him.

"I'm scared."

"Of what?"

"Of losing everything." Their eyes locked at his admission.

"So am I."

Annabel had slept soundly for the first time in days. Her boys were back home where they belonged. She'd sat side by side with Henry without the urge to strangle him. And it felt nice, once again, to eat like a normal person without counting every calorie and each gram of fat. So when Mackenzie's call came in at seven in the morning, Annabel was already awake and alert, flipping through a copy of *Good Housekeeping* while she waited for Harper and Hudson to bound through her bedroom door and hurl themselves onto her bed.

"I'm so sorry to call this early," Mackenzie apologized even before saying hello. Annabel could tell immediately that something was wrong. Her voice sounded different, strained, reminding Annabel of when Mackenzie had lost her baby.

"It's fine. I was already up. What's the matter?"

"He's cheating."

"I know. We've already been down this road. Honestly, I've come to terms with it. Okay, so maybe not completely, but I'm working on it. I'm channeling your advice. *Namaste.*"

"Not Henry. Trevor." Mackenzie sniffed before releasing a sob. "With Lucy!"

"What!?" Annabel sat up straight. "Hold on. This doesn't make any sense."

"You're telling me!"

"How do you know?" Annabel placed her magazine on the nightstand. This was the last piece of news she'd expected to receive. Trevor Mead stepping out on his stunning and kind wife with Piper's office assistant. It was absurd. Almost laughable.

"I caught them in the act!" Mackenzie

screeched into the phone.

"When? Where?"

"The night you found out about Henry. The night we were all at the hospital for Fern. I went to the office to pick up that work for Piper. And there they were, making out on Piper's desk. On her desk! I'm such a fool."

"Listen to me. You are not a fool. And you shouldn't be alone right now either. I'm going to see if I can get my babysitter here. If you don't hear from me, I'll be there in an hour." She hesitated. "Where's Trevor now?"

"I have no idea. I texted him to say that he is unwelcome at home. He's been trying to get in touch to talk about things. But what is there to talk about, right? I mean, what the fuck is there to talk about with him?"

"Hang tight. I'm jumping in the shower. I'll be there soon."

"Thank you, Annabel," she whispered. "I'm just not myself."

Forty-five minutes later, Annabel and Mackenzie were curled up on her couch under a blanket-sized pale green cashmere throw. Mackenzie's face was pallid and her typically silky blond hair appeared tangled, even a little greasy.

"Okay, start from the beginning. Tell me exactly what happened," Annabel coached. It was strangely ironic to be on the opposite side of a conversation they'd had so many times over the past few months. First Henry. Now Trevor. Were all men really dogs, desperate to gnaw on a fresh cut of meat as soon as the opportunity presented itself?

"So, I drove to the office, and when I got there, I noticed the door was unlocked. It *never* occurred to me that Trevor would be there. He was supposed to be at a dinner for work." She inhaled and then exhaled, squeezing her eyes shut for a moment while she tried to keep the tears at bay. "What an asshole. Anyway, I was creeping around the place like a serial killer was going to jump out at me if I looked in the wrong direction. Ridiculous, I know." Her shoulders quivered.

"It's okay. Just tell me slowly." Annabel placed her hand on Mackenzie's for support and encouragement.

"Right. So, I noticed that Trevor's office light was on, but when I went in, the room was empty. Piper's office light was also on. And do you know what I thought?"

"What?"

"I thought it was funny, because Piper can

be so absentminded sometimes. I figured she'd forgotten to switch it off."

"That makes sense." Annabel smiled kindly. "I probably would have thought the same thing."

"Only that obviously wasn't the case. Because when I went in to get her red folder, there they were. On her desk. Kissing."

"Kissing?" Annabel tried to hide her surprise. For whatever reason, she'd imagined them naked. Doing way more than kissing. It wasn't nearly as bad as she'd thought. Although didn't that make her a bit of a hypocrite? When it had been Henry and Lillian in a lip-lock, she'd completely lost her shit. Yet when it was someone else and she was an outsider looking in, a simple kiss didn't seem like the end of the world. Or, for that matter, like it had to be the end of Mackenzie and Trevor's relationship.

"Yup." Mackenzie nodded firmly, as if she'd just announced that Trevor and Lucy had been caught in the actual act of unbridled passion.

"And then what?"

"It's all a blur after that. I think Lucy tried to leave. Trevor tried to suggest it wasn't what I thought. I mean, is that insulting or what? I have two working eyes."

"Maybe he was telling the truth. It could have been an impulse," Annabel offered, barely believing her own words.

"Annabel, please. He lied to me about where he was. And it didn't look impulsive. It looked . . ." She paused, searching for the right explanation. "Comfortable. Like it wasn't the first time."

"Jesus." Annabel shook her head. "I didn't even know they knew each other."

"Neither did I. This is the girl that was helping us trail Henry, and all the while she's screwing *my* husband?"

"Does Piper know?"

"Yeah. I wasn't going to upset her, with everything she has going on with Todd and Max, but I guess Lucy told her."

"What did she say?"

"She was horrified. Apologetic. Clearly it's not her fault in any way, but she was trying to take some of the responsibility for her assistant's involvement. She said she was going to fire Lucy, but I told her not to do that."

"Why?"

"Well, I doubt Trevor will stand for that. What with her being his girlfriend and all."

"Let's not get ahead of ourselves here," Annabel advised. "I'm going to tell you exactly what you told me when I was first going through this. One, you do not know that anything more than one kiss transpired. Two, you don't know the circumstances of that kiss. Not that it's right. In any way, shape, or form. But don't you think you should at least hear him out?"

"I don't know. I'm not really in a 'hear him out' place at the moment."

"I can understand that."

"How can I even think about staying with someone who lied to me and then betrayed me? And do you know the worst part?"

"What?"

"He didn't even run after me! He stayed there. With her."

"He was probably scared."

"Who gives a shit if he was scared? I'm his wife."

"You're right, sweetie. You're right." Annabel tried to soothe without placating. There was nothing worse than being placated by someone when you felt completely vindicated in your anger.

"The press is going to have a field day with this. I can already see the headlines. 'Mead Media Heir Fucks over Wife by Fucking Office Assistant.'"

"You can't think about that." Annabel hadn't even considered the public ramifications for Mackenzie. Suddenly she felt thankful that her own situation was private.

"How can I not? If even one person outside of you and Piper finds out, I'm totally screwed." She laughed sardonically. "No pun intended."

"Well, you know our lips are sealed."

Mackenzie tilted her head downward and began to weep softly, dabbing the corners of her eyes with the sleeve of her flannel pajama top. "We were trying to have a baby."

"I know." Annabel hugged her close, allowing Mackenzie to cry on her shoulder.

"No wonder he didn't want to see the fertility specialist."

"Oh, sweetie."

"What am I supposed to do now?" Mackenzie looked up with an expression of utter despair. "What the hell am I supposed to do now?"

"We'll work through this."

"What if I can't?"

"You can. And you will. I promise." Annabel released Mackenzie from her embrace and held both of Mackenzie's hands in hers. "Do you remember what you told me when I was freaking out about Henry?"

"No."

"Well, I do. You said, 'You're stronger than you think.' And now I'm telling you the same. You are so much stronger than you think and so much stronger than I ever was." Annabel's eyes locked with Mackenzie's and she squeezed her hands. "We'll work through this. Together."

TWENTY-THREE

Finally, spring had sprung. The air was laced with the sweet scent of freshly cut grass and budding flowers with a dash of moist soil for good measure — a potent perfume that no amount of chemical sorcery could replicate. The songbirds had started singing, and the woodpeckers had commenced their incessant drumming, a sound that might have been grating, save for the chirpy season it represented in Piper's mind. Everything around her was vibrant and inviting, but it was all Piper could manage to wade through the motions of her day. To make it from the moment her alarm went off in the morning to the moment her head hit her pillow again that night. With as few nonessential social interactions as possible.

Fern had finally returned to school after the required bed rest prescribed by her doctor on the heels of her concussion. Piper had been forced to juggle work and a child who was home alone and needier than she normally was. She never thought she'd say as much, but Max had been a godsend while Fern was recovering. He'd spent most days at her house, attending to Fern's every whim, while Piper had been tied to her desk at Mead, attempting to get her job done while stewing about Lucy's betrayal inside her office. They hadn't spoken in depth about it yet. Her fling with Trevor. Or whatever it was. Piper couldn't even look at her. Of course, Lucy had tried to talk to her, to explain, as she'd put it. But Piper had wagged her finger and avoided eye contact. Because as far as she was concerned, there was no explanation. At least not a good one. Nothing she could say would ever be sufficient for Piper to have faith in her again. Beyond Piper being horrified on Mackenzie's behalf, she felt betrayed and even somewhat guilty.

She'd hired Lucy, after all. She'd given her more responsibility than almost any other assistant in the company. She'd trusted her with personal business. For Christ's sake, she'd had her tracking Henry Ford. Piper had also been the one to suggest that Lucy work alongside Trevor when he'd sent a company-wide e-mail asking if anyone could spare an extra helping hand on a big project he'd launched. Had they already been having an affair at that point? If so, she'd fallen right into that open trap. If not, was she in any way responsible for encouraging them to spend time together in close proximity?

And then there was Todd. He still hadn't moved back in, although most of his stuff remained at Piper and Fern's house. The neatly ironed dress shirts that hung in a tight row in her closet — *their* closet. Before she went to bed, she often found herself pressing her nose to those shirts, just so she could recall his distinctive scent — a heady combination of orange, lemon, jasmine, and lavender with warm, musky base notes. His black and brown polished shoes, in varying designs, were arranged in an ordered fashion on the closet floor below his suit pants. And in the bathroom, his toothbrush remained next to hers by the sink, and their razors lay side by side in the shower, although clearly he had others to spare.

He'd told her he needed time to think. That he loved her more than anything. Fern too. However, he wanted to work out the mechanics of things in his own mind before they could fall back into their old life. An old life that, he'd added, was no longer really possible, given that Max had insinuated himself into their family of three. Piper had thought about begging Todd to return. She'd thought about promising him she'd tell Max to leave and never come back. But Mackenzie had cautioned her. She'd said that Piper had to afford Todd the space he'd requested if she wanted him to be happy. More to the point, if she wanted them all to be happy. The thing was, it wasn't only Mackenzie who'd held her back. It had been nice having Max around at times. Unnerving, but still nice. In so many ways, he felt like home to her. He knew who she was from before she'd become Piper the crime reporter. Or Piper the single mom — even though he'd sort of created that title. He knew her entire family and her old friends, even ones she'd barely spoken to in the past ten years. He knew her in a way that Todd did not.

Of course, in turn, Todd knew things about Piper that Max did not. Like the fact that she hated peanut butter, but loved peanut butter ice cream. Or that she and Fern always spent an hour reading together on Sunday afternoons. Todd also knew that Piper used to be closer with her parents, but that she rarely spoke to them on the phone anymore, because they were both a little hard of hearing. And that it bothered her not to be able to check in with her mother as often as she used to. Todd knew that she liked the idea of skiing, but that once they hit the slopes, she'd inevitably be too cold to do more than a few runs. And, above all, he knew that the most important thing to her in the world was Fern's happiness. Perhaps Max could have assumed that, but — unlike Todd — he hadn't been around to witness its utmost importance to her firsthand.

Were there romantic sensations lingering between Piper and Max? Annabel had asked that particular question, which was hard for Piper to answer. She certainly didn't want to be with him in that way. Not anymore. But was there still an attraction? Unfortunately, yes. Still, it didn't change her feelings for Todd. Sweet and giving Todd, who'd offered his promise to devote his life to her and her daughter. He was the man she wanted to spend her life with.

When Todd had finally called on Monday to say he'd like to take her to lunch, Piper had replied instantly with an enthusiastic yes. She needed to see him, to touch him, to hold him close, if he'd allow it. Now, though, sitting alone at their favorite table for two in the back left corner of Avery's

Grill, Piper couldn't help but feel anxious. What if he'd asked her there to break up with her, to let her down easily in person? That was the kind of man Todd was. He'd never dump her via phone or e-mail or, God forbid, text message. He was far too considerate for that. And there was far too much history at stake.

"Hey." Todd appeared without warning and Piper stood up, waiting for him to open his arms first, which he did. She practically fell into his soothing embrace. "Easy there. You almost knocked me over." He smiled, and suddenly any anxiety she'd been experiencing faded away.

"Sorry." She sat back down across from him. "It's just that I've missed you so much."

"I've missed you too." He took her hands in his, and she exhaled for what seemed like the first time in weeks.

"So you'll come home?" She couldn't hold back, even though she was ignoring Mackenzie's advice not to sound desperate.

"I don't know." He hesitated, as if he were about to say something else, but then he remained quiet.

"What do you mean?" Panic set in. He'd just said he missed her. He'd smiled. He was still holding her hands. All the signs of forgiveness were there. Then why the doubt?

"Piper, I love you. You know that," he started.

"I love you too." She nodded impatiently.

"I know." He took a deep breath. "The thing is, sometimes love isn't enough."

"It *is.*" Her tone was urgent. "It is enough. Our love is enough. It's more than enough."

"I hope so." He spoke more slowly than she was used to from him. It was all she could do not to reach into his mouth and pull the words out.

"I *know* so."

"Well, I'm glad to hear you say that."

"You proposed. We were going to get married," she added, on the off chance he'd forgotten.

"I remember the proposal." His gaze dropped toward the table.

"I can't apologize enough for how I behaved that night. I have no idea what got into me. The call that Fern had fallen, that she had a concussion, it was just so —"

"Piper, relax." He cut her off, but not disrespectfully. "What I've realized in these past couple of weeks is that your walking out on the proposal wasn't the issue. I thought it was at the time. Bit of an ego squelcher there."

"Todd, truly, I'm so sorry." After weeks of

reliving it in her mind, she knew she still couldn't even begin to understand how he'd felt down on one knee, ring in hand, as she'd raced out of the restaurant. In response to a call from her ex-boyfriend and the father of her child.

"You don't have to say you're sorry anymore. I know it. And I believe you. What I'm trying to say is that ever since Max arrived, things have changed. The dynamic has changed. Between us. Between you and Fern. Between me and Fern. It's affected all of us. We can't continue to ignore that."

"I'll ask Max to leave." There — she'd said it. Even though she had no idea if that was actually possible. She'd figure it out.

"You can't do that. As tempting as it sounds. He's here. He cares about Fern, whether we think he has a right to or not. Above all, Fern cares about him. She wants him in her life. Dare I say, she needs him in her life."

"You're her father."

"Piper, I wish I were, but I'm not. She's the only daughter I've ever had. But I'm not her father. Not in her mind, which is all that really matters in this case. And I think if we can find a way to define our roles for Fern — for all of us — that will be the only possibility of moving forward."

"And then you'll come home?"

"Let's take it step by step."

"I need you to come home." Piper began crying softly just as the waitress approached.

"We'll need another minute, please," Todd alerted the waitress, and she retreated immediately. "Don't cry, Piper."

"I can't help it." She sniffed and blew her nose into a paper napkin. "Just tell me everything is going to be okay," she pleaded with him. So much for her pride.

"Oh, Piper, I wish I could." He squeezed her hands. "I want nothing more than to return to the life we were building together. But that same exact life is not a reality anymore."

"Then we'll find our new reality. We will. I know it." Her voice cracked. "We have to."

"Can someone tell me why it is that the good, healthy people are always the ones who die young?" After Piper's lunch with Todd, which had gone no further toward convincing her that everything would eventually be okay, she'd decided to invite Mackenzie and Annabel over for dinner as a distraction. And for moral support. "I mean, look at this guy. He was forty-eight, a marathon runner, and a father of four. Oh, and he was on the board of about five charitable organizations. Completely awful. Those poor children."

"I'm pretty sure it's because no one ever writes an obituary that says, 'Fat asshole kicked the bucket today from eating his way to a heart attack. His funeral will be held Thursday for a group of people who couldn't stand him when he was alive. Flowers welcome,' " Annabel deadpanned.

"You're funny." Mackenzie laughed and reached for a second slice of pizza. "When I die, you two had better say nice things about me. But feel free to mention that my ex-husband was a dickhead."

"You're already calling him *ex*, huh?" Annabel raised an eyebrow. "Impressive. I haven't even gotten there yet with Henry."

"I guess you're a more forgiving person than I am." Mackenzie shrugged. "My rule is no tolerance. Thank God we didn't have kids together." She sighed. "Hey, there's one sentence I never thought I'd say."

"Would you look at how pathetic we are?" Annabel shook her head. "Two of us have husbands who've cheated on us. And the other one is hanging on to her relationship by a thread."

"Gee, thanks." Piper shot her a dirty look. She'd told them about her conversation with Todd at lunch.

"Sorry, my friend, but we're at the point where there's no sugarcoating anything." Annabel turned to Mackenzie. "How are things with you and Trevor? I take it not so hot?"

"I wouldn't know, since I still haven't spoken to him." Mackenzie tipped the bottle of Sprite into her glass.

"Wow. You're avoiding him at work too?" Annabel nibbled on a garlic knot.

"He's barely made an appearance at the office since I discovered the affair. I gather it's a smidge complicated, what with his wife, girlfriend, and mother all working there. As far as I know, he's been out of town a lot. I'm assuming he's bought himself new clothing and toiletries, since I haven't let him back in the house."

"You know you can't go on like this forever," Piper interjected.

"I know, but right now I'm too pissed off to deal with it." She groaned. "I don't want to talk about it anymore. What about you? How are things with Henry? Shouldn't the divorce be final any day?" she asked Annabel.

"It should be. I think we just have to sign the papers." Annabel was suddenly very quiet.

"What is it?" Piper knew that silence typically meant that there was more to the story. There was always more to every story; she'd learned that day one on the job.

"Okay, so I'm sure this will sound crazy to you, but when he was over the other night, dropping off the kids, we really connected."

"You'll always be connected," Piper reassured her. "At the very least through the kids."

"No, this was different. He confided in me."

"About what?" Mackenzie smirked. "Sorry — I'm nosy."

"He said things are going sour with that deal Lillian is supposed to be helping him with. Turns out she's not the superstar he thought she was. Either that or . . ."

"Or what?" Piper watched Annabel's expression grow more thoughtful.

"Or there's something fishy going on."

"What do you mean?" Mackenzie's voice rose, showing she was intrigued.

"I mean I think there's something weird about this whole thing with Lillian. And please don't assume I'm in denial about the divorce or anything like that. I've come to terms with it. Pretty much. It's just that I know Henry. He's not the type to get romantically involved with someone he's working with. Especially when there's such a big deal at stake. Plus, and this may sound silly, he always wins. Never once in the history of our relationship has he let a deal fall through, much less let one crash and burn."

"I did read an article about his company this morning in our competitor's newspaper," Mackenzie admitted. "I wasn't going to say anything, but it seemed really positive. Like things were going in the right direction with the deal. I mean, it's public knowledge that he's trying to take over Digitcorp."

"People believe anything they see in print," Piper declared.

"I'm a little savvier than most people." Mackenzie balked.

"No, that's not what I meant." Piper thought for a moment. "Fern quoted that to me this morning. I can't even remember why. But I distinctly remember her saying it: 'People are very gullible. They'll believe anything they see in print.' It's from *Charlotte's Web.* She's always spouting little bits of wisdom from her favorite book, but I've learned to tune them out, to some degree."

"I'm not really following you." Annabel appeared confused, as did Mackenzie.

"Okay, so hear me out." Piper cleared her throat. "What if that article is exactly what they want the public to believe?"

"Who's they?" Annabel narrowed her eyes.

"*They* is Digitcorp." Piper spoke slowly. "They want the public to think everything is going swimmingly, and that includes everyone at Henry's company, with the exception of Henry, who knows otherwise. This way, no red flags will be waved before the deal goes belly-up."

"Wait —" Annabel tried to interrupt.

"Hold on a minute." Piper held up her hand as she continued to speculate aloud. "And what if Lillian is actually *not* on Henry's side, but, rather, is manipulating him on behalf of the enemy."

"That's crazy." Annabel was clearly dubious.

"Actually, it's not crazy," Mackenzie countered. "It's not crazy at all. One of the other things the article said this morning was that — rumor has it — Lillian used to date the CEO of Digitcorp a million years ago."

"Very interesting." Piper stood up, walked over to the desk in the kitchen, grabbed her laptop, and sat back down. She typed Lillian's name into the search window, and turned the screen so all of them could see. Then she clicked on the images tab and started flipping through every photo available, to the tune of Annabel's retching sounds. Unfortunately, their preliminary search turned up nothing.

"Look under his name," Mackenzie suggested. "Brett Myland. He's the CEO of Digitcorp."

"Good idea." Piper did as she said.

"Hold on a minute." Mackenzie pointed at a small snapshot of what appeared to be Brett Myland at his birthday party, flanked by his minority partners. "When was this taken?"

Piper checked the date. "Last week."

"It's just a group of guys." Annabel frowned.

"Yeah, but look right over here." She touched the screen with the tip of her finger, indicating the somewhat blurry silhouette of a woman in the background.

"Zoom in," Mackenzie ordered, and Piper obliged. "That's no guy, my friend. *That* is Lillian Duffy at Brett Myland's birthday party. Just last week. Obviously, she was trying not to be caught on camera."

"Holy shit." Annabel's eyes widened with excitement.

"Holy shit is right." Piper nodded and then grinned at the two of them meaningfully. "Ladies, I think we're about to blow the lid off a major story."

TWENTY-FOUR

At first, Mackenzie had been furious, bitter, and humiliated. Once she'd had some time to adjust to her new reality and the primal rage had subsided, she'd just felt sorry for herself, sinking beneath the surface of the pity pool that had become her life. It was unlike anything she'd experienced before. She'd always been a floater. Someone who rose to the surface. Someone who not only splashed around in the water, but, when she decided to jump out, did it with vehemence. Someone who pulled others out with her so they didn't drown in their own sorrow. Because playing the victim had never been her style. There was too much to look forward to in life. Too many milestones to anticipate. Too many joyous occasions to celebrate. She was a glass-half-full kind of girl. No. She was a glass-*completely*-full kind of girl, because her glass had always runneth over.

Was she being punished for that now? She'd often wondered, whenever anything good or bad had happened to someone she was close to, whether life events were meant to achieve some sort of universal balance among all mankind. For example, if you'd had an easy childhood, were you doomed to divorce? Or if you were in a happy, secure marriage, would you have trouble conceiving? What if you'd had an easy childhood, were in a happy marriage, and had a brood of four beautiful, healthy kids? What then? Was there a cataclysmic tragedy in your near future? Like the loss of a spouse or — heaven forbid — the death of a child.

Admittedly, there were people who seemed to be eternally unlucky. They were the ones who broke off the shorter end of the wishbone and whose cars got towed when they were parked in a perfectly legal spot with a paid meter. The ones whose homes were flooded every time there was heavy rain. Mackenzie's father had always taught her that most things in life had nothing to do with luck. He'd instilled in her the idea of the self-fulfilling prophecy, and had explained more times than she could count on both hands that you forged your own path, designed your own destiny. That everything happened for a reason. And that reason was not due to some divine intervention. Rather, it was a result of the way you conducted yourself and the choices you made. In essence, it was an extension of the golden rule: do unto others as you would have them do unto you. Only his philosophy went beyond that to suggest that everything you did, every decision you reached, and every action you took was the first in a domino effect that could impact not only your fate, but also the fates of everyone around you.

For her part, Mackenzie hadn't subscribed to his theory entirely. She'd maintained the belief that sometimes awful things happened without anyone being to blame. Although now, the more she thought about it, he may have been on to something. Perhaps she could have been a more attentive wife. Perhaps they could have talked more, really opened up to each other. Often it felt like she and Trevor were a married couple, yet neither of them actually knew who the other one really was or even what they each did all day, despite working for the same company. They were like two planets orbiting each other. Two planets who attended events together, occasionally had dinner together, and slept in the same bed at night. But if you asked either of them what the other one's hopes and dreams were, what their favorite color was, or something seemingly insignificant like what they'd had for lunch the day before, neither of them would have a clue. Maybe that should have been a sign that their relationship wouldn't last. Mackenzie knew firsthand that it worked for a lot of couples, as it always had for them. Or so she'd thought.

She'd lived through one near divorce already with Annabel. She'd seen how profoundly it had hurt her, how stung she'd been. Whether Annabel admitted it or not, Mackenzie suspected her friend still hadn't truly come to terms with the idea of living her life without Henry. As livid as Mackenzie had originally been, the more time that had elapsed — the more time she'd had to acutely analyze her situation, to peel back the layers of the onion until she'd reached the root — the more she realized that she may never have actually been in love with Trevor. She loved him, of course. Until now, he'd never done even the smallest thing to injure her. He'd always been kind and generous. He'd been the husband she'd expected him to be. He hadn't failed her in that way. But he'd never been a true partner. Someone she could wake up in the middle of the night to convey a random thought to or even to discuss a problem that was nagging her. And it wasn't because he was insensitive; it was because that simply wasn't the manner in which they interacted.

For those reasons and so many others, she'd finally texted Trevor and said she was willing to talk. He'd suggested they do it in the privacy of their own home. She'd replied that the office would be fine, behind closed doors of course. *Her* closed doors. Mackenzie wanted to be in a public place so that emotions wouldn't run high, but not too public of a place where strangers would be trying to eavesdrop on their conversation. Trevor had relented — she hadn't given him much choice — and now, sitting behind her desk, while her soon-to-be ex-husband fidgeted in the chair across from her, she felt even more resolute in her decision.

"If it's okay with you, I'd like to start." His eyes were bloodshot, his face unshaven, and his overall appearance unkempt. It seemed as though he'd had a rough go of it since Mackenzie had caught him in the act. Rightfully so.

"Go ahead." She nodded.

"First of all" — he cleared his throat — "I am so sorry. So, so incredibly sorry."

"Okay." Mackenzie couldn't help but roll

her eyes. He was going to have to do better than *sorry.*

"I'm sure that falls completely flat." He looked at her hopefully.

"It does." Her tone was clipped, and his expression wilted.

"I want you to know that what you saw in Piper's office is all that has ever happened between me and . . ." He paused. Mackenzie could tell he was afraid to say her name. "Lucy," he whispered. As if it were some sort of secret. As if she hadn't seen Lucy's lips pressed to his.

"I have a hard time believing that."

"I'm sure you do. But it is the truth. I'm not saying that makes it okay, but it's the truth, for whatever that's worth to you."

"Okay." Mackenzie nodded. Her truth was that it didn't actually matter. If anything, she'd come to realize that he'd done her a favor.

"And it will never happen again."

"Sure it will."

"No." He shook his head. "You have my word that it will not."

"Do you love her?" Mackenzie's expression remained neutral. She wasn't prepared to reveal her cards until he'd revealed his.

"What?" he asked, as if she'd sucker punched him in the stomach.

"Do you love her?"

"I love *you.*"

"That doesn't address my question." She spoke slowly. "Do. You. Love. Lucy?"

"I don't know." He dropped his head. He couldn't even look her in the eyes. Which was her answer.

"Yes, you do. And, at this point, I think you owe it to me to be honest." She exhaled. "One more time. Do you love her?" He nodded without speaking. "When?"

"When what?"

"When did this happen?" Mackenzie wasn't sure why it was important. But suddenly she wanted a sense of the timeline. To understand at what point things had gone wrong. At what point she'd lost him without even knowing it.

"I — I'm not sure," he stammered.

"Yes, you are. I need to know." She refused to let him get away with being a coward.

"It was a slow progression, I guess. She helped me out with that project a while back."

"I forgot about that." She circled her hand in the air to indicate that he should continue.

"And we got along really well." He hesitated. "Then she was on my plane home from a business trip to Boston. She grew up outside the city and was coming back from visiting family. Randomly, she'd been upgraded to the seat right next to me in first class. We ended up just talking the whole time. It was so easy. Like nothing I'd ever experienced before. With a woman."

"The trip to Boston, when I lost the baby?" Her throat felt like it might close up.

"Yes." His face fell. "That's why I didn't say anything then. Somehow I knew immediately. I had these instant feelings for her and —"

"So this has been going on for months, then."

"*No.* I mean, yes. But there's been nothing going on. We just . . . talk."

"You were doing more than talking when I saw you that night on top of Piper's desk."

"As I said, that was the first time."

"The first time what?"

"The first time we kissed."

"And then?"

"And then nothing! I swear to you."

"I believe you. I think." She felt sorry for him. He hadn't even been man enough to take her to bed.

"Now what?" Trevor was waiting for her to decide. He knew he was powerless, which in and of itself made him seem that much more pathetic in her eyes.

"Now we go our separate ways. We say good-bye."

"Good-bye?"

"Yes." She stood up, walked toward him, and kissed him on the cheek. "You're a good man, Trevor. I wish you'd had the courage to come to me with this. And I hope you have the courage moving forward to find true happiness."

"Mackenzie . . ." He reached out to touch her, but she recoiled.

"We're not there yet." She shook her head. "But who knows? Maybe one day we'll be friends."

"I hope so." He smiled weakly and took his cue to leave.

Once he'd closed the door behind him, all she felt was a little sadness and a lot of relief.

Mackenzie returned from lunch to find a note on her desk from Angela, CeCe's assistant, saying that CeCe needed to see her urgently and to come by as soon as she returned. When CeCe Mead used the word *urgent,* you listened.

As she approached her mother-in-law's office, Mackenzie could hear her haranguing someone over the phone for whatever offense they were guilty of this time. It was remarkable how much of her day, week, month, and year was devoted to berating, lecturing, and ranting, in no particular order. With any luck, she was taking out all of her frustrations on whomever was on the other end of the line, thereby leaving Mackenzie to face the most pleasant version of CeCe that was realistically possible.

"You can go ahead in," Angela encouraged, and smiled anxiously. Angela was one of those nervous people who spent her life on guard, waiting for the other shoe to drop. Now in her late fifties, she'd been working for CeCe for nearly three decades, since the minute she'd taken the helm as CEO of Mead Media in the aftermath of Trevor's father's death. It was hard to imagine that anyone could stay on such a violent emotional roller-coaster ride for that long, but Angela had a stomach of steel. And if she didn't, she certainly did a bang-up job of pretending she did.

"Are you sure? It sounds like she's still on a call." Mackenzie was more than content to wait until CeCe was finished. It was a well-known fact in the office that she did not appreciate being interrupted under any circumstances.

"Yup." Angela nodded. "She said in no uncertain terms that she wanted to see you the second you got back. No matter what she was doing."

"Great." Mackenzie rolled her eyes and then filled her lungs with air, puffing out her chest before exhaling. She should have had a shot of vodka with her Cobb salad at lunch. "Here goes nothing." She pushed open CeCe's door, and instantly CeCe swiveled around in her chair.

"Marco, I have to go. My daughter-in-law has just walked in." Mackenzie could hear a frantic, muffled voice through the receiver. "Well, I'm sorry. You'll just have to figure it out for yourself," she growled, and slammed down the phone.

"You wanted to see me?" Mackenzie walked toward CeCe's desk, on which a spray of white lilies sprouted from a massive ceramic vase — a bouquet so elaborate, it looked more like a small tree. "Wow, those are beautiful." She pointed to the flowers on steroids.

"Have a seat." CeCe ignored Mackenzie's observation and motioned to the chair facing her. She leaned forward on her forearms. "Now tell me how the baby making is going. Did you see Dr. Billingsly?"

"Um, no." Mackenzie was confused. Surely Trevor had told her about the situation with Lucy. Weeks had passed since she'd walked in on them. And she'd thought all this time that Trevor might have been staying at his childhood home. Plus, it was unlike him to keep anything from his mother. "Remember, Trevor didn't want to see a fertility specialist?"

"Then go without him." She flicked her wrist in the air like it was no big deal. As if she were suggesting that Mackenzie go supermarket shopping and leave Trevor at home.

"It's not really that simple. *Anymore.*"

"Why is that?" CeCe focused her beady eyes on Mackenzie.

"Honestly, CeCe, I think this is a conversation you should have with your son. There have been . . ." She searched for the appropriate word. "Developments."

"Please don't tell me you're talking about his *interaction* with that assistant girl." So she did know.

"It wasn't really an *interaction.* It was a kiss. At least, that's all that I saw."

"And?" CeCe didn't appear the least bit ruffled by Trevor's dalliance. Maybe she thought it was okay for men to step out on their wives.

"And he kissed another woman. Who's not me. His wife."

"I understand that." CeCe spoke deliberately, as if she were explaining something to a small child. "I just don't see what the big deal is. It's not like he's actually going to *be with her.*"

"Actually, it is like that. It's exactly like that. He loves her. Trevor loves Lucy."

"That's preposterous." CeCe laughed out loud. "You can't be serious."

"Oh, but I am. I just spoke to Trevor."

"He has no idea what he's talking about. I assure you, he's confused." She shook her head. "Now, let's get you an appointment with Stanley. Only the best for my future grandchild." She reached for the telephone.

"CeCe. We're getting a divorce. It's over."

"Like hell it is." Her expression hardened and her eyes glinted with fury. "Now, you listen to me, young lady. I will not have my son attached to some lowly worker bee who's quite obviously after him for his money and his stature. You will fight for him. Do you understand? You will fight for him until he changes his mind. Because if you don't . . ."

"Then what?" Mackenzie challenged calmly, well aware that it would set CeCe off even further.

"Then you, my dear, will walk away without a single penny." Her scowl softened before her lips curled into a wicked smile. "Do we understand each other?" She didn't wait for an answer. "Good." She turned away from Mackenzie. "You'll let me know when you've made that appointment."

"I'm sorry, CeCe." Mackenzie inhaled a dose of courage. For once she was going to have the last word. "At this point, I have to do what's best for me."

TWENTY-FIVE

Mackenzie had confirmed their suspicions. Annabel wasn't sure how exactly. All she'd mentioned was something about using one of CeCe's sources unbeknownst to her. But, either way, Piper had been right. Lillian Duffy was playing for the other team. She wasn't Henry's ace in the hole. She was Digitcorp's. And she wasn't in a romantic relationship with Henry — although who knew how far she'd taken her deception? She was, quite to the contrary, Brett Myland's girlfriend. Brett Myland, the CEO of Digitcorp.

Annabel almost felt sorry for Henry. Almost. Certainly she didn't want Lillian and her cohorts to destroy his company. That said, if he'd taken her to bed, it would be a wee bit challenging for her to sympathize with his predicament. In any case, she'd called Henry early that morning. He'd been alone, or so it had sounded. She'd asked him if it would be possible for his sister to take the kids for the night so that they could talk privately. Annabel had been surprised that he'd seemed eager, if not excited, to do so. He'd even offered to bring over dinner, which she'd said would be fine with her.

If she were being honest with herself, she wasn't sure what she expected as the outcome of their conversation. Or, more to the point, what she wanted the outcome to be. A few months ago, she would have jumped at the opportunity to share this kind of salacious information with Henry. Even if it meant implicating herself and her friends as stalkers, it would have been worth it in order to incriminate Lillian. To stick it to her for duping Henry into God knows what. She'd had nothing to lose back then. Only now things felt different. *She* felt different. Annabel was no longer desperate to hold on to him at all costs. Nor was she delusional enough to believe that he'd come running home to her so they could resume their lives as a happyish family of four, merely because she'd helped him out. If anything, he'd be presenting their divorce papers along with their takeout tonight. He'd had them for weeks, though, and, for whatever reason, had forgotten to bring them with him every time they'd seen each other to exchange the kids. All she had to do was sign on the dotted line to officially pronounce herself single and unattached, although, truth be told, she'd been feeling that way for a while now.

There was also the possibility that Henry could be angry with her. Or, perhaps, think she was lying in order to delay the finalization of their split. After all, she had spent the better part of the past six months having him trailed by a couple of amateur sleuths. Still, those amateurs had discovered what no one else had. And that in and of itself should be worth its weight in goodwill.

The primary thing Annabel was thankful for was the fact that with the passage of time, she'd finally moved past her anger to discover that all of her cursing, all of her tears, all of the times she'd punched her pillow in rage had been cathartic. She'd needed a means of releasing her inner demons, a way of cleansing and purifying. That said, she realized she couldn't go on like this forever, although it had seemed unlikely that she'd ever turn a corner. Yet she had. She'd stepped out of the darkness and into the light of her future.

At the moment, Annabel had no idea what her next steps would be. Whether she should return to work in some capacity. Or if she'd ever meet someone new and have a second chance at love. But, for the first time in a long time, she didn't care. She'd made peace with her reality, thanks, in large part, to Mackenzie and Piper's friendship. Of course, the irony wasn't lost on her that her older friends — the mothers at Harper and Hudson's school, the women she'd known for five, ten years from various chapters in her life — had crawled into the cracks of the woodwork during her separation, never to appear again, while her new friends had stepped up to support her. Piper and Mackenzie had become her people. The ones she called crying in the middle of the night. The ones who materialized at her front door at a moment's notice when they detected even the slightest note of sadness in her voice. She'd learned so much from leaning on them. She'd learned to be her own person. To take responsibility for her mistakes and to face her fears, even if it meant stumbling like a fool along the way.

She had no idea why she hadn't noticed how lost she'd been the past few years. To give him some credit, Henry must have seen it. In his own selfish way, he'd known that things weren't right. And he'd done something about it. Maybe not in the most gentle way, but perhaps he'd given her the push she'd needed, albeit in the only way he could manage. And now she could do him a favor in return.

When the doorbell rang, Annabel was putting the finishing touches on a peach cobbler Mackenzie had taught her to make. She'd been shocked by how simple it was to create something that looked and tasted so professional without a lot of effort. And she'd figured that since Henry had offered to bring dinner, the least she could do was whip up something for dessert. Plus, it couldn't hurt to ply him with sweets before delivering such sour news.

"Come in," she bellowed as she slid the cobbler into the oven, and set the timer for thirty minutes. She heard the door close, and soon after Henry appeared before her, looking disheveled and downtrodden. Annabel could always tell he was really worried about something when his forehead remained steadily furrowed.

"Hey." He hoisted the plastic bags he was holding onto the kitchen island and dropped himself onto one of the barstools, instinctively hunching his back.

"What's wrong?" Annabel slipped the pot holders off her hands and sat down next to him, turning her chair to face his.

"It's all falling apart, Annie." As soon as

he finished speaking, he pressed his finger-tips into his closed eyelids. "I'm going to lose everything. And for once I can't figure out why. For the life of me, I can't fucking figure out what's going on."

"I assume you're talking about work?"

"Mostly." He looked up at her, and she could see the pain behind his gaze. She hadn't planned to bring it up first thing. She'd figured maybe they could eat first. Partake in a little cobbler, and then she'd broach the difficult subject. Henry was typically more forgiving when his stomach was full.

"Can you tell me about it?"

"There's not much to tell. Digitcorp has managed to get their hands on information that was completely confidential, and I have no idea how. I practically strip-searched everyone at the company." Annabel cringed at the thought of him strip-searching Lillian. "Well, not really, but you know what I mean. I had to."

"Listen, I need to tell you something." Annabel started to unburden herself.

"Right, sorry. But is there any way it can wait? Just ten minutes. I need to clear my mind, if that's even possible."

"Actually, not really. It has to do with this," she continued, treading carefully and watching his reaction.

"With my Digitcorp deal?" He was rightfully confused.

"Sort of." Annabel crinkled her nose and pressed her lips together before she started speaking again. "I mean, yeah. It does."

"Annie, what are you talking about?"

"I know who the mole is."

"Excuse me?"

"I said, I know who the mole is. The person who's sabotaging you and the company."

"Okay." He was dubious, she could tell.

"It's Lillian." There — she'd said it. She'd expected the unveiling to be more gratifying, but it wasn't.

"Lillian Duffy?"

"The one and only."

"Dare I ask why you think this?"

"It's kind of a long story."

"I'm ready to listen." And so he did. Intently. As she outlined everything for him, from the day she'd decided to enlist Piper and then Mackenzie to catch him in the act of an affair right up to her suspicions about Lillian, which had led to Piper's hypothesis and finally Mackenzie's confirmation.

"So, there you have it." At first he was quiet. Eerily so.

"I don't know what to say." He shook his

head. "First of all, I want you to know that I never cheated on you. I would never . . ." He trailed off, presumably still scandalized by the totality of her discovery and all that she'd admitted to him.

"Piper saw you kissing Lillian in the parking lot of Templeton's." She shrugged. "It's okay, Henry. If that was the first time, you didn't do anything wrong. We were already separated. I'm over it," she lied.

"Oh, Annie." He took her hands in his. "Not only was that the first time; it was the one and only time. And let me say I was caught completely off guard. I never had any romantic intentions toward Lillian. For lack of a better word, she kind of mauled me. I guess now I know why."

"That's nice to hear." Annabel smiled. She still didn't like the mere idea that Henry's lips had so much as touched another woman's. But she'd come to a point where details like that were no longer destructive to her ongoing evolution as a more understanding person. "I thought you might be pissed about the stalking."

"I'm not thrilled about it," he laughed. "But do you have any idea what your discovery means for me? For us?"

"I'm not entirely sure."

"Let me tell you, then." He leaned in

toward her. "You, Annabel Ford, have just saved my company. You have, quite literally, obliterated every negative thing that's been going on for the past few months." He paused. "Well, all except one."

"What's that?"

"Our divorce."

"Do you have the papers?"

"I do."

"I'm ready to sign." One involuntary sob caught in her throat and she pushed it back down. She wouldn't cry. She'd promised herself that much. At least not until he was gone. Annabel had thought she'd made peace with the situation. After all, she'd come so far since the day Henry had declared their status as a married couple over and done with. To both her astonishment and gratification, she'd learned to exist in the moment more with her family and friends, to balance the stresses and responsibilities of raising two children with moments of joy. And she'd learned to slow down and to relax her standards for household perfection by acknowledging to herself that if everything wasn't perfect all the time, the world would not come to a screeching halt. What was more, she'd realized that she was overlooking the things in her life that deserved a lot more of her attention and appreciation, like spending quality time with her husband and children. But that didn't matter now. Regardless of how far she'd come, this was still where they had ended up.

"I don't want you to." Without warning he cupped her face in his hands. "I love you, Annie. I made a mistake. I never should have left."

"What? No, you're just happy about the stuff with the company. I don't want you to confuse the two things."

"Oh, I'm not confused. I'm not confused at all. I've been feeling this way for a couple of months now. Why do you think I keep forgetting to bring over the papers?" He kissed her on the lips. "I've been so wrapped up with everything at work that there never felt like the right time to tell you. And you seemed so independent and content without me. But I know how much I love you. More than ever. I don't want to lose you, Annie. I don't want to lose our family." Then he kissed her more passionately, and for a moment her head spun.

"I'm . . . not sure how to respond."

"Tell me you love me too."

"I do. I love you too." She let him hug her close.

"Music to my ears." Henry was nearly

giddy. "I'm not exactly sure where to go from here, but we'll figure it out. I promise you that. For now . . ." He paused briefly.

And allowing herself the freedom to let things play out as they would, she finished his sentence. "We eat cobbler."

"So the cobbler was yummy?" Mackenzie shoveled a heaping spoonful of granola into her mouth.

"That's your takeaway? Really?" Piper tilted her head to one side as if analyzing her. "Annabel just told us that she and Henry are back together and that, for all intents and purposes, he never actually cheated on her."

"Well, I'm obviously thrilled about that." Mackenzie rolled her eyes. "Is it so wrong that I want to make sure my recipe was up to snuff?"

"For the record, it was delicious," Annabel confirmed. "We skipped dinner altogether. I think Henry was pretty surprised that I'd actually made it, but aside from that, it was perfection. And super easy. I had no idea baking could be so fun."

"Welcome to my world." Mackenzie spoke through a full mouth.

"Was it me, or was that instructor tougher than usual?" Piper picked at a piece of her blueberry muffin. They'd all decided to meet for an exercise class at eight in the morning and then have breakfast afterward at Café Crunch, their regular stomping ground.

"Totally. She's the new weekend girl. I heard she used to teach a spin class in town. My ass already hurts." Mackenzie shifted in her chair.

"I could never spin." This from Annabel. "It's too cultish."

"Completely," Mackenzie agreed. "One of my old friends from New York City used to do it. They all have their specific bikes and, apparently, if you're new and you take someone's spot, it's tantamount to holding them at gunpoint and mugging them."

"I could never be that serious about working out," Piper declared. "It's a minor miracle I've committed myself for this long."

"Well, it's good that your mind is more motivated than your body." Annabel took a slow sip of her coffee. "You saved Henry's company."

"It was a team effort," Piper offered modestly, despite her huge, proud grin.

"Maybe so, but you were the one who connected the dots."

"Actually, I'd say we have Fern's obsession with *Charlotte's Web* to thank for that!"

"Speaking of people believing everything they see in print . . ." Mackenzie smirked. "I have a little idea of my own."

"Do tell!" Annabel was immediately intrigued.

"Okay, so I was thinking that Piper should write an article for the *Journal* about Henry's company and how the Digitcorp deal went down the tubes as a result of their underhanded deception."

"I like that!" Annabel's eyes widened with anticipation.

"I like that too," Piper agreed. "As long as you think I can do it justice."

"Are you kidding?" Mackenzie asked. "You're an amazing journalist, and what better way to flex your creative muscles than to expose your friend's husband's sworn enemy?'

"Sworn enemy?" Annabel laughed.

"I told you I watch a lot of crime shows on television." Mackenzie pilfered a piece of bacon off Annabel's plate.

"Hey, watch it," Annabel teased.

"What? I'm saving you calories."

"I'm not counting calories anymore. That was stupid and pointless."

"Well, I'm glad you finally came to your senses there."

"Seriously, though, it would be nice to

stick it to Brett Myland. Not to mention Lillian Duffy."

"What a bitch," Piper interjected. "By the way, how can we be sure that the *Journal* will publish the piece?"

"Have you forgotten that I'm married to the heir apparent?"

"No, but . . ." Piper hesitated. "I wasn't sure if you were really in that place with him. You know, given the circumstances."

"Don't worry about that. Just leave it to me."

"Thank you." Annabel nodded. "Thank you both."

"Can you believe this all started at this same table in this same café, with you telling me you were absolutely certain that Henry was cheating on you?" Piper mused.

"No, I cannot." Annabel shook her head. "I may have the jumped the gun on that one."

"Too bad I didn't," Mackenzie added. "I feel like one of those women."

"Which women?" Annabel took a bite of her vegetable omelet.

"The ones you used to talk about. The ones who thought their husbands would never have an affair and were shocked off their rockers when they found out they were."

"Honestly, I never would have suspected Trevor either. And I'm usually the first to accuse." Annabel reached across the table and placed her hand on Mackenzie's. "I think this could wind up to be a good thing for you, though. I know what an upheaval like this can lead to. And you may not want to hear this now, but you'll find someone new and even more wonderful."

"You're right," Mackenzie relented. "It still feels shitty, though. I wish he'd just told me."

"Men are cowards," Annabel professed.

"Ain't that the truth?" Piper agreed.

"What's going on with you and Max?" Mackenzie turned toward her. "No signs of him fleeing the coop anytime soon?"

"Nope."

"And you're cool with that?"

"I don't really have a choice." Piper thought for a moment. "I guess I finally came to the conclusion that I can't hold a grudge forever. It's not healthy for me, and it's not fair to Fern. Or to Todd. If Max really wants to have a place in his daughter's life, then he deserves a chance. I just need to figure out how we're going to work it all out. So that everyone's happy."

"Wouldn't that be nice?" Annabel smiled at her friends.

"Amen to that," Mackenzie concurred.

"We'll get there," Piper avowed. "I have a feeling happiness is just around the corner. For all of us."

TWENTY-SIX

For more than a decade she'd been nurturing her anger, nourishing the pain over Max's abandonment that had cemented its place in her heart. Although she hadn't thought about Max often, in a manner of speaking, her bitterness toward him was like a disease — the kind that killed you slowly but surely, rotting your mind and then your body until you were no longer the person you'd once been. Or the person you wanted to be. Of course, she hadn't realized anything of the sort until he had shown up at her door unexpectedly. She'd felt justified in her animosity. She'd worn her resentment as a badge of honor, as she'd gone about her life as a single working mom.

Sure, she'd known that there were plenty of parents out there who were going it alone, as she was, whether due to divorce or, God forbid, the death of a significant other. Still, she'd told herself that she had it the worst. She'd been abandoned by the love of her life. Only now that she'd been able to release some — if not all — of her hostility toward him, her previous position seemed completely shortsighted. How had she ever thought it would have been easier to be a widow? How had she even begun to rationalize that losing someone to an illness or a tragic accident was better than having someone walk out on you intentionally? It was ridiculous and selfish.

That wasn't to say that she thought what Max had done was at all justified. But life wasn't fair. If she'd learned one thing and only one thing through the years, it was that. And maybe, just maybe, she was finally ready to forgive, if not forget.

At Annabel's suggestion, she'd called Max over the weekend and asked him to come to her house to talk first thing Monday morning, after the bus had picked Fern up for school. She'd sent Lucy an e-mail to let her know she'd be at the office an hour or so late, since their verbal communication had disintegrated to monosyllabic discourse. Even Mackenzie had urged Piper to let it go. She'd said that Lucy was young and naive and that most women in her position would have allowed themselves to be courted by someone who was not only their boss, but someone who was in line to take over the entire company they worked for. She'd gone so far as to say that she didn't blame Lucy and that, in some strange way, she'd done Mackenzie a favor. Piper had been more than a little astonished at the ease with which Mackenzie had been able to exonerate Lucy, especially since Piper was still stung by her assistant's betrayal, and it wasn't like Lucy had set her sights on Todd.

But instead of trying to rile Mackenzie, she'd decided to heed Annabel's advice and take a page from Mackenzie's book of clemency. She wasn't entirely sure what she was going to say to Max. She just knew she had to tell him how she felt. How he'd made her feel. And afterward they needed to move on. Somehow. So that Piper could finally convince Todd to come back home.

Max arrived early, just as Piper had put the final touches on her article about Digit-corp's deception and sent it to Mackenzie. The piece was strong. It was bold. If it didn't make a splash, she wasn't sure what would.

"Hey. Come on in." Piper held the front door open for Max to walk through and closed it behind him, after noticing that the seal at the top had unstuck. Those were the sorts of things that happened when Todd wasn't around. Along with the washing machine making strange noises and the freezer leaking.

"Thanks." He followed her into the kitchen, where she motioned for him to take a seat at the table.

"Do you want some coffee?" she offered. It seemed like the polite thing to ask, since she was already pouring herself a cup.

"Nah, I'm fine."

"Okay." She sat down across from him, cradling the steaming mug in her hands. "We need to talk." *No sense in beating around the bush.*

"I agree." He nodded. "Piper —" he started.

"Sorry," she interrupted him. "What I should have said was, I need to talk. And I need you to listen."

"All right, then."

"The good news is that I don't despise you anymore."

"I'd say that is good news." He smiled.

"The bad news is that you've hurt me and, although she may not want to admit it, you've hurt Fern too."

"That was never —" he tried to interject, but she didn't give him a chance.

"Please let me finish." She took a deep

breath and then a small sip of her coffee. "What you did all those years ago was horrible. I'm sure that goes without saying. Do you have any idea how it felt to have you leave?"

"No, I don't." He shook his head.

"I thought you were coming back, Max. Every single day. Every single week. Every month that passed. I told myself there was no way that you could have walked out on me and our unborn child for good. Hell, even after Fern was born, I thought, *The news will reach him. He'll find out that he has a daughter and he'll change his mind. He'll want to meet her. Even if he doesn't want me anymore.*"

"I honestly thought I was going to come back too." He looked up at her with a wounded expression. "I kept tabs on you through a few friends in the beginning. But then it got too painful. Every time I saw a baby, I thought about Fern. Every time I saw a woman who even remotely resembled you, I followed her to make sure. I thought about both of you all the time. For what it's worth."

"Honestly, it's not worth much." Piper wasn't sure whether to believe him or not. But she realized it didn't matter so much to her anymore.

"I understand."

"My intent isn't to try to punish you now. What I've come to terms with is that missing out on the first ten years of Fern's life is penance enough for you."

"That's for sure."

"Although I'm sure you can see why I find it hard to feel sorry for you."

"I don't want your pity, Piper."

"That's good, because you're not going to get it." She took a large gulp of her coffee, which had finally cooled down, and set the mug on the table. "I'm not looking to rehash everything that happened back then or even what's happened since. You're here now, and we need to find a way to move forward. We need to put a system in place so that, as long as you're committed, you can be the kind of father to Fern that you should have been all along."

"That's very generous of you. You have no idea how much this means to me."

"I'm not doing it for you. I'm doing it for Fern. And for me. And for Todd. *We* deserve to be happy."

"Yes, you do." Max nodded. "Is it my turn?"

"Go ahead," Piper allowed.

"I love you."

"Excuse me?" That was not at all what

she'd expected him to say. Not even a little.

"Don't get upset. I know you're in love with Todd." He paused. "It's just important that you know. At least to me."

"Okay." She wasn't sure where he was going with this revelation.

"I've always loved you. Even while we were apart. I still love you, Piper. I was terrified about finding out I was going to be a dad. Believe me, I'm not trying to make excuses for what I did. I was just so scared. I know I've been a coward. I never even got in touch until Fern reached out to me. I . . ." He stopped himself.

"What?"

"That day. The day I came to your house and told you I was leaving."

"Yeah?"

"I'd planned to propose to you." His eyes met hers. "I had a ring and everything. It wasn't much. But . . ."

"But something changed your mind."

"Yes — fear."

"Fear of marrying me?"

"Fear of everything changing in my life. We were so young."

"I know."

"The joke of it is" — he laughed — "I'm the one who ended up with nothing."

"Not nothing. You do have a beautiful

daughter." She touched his arm.

"Who doesn't know the first thing about me."

"You can fix that. You have a second chance."

"I'm moving to California, Piper," Max announced, catching her off guard for the second time.

"California?" A month ago, she would have been thrilled to receive such news. She would have screamed it from the rooftop. Done a jig on the kitchen counter. But now it felt wrong. Like a second betrayal of sorts. "I should have known you wouldn't stick around for long."

"It's really not like that."

"Well, then, what is it like?"

"I've thought long and hard about this. I have a few friends in San Diego. I was living there for a while. And one of them offered me a great job. It's nothing earth-shattering, just sales for a pharmaceutical company. But it will pay the bills."

"Certainly you could find a job here, no? Closer to Fern."

"I could, but I don't want to be a tag-on to your life. I guess I thought . . ."

"You thought what?"

"That there would be a chance for us too."

"I'm sorry."

"Don't say that. You have nothing to be sorry for. Ever." He smiled. "I'm actually happy for you. Todd seems like a great guy, and I know Fern adores him."

"That's nice to hear." Piper was still trying to digest everything Max had said. "Fern's going to be upset. That you're leaving."

"I already told her. I wanted her to hear it from me."

"And?"

"And I have an idea I want to run by you."

"I'm all ears."

"What would you think about Fern coming to stay with me for a couple of weeks this summer?" He looked nervous. Like he was prepared for Piper to shut him down immediately. "I've already rented a two-bedroom apartment there. My friend checked it out and he says it's really nice. Right by the water. I know it's a lot to ask. And I'll still visit her here as often as I can, but to have that one-on-one time with Fern would mean the world to me. Think about it, Piper. Please."

"I will." She nodded. "I promise."

"Thank you."

"You're welcome."

"This is *amazing.* I can't believe you wrote

it so quickly. It's so thorough." Mackenzie looked down at the stack of printed pages in her hand — Piper's article about Digit-corp's dirty scheming and near destruction of Henry's company. She'd nailed it.

"I do have a little experience with quick turnarounds." Piper was sitting across from Mackenzie in her office, waiting for Trevor to materialize.

"I sent it to Trevor last night. I'm not sure if he's read it yet, but I know he's going to love it as much as I do. This could mean a lot of visibility for you, Piper. If it has the impact I think it will."

"I know." She fidgeted with the paper clips on her desk. "I'm not sure whether to be excited or terrified."

"Definitely the former." Mackenzie nodded as Piper's phone rang. Piper checked the number. Just one of the many publicists who tried to pitch her stories every day. She'd asked Lucy to make herself scarce for an hour, so that neither she nor Mackenzie had to shoulder the awkward burden of watching Trevor interact with her.

There was a knock at the door, even though it was slightly ajar. "Come in," Piper called out, and Trevor appeared in front of them. "Make yourself at home." She motioned to the chair next to Mackenzie's. It felt strange to be the one in the driver's seat, especially when the heir to the company that employed you was sitting opposite you. Part of her wanted to leap across the desk and strangle him with her bare hands, on Mackenzie's behalf, of course. But that wasn't the purpose of their meeting.

"So? Did you read it?" Mackenzie asked eagerly.

"I did." Trevor nodded. Piper could tell he was uncomfortable, although she didn't really care. *Let him squirm,* she thought.

"And?"

"And it's major." He smiled at Piper. "Really excellent work."

"Thank you." The praise felt hollow coming from him, but she accepted the compliment nonetheless. It still confounded her how Mackenzie could sit beside him like nothing had happened. Like he hadn't made out with Lucy on the very desk they were conversing over. She considered all the anger she'd harbored toward Max for ten years, and he hadn't even cheated on her.

"Can I assume you've done your homework? Verified the story? Checked sources?"

"Absolutely," Piper confirmed. "One hundred percent."

"And we have the exclusive on this, right?"

"Yes," she stated plainly. He was doing his

due diligence, which wouldn't have annoyed her coming from someone else. "Honestly, I don't think anyone even knows that the story is about to be blown wide-open. Including Brett Myland, Lillian Duffy, and everyone else who works for Digitcorp."

"Excellent!" He puffed his chest. "I'm fairly certain that what Lillian has done is illegal in more ways than one. Especially if, as you say, there was a contract in place on Henry's side. Either way, she'd have a damn hard time proving it wasn't. This could be a real coup for Mead Media."

"And for Piper," Mackenzie clarified.

"Sure, of course." He didn't care about whatever accolades she might receive. That was obvious. But regardless of Trevor's feelings, she wasn't doing this for the notoriety. She was doing it for Annabel.

"So, we're all set? You'll publish it in tomorrow's paper?"

"You know I have to pass it by my mother first."

"I do," Mackenzie acknowledged. "I've been meaning to thank you, by the way."

"For what?"

"For taking care of explaining our situation to her."

"It was the least I could do." Trevor avoided any eye contact with Piper. He had to figure she knew everything at this point. And that she didn't think much of him because of it. Certainly she would never say as much, for fear of losing her job. Still, Trevor was a smart enough guy to understand that when you stepped out on someone's best friend with their assistant, it kind of rendered you persona non grata for the foreseeable future.

"True, but I'm sure it wasn't a fun conversation."

"No, it wasn't." He exhaled. "I'm going to take this to her now." He reached for the pages Mackenzie was holding. The three of them were well aware that CeCe read things only in hard copy, as she insisted she couldn't edit on the computer. Not that she really edited anything these days. Her job was to be the overseer. To be the one who took all the credit when things went well and also the one who shouldered the responsibility when things went wrong, even if she did try to blame everyone else first. Piper didn't envy her position.

"Thank you again." Mackenzie smiled genuinely

"As I said, it's the least I can do." He stood up and, before speaking, he seemed to stop and think for a moment. He looked at Mackenzie. Really looked at her for the first time since he'd entered Piper's office. "You can count on me. I promise."

Once he'd gone, Mackenzie turned back toward Piper and released a shriek. "This is going to be huge! I can feel it."

"From your mouth to God's ears." Piper laughed nervously.

"Oh, trust me, you don't need divine intervention on this one. You earned whatever comes your way."

"With your help."

"That's what friends are for, right?" Mackenzie grinned.

"It sure is."

As time went on, and the months and years came and went, he was never without friends.

— Charlotte's Web

TWENTY-SEVEN

"First, the front page of the *Journal*. Now lead story in the business section of the *New York Times*. I still can't get over it," Mackenzie gushed. "Piper, my friend, you have arrived."

They were back at Café Crunch to celebrate for roughly the fifth time in the days since the article had been published on the front page of the *Journal,* against CeCe's will. Apparently, she'd put her foot down with Trevor. She'd said she didn't care if the Pope had run naked down Main Street in Eastport; since the story had originated with Mackenzie, she wanted it blocked.

In a rare display of valor, Trevor had gone behind her back in order to take just one small step toward making things right with Mackenzie. Fortunately, for his sake, CeCe had forgiven him once all of the hype had ensued surrounding Piper's exposé. She'd also offered Piper a promotion in title and a substantial raise in salary.

"And it was all over the AP wire! Henry said he owes you his life," Annabel enthused.

"I wouldn't go that far." Piper feigned modesty. "Okay, fine. It is really awesome." She squealed. "I actually have some unbelievable news."

"You're pregnant?" Mackenzie smirked.

"God, no. Please don't even put that out in the universe." Piper laughed. "I'm very happy with Fern and Fern alone. She's enough of a handful at this point."

"Just you wait until she's a teenager. My friend Rachel's daughter turned thirteen last month and she's driving her to drink. Literally." Annabel took a sip of some green concoction Mackenzie had convinced her to try. "This is actually pretty tasty."

"It's green apple, celery, spinach, and some other stuff that's good for you," Mackenzie explained. "So, what's the word?" She turned toward Piper, who was sitting next to her.

"I got a job offer to be a writer for a new crime show coming to Fox this fall!"

"Holy shit! That's amazing!" Mackenzie hugged her.

"Congratulations, Piper." Annabel reached across the table to give her arm a tight squeeze. "No one deserves it more than you do!"

"I mean, that's like your dream come true, right?" This was Mackenzie. "You know I want every single detail. What's the show called? Who's the producer? Is it Mark Burnett?"

"Well, it's as-yet-untitled. I know that much. They said it's sort of a cross between *America's Most Wanted* and *American Idol,* whatever the hell that means. No idea who the producers are. They couldn't tell me too much, since I have to sign some confidentiality agreement first, but it sounds like exactly the opportunity I've been waiting for pretty much forever." She paused. "As a bonus, the job is bicoastal between New York City and Los Angeles, which means I'll get to take Fern out West with me a lot. And LA isn't far from San Diego, where Max will be, which Fern is thrilled about. She thinks I'm going to be a celebrity."

"So I take it you're not accepting CeCe's offer?" Mackenzie asked.

"You've got that right." Piper nodded definitively. "I need a change. I've been working at Mead for so many years now, and with everything that's gone down with Lucy and Trevor, I just think it's for the best for everyone. What about you?" She looked at Mackenzie.

"I already told CeCe I'll be resigning. It makes no sense for me to stay."

"What will you do next?" Annabel probed.

"I'm not really sure, to be honest." Mackenzie shrugged. "Trevor went to bat for me in the divorce settlement. Let's just say I'll be financially secure for a while. And then some. Although I do want to find something I'm passionate about, when the time is right."

"Lucky girl." Annabel tore off a piece of her croissant. "In the end, Trevor kind of stepped up, huh?"

"He really did," Mackenzie acknowledged. "It's puzzling even to me that I never realized I wasn't happy in our marriage. I think somehow I confused contentedness with happiness. Does that make any sense? It was like all of the right boxes had been checked. Trevor was handsome, kind, generous, and obviously very wealthy — although that part never really mattered to me. He was the guy every girl dreamed of marrying. And then there was the proposal and the ring and the extravagant wedding. It was all so consuming and over-the-top fabulous while it was happening."

"But?" Annabel prompted.

"But the burning desire wasn't ever there

between us, nor was the intimate companionship I've realized I deserve in a husband. It was like I was wrapped up in this life he'd enveloped me in, even though we never truly got each other. We're so different in almost every way." She thought for a moment. "Oddly enough, I feel thankful now that he and Lucy met. It forced me to see what was right in front of my eyes all along. I need someone who shares my interests. Someone with whom I really want to have and raise children. And, most important, someone I want to throw down on the bed and have my way with. The bottom line is that Trevor felt more like a friend."

"Do you think you'll start dating again soon?" Annabel couldn't help herself.

"Funny you should ask." Mackenzie grinned knowingly.

"I knew it!" Annabel announced. "What did I tell you?" She pointed to Piper.

"You were right; I'll give you that," Piper admitted. "She said you'd find someone in no time."

"Well, let's not get ahead of ourselves." Mackenzie held her hand up to stop them from jumping to conclusions. "The ink on the divorce papers has barely dried."

"And may I say it was the quickest divorce in the history of divorces," Annabel commented.

"I can give CeCe credit for expediting it. Once something has been decided on, she wants it done and over with so she can spin it to her favor and move on. Unexpectedly, this time it worked to my advantage." Mackenzie picked at her chocolate chip muffin.

"So, who's the guy?" Annabel arched an eyebrow.

"Do you remember James? That doctor we met the night you took me to the hospital?"

"Vaguely." Annabel hesitated. "Super hot, right?"

"Kind of." Mackenzie blushed. "Anyway, he asked me to go to the opera with him next Saturday night."

"He doesn't waste any time." Piper laughed.

"Actually, he was really respectful about it. He heard about the divorce. He said he just wants to get to know me better, whether as just friends or something more. We're going to take it slow; see where things go from here."

"But you like him." Annabel stated the obvious.

"I do," Mackenzie confessed.

"Oh, sorry, that wasn't a question. I can tell. It's written all over your face."

"Is that tacky?" Mackenzie scrunched her nose. "So soon after? I mean, I'm not saying he's the one. I guess I just want to find true love. Eventually."

"If it feels right, that's all that matters," Annabel affirmed. "Speaking of which, what's going on with you and Todd?" She shifted the conversation back to Piper.

"Things have been good. Really good. He moved back in. And not only is he supportive of my new bicoastal career plans, but he seems legitimately excited for me."

"And all is friendly between Todd and Fern?"

"Thankfully, yes. Not to mention that she's cool with Max's decision to move to California, now that she knows we'll be traveling there pretty often."

"Wow. Seems like everything is as close to perfect as it could be. Although no more mention of marriage from Todd?" Annabel and Mackenzie exchanged glances.

"Nope." Piper looked down at her plate of eggs and potatoes. "I guess he's not there yet. For the second time."

"Are you sure?" Mackenzie stood up, as did Annabel. They both backed away from the table.

"What do you mean, am I sure? Where are you guys going?" Piper stared at them

405

blankly. And before she knew what was happening, Todd and Fern came out from behind her. "What's going on?" Suddenly Todd knelt down on one knee in front of her, in the middle of the café. "Oh, my God!" Piper's hands flew to her mouth.

"Did you really think I'd let you get away that easy?" Todd opened up the black velvet ring box in his palm to reveal the same sparkling, pave-encrusted diamond band with the same oval-shaped emerald stone he'd presented to her on their second anniversary at Templeton's. "Let's try this again. Piper, will you marry me?"

"Yes!" she cried. "Yes, yes, yes!" She jumped out of her chair, knocking it to the ground and sending her purse and its entire contents to the floor. Todd got to his feet too, and slipped the ring onto Piper's finger before kissing her passionately, as the entire café full of patrons erupted into applause. Once they broke apart, she hugged Fern close. Then Mackenzie and Annabel too. "So, you all knew about this?"

Fern nodded enthusiastically, her smile wide and proud.

"We may have played a small role." Annabel winked at her.

Todd wrapped his arms around Piper's waist. "So, everyone finally happy?"

"We sure are!" Piper beamed. "You know I'd hate to say I told you so."

"But?" Mackenzie encouraged.

"Fine. I told you so!"

EPILOGUE

"Who wants Daddy's superduper delicious pancakes?" Henry's bellow echoed throughout the house. It was only ten in the morning and he'd already gone for a jog and stopped on the way home to pick up a dozen eggs and Annabel's favorite fresh-squeezed orange juice from the farmers' market. They'd invited Mackenzie and James and Piper, Todd, and Fern over for a midmorning brunch.

"I DO!" Harper called down the stairs, racing into the kitchen with his brother not far behind him.

"I DO TOO!" Hudson echoed. Neither of them had mastered the art of what Annabel called their inside voices.

"And what about you?" Henry came up behind his wife, grabbed her playfully around the waist, and kissed her neck tenderly.

"I should have an egg-white omelet." She

smiled wryly, turning around to face Henry. "But homemade pancakes are just too tempting to pass up." She clasped his face in her hands and planted a kiss firmly on his lips.

"Pancakes all around, then," Henry announced triumphantly.

"With strawberries on top!" Annabel added. It had been just a few weeks since Henry had moved back in, but they'd yet to fall back into even one of their old habits. And she felt absolutely certain that their renewed passion toward each other and toward maintaining their family of four would only continue to flourish.

"Yay!" the boys cheered together as the doorbell rang.

"That'll be our guests," Annabel declared, and made her way toward the front door.

"Hello, hello!" Mackenzie smiled wide, as Annabel ushered everyone into the house.

"You guys have good timing." She hugged Mackenzie, then Piper, and shook hands with James before kissing Todd on the cheek. "Welcome." She leaned over to give Fern a tight squeeze. "Don't you look pretty?" She motioned to Fern's pink dress with embroidered flowers.

"Thank you." Fern curtsied before revealing a proud grin.

"Let's all migrate into the family room. Henry's making pancakes."

"Hi, everyone!" Henry called from the other room.

"We've also got eggs, bagels, and fruit salad," Annabel continued. "Whatever strikes your fancy."

"Sounds delicious." James nodded approvingly. Annabel didn't know him that well yet, but she could see how happy he was making Mackenzie. And that was what really mattered to her. After all, Mackenzie had always been the first one to steer her and Piper toward finding their own happiness in her wise but gentle way.

"Take a seat — make yourself at home. I'm going to check on Henry's progress."

"I'll help you." Piper stood up.

"Me too." Mackenzie followed suit.

"No, you will not. We've got everything under control."

"Really? There's nothing we can do?" Piper sat back down reluctantly.

"Nothing?" Mackenzie repeated.

"Nothing. Just relax," Annabel insisted.

"I'm not particularly good at relaxing," Piper added.

"Todd, can you please tell your fiancée to chill out?" She laughed. "I assure you, we're on it."

"I can try." Todd shrugged. "You know. *Some women.*"

"I sure do." Annabel rolled her eyes good-naturedly and then retreated to the kitchen, where Henry was cracking eggs into a hot pan, with the boys a captive audience.

"Mommy?" Harper widened his eyes at her.

"Yes, sweetheart?"

"I like having Daddy home. Is he going to stay?"

"I think you should ask Daddy that." Annabel winked at Henry. "But I'm pretty sure I know the answer."

Henry walked toward his sons, who were standing side by side, looking more distinct with each passing day, despite the fact that they were supposed to be identical. He knelt down in front of them and took one of their hands in each of his. "I promise you I'm not going anywhere. Ever again. I love your mommy. And I love both of you . . ."

"To the moon and back," Hudson said, finishing his thought.

"To the moon and back." Henry nodded and hugged them close.

Annabel closed her eyes. And finally exhaled.

■ ■ ■ ■

READERS GUIDE: SOME WOMEN

EMILY LIEBERT

■ ■ ■ ■

A CONVERSATION WITH EMILY LIEBERT

Q: Some Women *takes place in Connecticut, where you reside. How much did your own town influence the fictional Eastport?*

A: I tend to write what I know. So yes, there are certain similarities in the overall culture and some of the stereotypes. My main characters aren't based on any particular individuals in my life, but there are always aspects of my characters that have been inspired by my friends, family, and occasionally people I don't particularly care for. If there's one thing I'm sure of, it's that everyone I know will ask me if (insert name of character) is them! But I'll never tell. . . .

Q: Your four novels have closely examined women's lives and the relationships we foster in our lives. Is this theme something you're passionate about exploring further?

A: Yes! I think there's endless material there.

I believe that women are ever-evolving throughout the course of their lives. I know I am. There are so many different relationships, life stages, struggles, experiences — both good and bad — to live through. And people deal with things in very diverse ways. I'm fascinated by this and definitely plan to dig deeper and deeper into what truly makes women (and men) tick.

Q: What inspired the story line for Some Women?

A: At the beginning of the book, the three main characters barely know one another. In fact, Annabel and Mackenzie have never even met. Ultimately, they're brought together by a barre class that they all take — it's a group fitness class which is a combination of yoga, Pilates, and ballet. (While Piper and Mackenzie do work at the same company, they hardly interacted before connecting through barre.) As it happens, I started taking the same sort of class at Pure Barre in Westport two years ago. I fell in love. Not only because it changed my body and made me infinitely stronger — physically and mentally — but because it became a sanctuary for me. A place where I could go and focus on myself (and only myself) for fifty-five minutes in class. Like the characters in the book, I made a few close friends there. They're not the friends who I typically socialize with or whose kids are friends with mine. Our husbands have never met. But we have a mutual bond. So that's where the original nugget of an idea came from. Beyond that, I knew I wanted to focus on three strong yet very different women, each of whom was confronted with a major life-altering change, and to depict how the ripple effects spread through their lives.

Q: Are these life-altering changes what draw each of them to the other two women?

A: Absolutely. Honestly, I don't know whether Annabel, Piper, and Mackenzie would be friends under normal circumstances. Yet once they're thrust into one another's personal lives unexpectedly, they form an immediate bond. It's almost as if the universe connected them at a time when they each desperately needed to find a way to fill a void. They're able to support and bolster one another in ways that the other people in their lives — people they've known for years — cannot.

Q. Do you think it's a challenge for women to make new friendships as adults?

A: I think it depends on the person. I moved

to a new town two years ago knowing not a single person. In that time, I've met so many inspiring women, many of whom have become close friends. That said, if you're not outgoing, it can certainly be difficult. Or if you're someone who doesn't like to get out and experience different things, it can certainly be challenging. Having school-aged children can make a big difference because it allows you to meet other moms with whom you definitely have at least one thing in common.

Q: *You're a mother to two young children. Did any of your parenting experiences inform the relationship between Piper and Fern?*

A: Since my children are younger (five and six years old) and they're both boys, my experiences are more closely related to Annabel's experiences with Harper and Hudson than they are with Piper and Fern's relationship. That said, I have friends with daughters who are Fern's age and I remember my own relationship with my mom, so that helped in depicting the nuances of their relationship.

Q: *What influenced you to choose* Charlotte's Web *as Fern's most beloved book?*

A: It's my favorite book! I write about

friendship and love. To me, the greatest literary depiction of those two things is the bond between Charlotte and Wilbur. It's so pure. So forgiving. And so poignant. I just read it to my kids recently and I was weeping by the end.

Q: What advice can you offer to burgeoning authors?

A: My advice is to write what you're passionate about. Also, you should aim to put words to paper as often as you can, even if you're not feeling it on a given day. I'm at my best when I write at least five days in a row. And, finally, develop a thick skin. There's a lot of rejection in this business. We've all been there. Just tell yourself quitting is not an option and when a door is slammed in your face, kick it in!

Q: What's next for you?

A: I'm hard at work on my sixth book. And already brainstorming for the many I hope to write after that. Outside of the literary world, I'm working even harder at being the best mom I can be to my five- and six-year-old sons — *that* is the most awesome (and most challenging!) job I could ever ask for.

ABOUT THE AUTHOR

Emily Liebert is the award-winning author of *Those Secrets We Keep, When We Fall, You Knew Me When,* and the nonfiction book *Facebook Fairytales.* She's been featured on *Today, The Rachael Ray Show, Anderson Live,* FOX News, in *InStyle, People StyleWatch,* the *New York Times,* the *Wall Street Journal,* and the *Chicago Tribune,* among other national media outlets.

Currently, Emily is hard at work on her sixth book. She lives in Westport, Connecticut, with her husband and their two sons.

The employees of Thorndike Press hope you have enjoyed this Large Print book. All our Thorndike, Wheeler, and Kennebec Large Print titles are designed for easy reading, and all our books are made to last. Other Thorndike Press Large Print books are available at your library, through selected bookstores, or directly from us.

For information about titles, please call:
  (800) 223-1244

or visit our Web site at:
  http://gale.cengage.com/thorndike

To share your comments, please write:
  Publisher
  Thorndike Press
  10 Water St., Suite 310
  Waterville, ME 04901